STRAY

STRAY

MONICA HESSE

HOT
KEY
BOOKS

First published in Great Britain in 2013 by Hot Key Books
Northburgh House, 10 Northburgh Street, London EC1V 0AT

A CIP catalogue record for this book is available from the British Library.

ISBN: 978-1-4714-0027-8

1

Typeset by Palimpsest Book Production Limited, Falkirk, Stirlingshire
This book is set in 10.5pt Berling LT Std

Printed and bound by Clays Ltd, St Ives Plc

FSC

Hot Key Books supports the Forest Stewardship Council (FSC),
the leading international forest certification organisation, and is committed
to printing only on Greenpeace-approved FSC-certified paper.

www.hotkeybooks.com

Hot Key Books is part of the Bonnier Publishing Group
www.bonnierpublishing.com

For my dad, who taught me to write,
and my mom, who taught me to read.
And for Rob.

"Don't forget about us, Lona."

"Of course not."

"If the Path is working it will be easy to forget, because We won't matter."

"That's not true."

"It is."

He was right. Lona knew. The Path was a cajoling teacher, a relentless force. "If" the Path is working. The Julian Path was always working. Fenn knew that as well as she did. The "if" was a gift to Lona. A courtesy. What he really meant was, "Don't feel bad about forgetting. It will happen. It is inevitable. But all will be forgiven between us."

Fenn reached over to Lona and did the thing that he had done once before. He brushed his fingers against her wrist, over the bones that joined her forearm to her hand. His touch was quick and light and furtive. Maybe he had figured out that this was abnormal behavior, better to be done in secret. This was behavior to be analyzed and diagnosed. Dealt with.

Lona felt a tear trickle from the corner of her eye down the bridge of her nose, mucousy and wet. This was also abnormal behavior. Lona was only supposed to cry in Julian's world. She was not supposed to cry Off Path.

The bell rang. Lona looked toward the door leading to the bay, and then back at Fenn.

"Go," he said. When she didn't, he nudged her arm. "Go," he said again. "Julian is waiting."

At her pod, the lights were already dimming. She thought about how amputated it had felt to enter the bay without him. How solitary Fenn had looked in his regulation clothing.

The recording began. It was a balm of a message, an ointment, doing what it was designed to do. It soothed. *The Path is for you*, it said. *The Path is in you.*

Lona tried to hold on to Fenn's face. She owed him that. *You are the Path.*

It was impossible. The conversation was already fading. The tears she had just shed were evaporating against her face, dry and tight. A membrane of sadness, a memento of disobedience.

This was as it was supposed to be, the great architecture of Lona's existence. The life she'd just been living ceased to be important. New colors appeared in front of her eyes, new sounds echoed in her ears. A brassy alarm clock. A lawn mower.

Lona's pod disappeared, until she was no longer in the bay, but in a familiar bedroom.

Lona was becoming Julian again.

1

First, the pool was cold. If it was below sixty-seven degrees, they weren't supposed to swim. But the thermometer obviously said sixty-five, and the coach hadn't done anything but assign a satanic warm-up. Then, Dan forgot he'd offered to drive Julian to school, so Julian was jogging the seven blocks from practice holding his backpack in front of himself like an hors d'oeuvres tray, trying not to crush the paper model inside. Capsaicin, it was called – the molecule that made peppers hot. On the fifth block, his mother called to say that his capsaicin molecule was sitting on the kitchen table. Julian opened his bag. Cheerios.

"Is this going to be a bad day?" the new manager asked, tapping the screen with his fingernail. The control room was a still, gray dark. Two Monitors sat at their desks, a patchwork of scenes running across their computers. Talia clicked on the tiny square now marked with an oily fingerprint, enlarging it and noting the number in the bottom right-hand corner. Then she opened a browser and typed the number into Julianbase.

Then she reminded herself that the new manager's name rhymed with skeevy, which was helpful.

"Day 6001 is a five-point-four, Mr. Greevey," she said. "In Path, that means it's classified as Mildly Downcast, but it's within the normal range. It's barely below average, which is six."

"I know it's six."

He sounded testy. New sector managers always sounded testy. Talia wished his testiness was not currently manifested as a greasy whorl pattern on her screen. Talia bet he didn't know it was six.

"Of course. I'm just saying that we usually only register days that are Moderate-Severe Depressed or worse – anything less than a three."

"So you're not going to call a Coping Technician?"

He sounded accusatory. New sector managers always sounded accusatory. The Coping Technicians hated when new managers started even more than Talia did – the worrying, the whining, the stupid rules that the manager would later realize were stupid and try to blame on someone else. CTs had started referring to new managers as FMs. They said it stood for Floor Manager. It stood for Fecal Matter.

The rumor was that this one got the job because he was somebody's nephew. He was slightly less competent and more execrable than the one before.

"No," Talia said. "I don't need to call a CT. Besides, Lona is the one in 6001. On her charts, she scores very high in resilience, which makes it easier for her to cope with anything Julian's coping with."

Talia liked Lona. This wasn't something you said out loud, not unless you wanted to spend a weekend in a remedial Monitor training seminar. It was unwise, the seminar would explain, to 'like' any of them, when they were all learning to become the same person. But Talia liked how, when Julian ran, sometimes Lona's feet moved, too, little twitches like a dog having a dream, which made her long hair come untucked and fall down her arm. There was something endearing about this. Talia also felt a bond with Lona for other reasons, but those reasons were mixed with unease. Those reasons were better ignored.

And then, because Talia could tell that Greevey was the kind of person who worried more when everything seemed fine than when something was wrong, she added: "But you might want to have one on reserve for later this week. Jynd is in 5724, and Julian's grandfather dies in 5727. That's always a hard day."

This pleased him. Greevey gave Talia an important nod. "I'll arrange that."

When he left, Talia turned back to her screen. Day 6001 was familiar. She'd monitored it just a few weeks ago, and she actually kind of liked it. It was a five-point-four, but a funny five-point-four – the kind where the things that went wrong could have been accompanied by a pre-recorded laugh track, full of chuckles and polite groans. After Julian realized he'd left the molecule at home, his mother would offer to drive it to him, but there would be a misunderstanding about which entrance they were meeting at. Julian would go to the south entrance, and his mother would go to the west. Later, Julian would misread his sheet music in choir practice and start singing with the girls.

Talia was convinced Julian would not have viewed this

3

day as a five-point-four at all, but as an even six, or maybe six-point-two. The day's cozy ridiculousness would have amused him, if not immediately, then a few days later, when he mulled it over in his private thoughts. No one had access to his real private thoughts, of course. But Julian's ability to get over things like forgotten molecules was, after all, part of what had made Julian such a likable selection.

For now, Julian was merely trotting into Mr. Orlando's Chemistry class and explaining how his pepper model was missing.

"Was it too *hot* to handle?" Mr. Orlando asked. Bless him, he thought his capsaicin pun was hilarious. The difference between Mr. Orlando and Ms. Shaw, the other Chemistry teacher, was that Mr. Orlando embraced his own dorkiness, which made everyone like him. He wore shortsleeved button-downs that never quite closed over his stomach; his belly button appeared as a triangle of pale flesh like the eye at the top of a pyramid on a dollar bill. He called his belly button 'The Seeing Eye.'

"Maybe *you* are too hot to handle," Julian said, and everyone laughed. This was the type of thing you couldn't get away with in Ms. Shaw's class.

"Go." Mr. Orlando rolled his eyes. "Go get your capsaicin. Come back ready to talk about ion bonding."

Julian obediently loped toward the school's south entrance, pausing to glance at his reflection in a hallway trophy case. It was a good year for Julian's looks. He was tall-ish but not too tall. He was handsome-ish, but not overly handsome. He had long limbs, doe-brown eyes. Right now his hair was still damp, darker than its normal color.

4

When it dried, it would be nearly the same shade as his skin, giving the impression that if he stood in front of a beige wall, he could blend in.

Julian didn't look at himself frequently, meaning that those in Path were not often confronted with a mirror image of a face that was not technically theirs. There was discussion, once, about whether Path should be modified so that Pathers saw their own faces when Julian looked in the mirror. It hadn't gone anywhere. Budget issues, probably.

The red light above Talia's computer screen began to flash, simultaneously emitting an atonal whistle. Noon. Time for midday rounds. Talia could see the entire Path bay from where she was, but just barely. From the control room, the evenly spaced pods looked like blobby, boulder-sized masses. On floor level, a neat path of footlights, the kind they had in movie theaters, lit an efficient walkway for the Monitors to follow. It was peaceful down in the bay. Once it had been the gymnasium part of a posh health club. The control room had been the welcome desk. The Calisthenics room had been the weight room. The showers had been the showers. Some things don't change.

There would have been basketball nets then, in the bay. It would have smelled like sweat and shoe leather. Now it smelled dry and electronic, and the only sound was a low whooshing, which was the sound of two hundred machines running. It sounded like breathing. Here in the bay, the boulders came to life.

In the beginning, when Talia first started her job, they used regular dental chairs, tilted back into reclining position.

The vinyl stuck to skin, though. Created too many bed sores. Now the chairs were coated with microfiber.

The patrolling was Talia's favorite part of her job – walking around her assigned Pathers, noting anyone who was growing faster than expected and needed to be fitted with a new pod. She rarely had to touch anyone. That was mostly a CT job – stroking the shoulder of a Pather who was having a particularly traumatic day. The pods could replicate most sensory experiences, but sometimes Pathers responded better to actual human touch. CTs used to be called Touchers before they unionized and decided the title didn't fully enough represent their skill sets. Not that Talia blamed them. Who would want to be a professional Toucher? The Monitors tried to remember to use the new title, with limited success.

To her right, a big redheaded Pather named Grni was somewhere in the 6300s. Julian was filling out college applications, his father plotting a road trip down to a university in St. Louis. To Talia's left, a smaller Pather named Dwnd must be in the mid 2000s. Julian had decided the swing set was a pirate ship and was annoyed his mom didn't remember to say 'Ahoy.' The sound from that pod was tinny; Talia made a note to have it checked. Further down, a young Pather, barely over 365, wearing his miniature visioneers and supported by a special headrest, played a singsongy game of Pattycake with Julian's parents while a Coping Technician changed his diaper. The diaper was a problem, but no one had been able to design a better stopgap solution for before young Pathers could go on the bathroom break schedule. Someone would think of

6

something. Path was only eighteen. It was getting better all the time.

Finally Talia came to Lona. Julian was done with Chemistry, running lightly to English. Lona's feet twitched in time. One foot bounced off of her chair and dangled to the side. Julian's loping wasn't effective; he went up and down as much as he went forward. He wasn't a great runner, Talia thought, but Lona might have been.

Which was a useless thing to think. There had never really been a Lona without Julian.

She lifted Lona's foot back onto her chair. She might have called a Toucher if it was anyone else, but Lona intrigued her ever since what had happened eleven years ago, and, if she was really being honest with herself, Lona scared her.

Talia finished her rounds and walked back up to the control room. The pods became boulders again. Peaceful boulders, neat rows, safe order, dim light.

"Lona was running again," she said to the second Monitor, a younger woman with cropped hair who sat in the other desk. Lona's twitchy feet were famous in the control room. "Also, I think Dwnd's sound needs to be checked."

"It's the new speakers. Supposed to be better, but last week I had to send out two Pathers for eardrum exams. One was the day after Julian lit off all those firecrackers in 4200s, so maybe that was supposed to happen?"

A current debate among Path overseers: if Julian got sick, did that mean the Pather in that day should also be sick? Some argued yes – Pathers were supposed to have a full range of human experiences through Julian, and experiences

7

included damaged eardrums. Others said the Pathers were put in Path to give them better lives than they ever would have had Off Path. How much was pain necessary to the ideal human experience?

"What do you think of the new guy?" Talia asked.

"Kind of an idiot. He made me call a Coping Technician for a stubbed toe today. As if he was actually worried about the toe and not his ass."

"How did that go?"

"The Toucher can kiss *my* ass. Did you hear they were *all* asking for Christmas off? What did they think this job—"

Before she could complete her sentence, a piercing sound rang through the cavernous bay – a horrible, hideous scream. It was much louder than any sound Talia's computer could make, and louder even than Julian's yells when he broke his left tibia in 4428 after a failed wheelie off the bicycle ramp. It was a sound that could not have been learned by any Pather through any experience in the Julian Path.

But it was a Pather who was making that terrified sound.

The other Monitor's fingers flew over the keyboard as she tried to isolate the origin of the scream.

"It's Ernd, in Quadrant 4," she panicked. "I don't know what . . . It doesn't make any . . . Ernd is Off Path."

There were emergency procedures for this. They were just pretend emergency procedures, though. No one ever expected to have to use them. No one went Off Path without permission, without the soothing mechanisms and dozens of meetings that went into preparing for such an event. Pathers did not go Off Path on their own, and so nobody needed emergency procedures.

But these procedures must have involved the overhead lights coming on, Talia thought, because that's what was happening. The lights were coming on. The visioneers were lifting, hours before Calisthenics were scheduled to take place.

In Quadrant 1, Lona Sixteen Always was heading into the choir room, watching Nick as he did an impression of the choral director and the way his bottom lip quivered. Lona was picking up Julian's folder of music from his assigned slot. She was listening to Mr. Santolar's quivering lip tell them that the concert was in just a week, and don't make him regret choosing such hard music for high school students. And then – then she wasn't.

Then she was in the bay with all of the other Pathers from Sector 14, and the shrieking sound she heard had nothing to do with choir music. One person was screaming, and then another, and then, as the visioneers lifted, the whole room filled with the sounds of terror.

Lona felt warm light on her face. Sunbeams streamed in the slender windows that surrounded the top of the bay.

Julian spent every spring break visiting his grandparents in Florida, and sometimes they went to Cocoa Beach. Julian belonged to the local parks and rec swim team, and in the summer they practiced outside for ninety minutes every night. Julian had more fresh air than most people of his generation, which was another reason that Julian had been chosen.

And yet, as Lona peered up at the slivers of light piercing in through the top of the gymnasium, she intuitively understood something: this was the first time she had ever seen the sun.

2

"We were so scared," a small girl with dark skin was saying. "It was like the time We locked ourselves in the bathroom when Melissa was babysitting."

"No," said an older, wavy-haired boy. "It was like when We had our tonsils out and We woke up and Mom and Dad weren't in the room."

"That hasn't happened to us yet," the girl protested, annoyed. "We aren't supposed to tell us."

Lona flexed the muscles her machine told her to flex and listened to the conversations around her. The Calisthenics hour had been lost to gossip about what happened in the bay. It – whatever it was – hadn't lasted more than sixty seconds. Then the visioneers started working again. A few minutes later the room flooded with CTs who walked between pods, gently stroking the arms of two children at the same time. More arrived throughout the afternoon (helicoptered in from neighboring sectors?) and by the beginning of Calisthenics, there was nearly one Coping Technician for every Pather. Stroking arms. Upper arms. The length between the shoulder and the elbow, with steady, even pressure. This was the Toucher's specialty. Stroking arms and saying "Sh-sh-sh-sh-shhhhhh."

Lona's current Coping Technician hadn't arrived until It – whatever it was – was long over. Now, since Lona's arms were locked in the bicep/tricep machine, the CT stroked her calf, from the side of her knee down to her ankle. It was an awkward fit, this asthmatic, porky man wedged between the pulleys and levers of her muscle strengthener, but he managed to give it some dignity.

Next to Lona, the older boy apologized to the younger girl for spoiling the news about the tonsillectomy – a clear violation of Path rules. "It's not that bad," he said. "We don't even cry."

We.

The only pronoun that a Pather used was 'We.' It hadn't been planned that way. Just a natural evolution. When Lona was in her mid-4000s, a graduate student had written her linguistics dissertation about the 'unique Pather dialect.' She came for research during Calisthenics, sitting near Lona, down by the calf muscle that the CT was currently comforting.

"Do you find that the first person plural pronoun gives you a greater sense of community?" she had asked, pen poised above her spiral notebook. She had narrow eyes like a bird, and freckles across her forearms and the bridge of her nose. "Or do you feel that it upsets your sense of individuality?"

Lona had stared at her. "We don't understand what you're talking about."

What a stupid question. What pronoun were they supposed to use? 'You' was just 'Me' yesterday, or would be tomorrow. They were all 'We's, dots at different points along the same line. They were all journeying together.

12

The only thing 'individual' about Lona was her name, and that was a random assignment. The L, the twelfth letter of the alphabet, represented the twelfth month of the year and signified that she had been born in December. The O meant her birth date was the fifteenth. The N stood for her sector, and the A was her quadrant. Her full name was Lona Sixteen Always. 'Sixteen' was her year signifier – last year she had been Lona Fifteen – and 'Always' was the age of the Julian Path when she entered it. It had been the project's third year. The first-year Pathers were called Beginnings. The seconds were Accelerates.

Not that this mattered. Lona's birthday might be December 15, but since her days were synced with Julian's, the only birthday that mattered was his, which was October 6. Lona's name was just a way to keep track of things. Wherever she was, someone could hear her name and know exactly where she belonged. The same year the linguistics student had come, six or seven months later, Lona met another December 15 born her year. This Pather's name was Losk; she was briefly in Sector 14 for reasons Lona never knew.

"You two can chat," a tiny, pixie-ish Coping Technician had cooed. "You both just had the same day.

The other girl was taller than Lona. She had pale hair – Lona's was sandy and rough – and brown eyes that looked like boardwalk fudge from Julian's vacations. They looked a lot like Julian's friend Sarafina's eyes. Lona wondered briefly whether Sarafina had ever noticed the similarity before remembering that Sarafina had never seen Losk's eyes.

"Well, today was gross," Losk said.

"It was?" Lona's reply had a question mark after it, but Losk didn't hear it.

"When We face-planted in gym and everyone saw and laughed. So awful."

"They weren't laughing in a mean way," Lona said, perplexed. "It was just funny. And then our team won anyway."

"It wasn't funny. We wanted to die. And what if We get chosen last for basketball next time?"

"Who cares if We do? We're the best at swimming anyway, and everyone knows that."

If Lona got to plan the gym program, there would be no basketball unit. Basketball unit would be banished to a cupboard with all of the other ball sports. Floor hockey could stay. A puck wasn't really a ball.

"But gym is *every day*," Losk protested.

"We don't even *like* gym." Lona was almost laughing now at having to explain this. "It's the most boring class all day."

"No it's not. It's the only fun thing We ever get to do."

Losk wasn't reassured by Lona's reasoning; in fact, she was getting even more upset. Bright pink spots appeared in the middle of her cheeks.

"We know," Lona said, not because she agreed, but because this conversation was unsettling and she wanted it to be over. "It wasn't the best day. Definitely not an eleven."

That appeased Losk. Her face returned to its normal color. "At least it got better when Seth de-pantsed Curtis," she said. "Then everyone was laughing at him, not us."

Lona nodded, but she was uncomfortable with this

memory. The other students hadn't laughed at Curtis the same way they had laughed at Julian. It wasn't a friendly laugh, but a mean one. Curtis was shy and quiet. He carried an injection kit around in a fanny pack in case he accidentally ate a peanut. When Seth pulled down Curtis's shorts in the middle of gym class, it hadn't made Lona feel relieved. It had made her feel sad.

The conversation had ended. Lona was still confused. They were paired together to talk about the events of their day. But they'd had the same events, and they each thought the day was something totally different. It didn't make sense.

At least on that day she had been able to talk to Fenn.

Her mind unfurled the same series of questions it always did when she thought of him. *Where is Fenn? What is he doing now? Does he wonder what I'm doing now? Where is Fenn? What is he doing now? Where is Fenn?*

They'd known each other forever. Sometimes people exaggerated when they said that. Julian and Nick hadn't really been friends 'forever,' as Julian's mom liked to say; they met in first grade. Lona had always known Fenn. In her first clear memory, he was barely in his 2000s, a careful, dark-haired boy who was taking too long at a flexibility machine. Lona saw why: he held a crumpled piece of paper in his hand. Contraband.

"What's that?" she asked – quietly so no one else would hear.

"It's our ones and elevens. We're not supposed to see."

The Coping Technicians kept track of monthly highs and lows for all of the Pathers. This paper contained all of Fenn's.

His CT must have dropped it; Fenn looked nervous about finding it. The creases in the paper were transparent with his sweat.

"Did We look?"

"We're not supposed to see," he said again.

Lona plucked the sheet from his hand. She couldn't read yet, but she knew her numbers. "We'll look for us," she said, meaning she would look for him.

He said: "We'll look for each other."

On the Losk day, he offered reasonable explanations. He always offered reasonable explanations. "Maybe Losk's sound was malfunctioning," he suggested when Lona sat next to him in quadriceps. "We remember that day, a little bit. It was sad when everyone laughed at Curtis. Julian is always nice to Curtis."

He chewed his bottom lip. Lona noticed all the older Pathers did this – some habit Julian picked up in high school. "It must have been Losk's equipment."

That didn't make sense. Part of the reason Calisthenics didn't happen in the bay was because Monitors used the time to examine the pods for potential repairs. The equipment was meticulously maintained. It never went wrong.

"Besides," he continued, "confusion like that doesn't sound like it would be prescribed with the Path." Fenn was like that, measured and methodical. He would eliminate possibilities, chew through arguments. He never spoke until he had complete sentences. "Path only has negative emotions that have been monitored, or that are there for a reason. Otherwise it would just be like Before, remember?"

Lona shuddered. She didn't technically remember – none of them did – but she had learned about Before, in one of the presentations that sometimes happened during Calisthenics. Path History. Emotional Well-Being. Proper Calisthenics. In this particular presentation, they learned about Before Path. Before Path, Lona would have been beaten or neglected by parents who had been declared unfit. If she were lucky she might have been put in something called 'foster care,' but even that was dangerous. The presenter showed pictures of a shrunken boy locked in a dog cage, staring through the bars with huge eyes. "That's how the authorities found him," the presenter said. "That's where his foster parents kept him. He didn't know how to read. He spent every day in his own filth. This is what it used to be like, for everyone like you. You have all been given a very special gift."

That gift was the Path, the man said. That gift was the fact that when these potentially unfit people disobeyed orders not to have children, the children were rescued and put into a life they never would have been able to have. A good education. Proper nutrition. When the Julian Act was passed in Congress, the CT said, people wept with joy.

"Fenn," Lona said. "What if it was a negative emotion only to Losk?"

"But it was the same day."

"We know. But what if . . . remember how Dad is always talking about 'personality differences'?"

"Steve and I here, we just have a little personality difference," Fenn mimicked. Julian's dad never wanted to believe anyone was mean, just that they all had different personalities.

"Right. What if that's what We have? A personality difference? From Losk?"

Both she and Fenn stopped using their machines. The air around them was silent. Fenn was staring at her. His eyes were green, she noticed, an even greener green than Losk's were a brown brown. He stared at her with his green eyes, not judging, but like she was speaking in another language and he wanted to understand it.

"We all," he began. "We all have the same personality. We all have Julian's personality. It is the ideal personality."

Lona's cheeks flushed. Of course. How could they have different personalities when they were the same? "Right," she said. "That was stupid."

Before he could respond, a CT with a clipboard walked by. "Rotate!" she barked. "Fenn, abdominals. Lona, shoulders."

Fenn started in the direction of the ab machines, but went only a few steps before turning and running back to Lona. Touching wasn't forbidden between Pathers; it didn't need to be. It never would have occurred to Lona to touch Fenn or anyone else. When he reached her left arm, he extended his fingers and stroked. Stroke, stroke, stroke, just like the Coping Technicians. But on the third stroke he did something they never did. He squeezed. Just a little. Gently. His hand was warm, and she could feel his pulse in his fingertips, faintly, like the heartbeat of a bird. He looked into her eyes and squeezed, before dropping her hand and walking away.

That was the first time he ever touched her.

The second was the last day she ever saw him.

That might have been what started it all.

Lona never met Losk again. She never met anyone with her birthday again. Path had been fixed, probably, to prevent it from happening. Path had also been fixed to prevent her from seeing Fenn.

That wasn't a fair description. Fenn left when he was supposed to leave, to the new center where all Pathers went at 6570 when Julian turned eighteen. Rumors occasionally floated down, blended with Pather speculation: Julian went to the University of Chicago. Julian spent a summer backpacking in Canada. Julian's roommate was hilarious.

People had seen Lona and Fenn on the day they said goodbye, the crying and the illicit touch. Grownups had seen. Lona heard the whispers. *Unexpected. Unfortunate. Re-immersed. Remmersed.*

They kept saying that. 'Remmersed.'

The whispers stopped when a pinched, hard woman – not even a CT but a Monitor – stopped them. "Have you thought," she said, not a little exasperated, "that maybe Lona being upset proves that the Path is working? That she's learned to form human relationships?"

"Maybe you'll be sent to my Eighteens center," he'd said hopefully, once, but after the whispers she knew that wouldn't happen. She would never see Fenn again.

She hadn't forgotten about him, though. He'd been wrong about that. She thought of him all of the time. Because she'd never forgotten about him, she'd also decided never to make another friend like him. Something she didn't have could not be taken away.

It was better to keep focused, to walk the narrow path, to never stray.

3

The Calisthenics room went silent, and after a second Lona understood why. It was Ernd, the Pather who'd screamed, the one whose visioneers first went blank.

Ernd hadn't been in Calisthenics at all this period – a team of Coping Technicians and Monitors had detained her in the bay. Here she was now, though, allowing herself to be led through the machines to an empty arm-stretcher near Lona. Ernd wasn't someone Lona had noticed much before. Pale, like all of them. Slender. Younger – maybe high 3000s.

Ernd let her forearm be strapped into the machine, then answered everyone's unspoken question.

"They wanted to know what happened. Exactly what happened. But it was hard to tell them. First, We were at Nick's house, getting out the garden hose. We were going to spray his sister when she got home."

"We were studying for an algebra test," said a female Pather with a button nose.

"We pottied, like a big boy," a tiny one volunteered.

"We were talking to Grandpa on the phone, about how he would be out of the hospital in no time."

"We didn't realize that aluminum foil couldn't go in the microwave."

Ernd nodded, solemnly. "We were just making sure there were no kinks in the hose, and then there was . . . nothing."

"Nothing," another Pather repeated, and the word spread through the group.

"Nothing."

"Nothing."

"They kept asking us, 'what did you see?'" Ernd said. "They didn't understand that there was *nothing*."

Lona understood what she meant. For a brief moment, nothing had appeared in her visioneers. Usually, a few minutes before Calisthenics, a low tone would begin in the Pathers' earpieces, a wavy tone, like the deeper registers of a flute. Over the tone, the soothing voice would say something. The words changed a little sometimes, but were mostly the same:

Good morning, Pather. It is time to step out of your rewarding Path in order to exercise your body. Discipline is virtuous. Compliance is virtuous. Empathy is virtuous. The Path is for you. The Path is in you. You are the Path.

The flute would fade away, and the screen would turn to a pleasant, neutral lilac before lifting from their eyes.

Whatever had happened today had been nothing like that. It had been jarring and sudden – falling into an abyss. *Like when the sea kayak tipped over and for a minute We couldn't get out*, someone had said earlier.

But it wasn't like that, not at all. On all of those occasions – the bathroom locking, the tonsils – the Pathers had never been alone. Even in the sea kayak, when the bubbly water churned so violently that it was impossible to tell which way was up and which was down – even then, they had not been alone.

22

They had been with Julian. They had been Julian, but also been with him.

Lona knew what made the bay interruption so terrifying. It wasn't just that the Path stopped. It was that every person in the Path had been left totally and completely alone.

The intercom light on the Calisthenics room flashed. "It is time to return," the neutral voice said, "to the Path."

Lona waited as her machine stopped vibrating before lining up for Toiletry, taking a clean set of baggy clothing from the 'Girls (Medium)' stack and stepping into a shower stall.

Back inside the bay she walked to her pod, which was designed to mold to all of her muscles and every hair on her head. She was exhausted. Julian hadn't slept well the night before. He'd stayed up to finish a paper, then watched time pass on his alarm clock.

"Good morning, Pather," the voice said. "You are about to embark on another fulfilled day in the Path. We apologize—" *an apology was new*— "for the power outage that earlier caused a disruption on your journey. The problem has been resolved."

The other reason Lona was exhausted had nothing to do with Julian's REM cycle. It was that this thing – whatever it was – kept needling at her.

Whatever it was. Why did she keep thinking that? She knew what it was. They just said it was a power outage.

She tried to calm her breathing.

But didn't that sound a little weird, a power outage? Shouldn't that have meant that the whole system failed at once, instead of pod by pod? And if it was a power outage, then how was it that the lights all came on and the visioneer hoods lifted? Wouldn't a power outage have prevented that?

The fade-in to Path was a soft, burnt-orange color that gradually brightened in intensity. The tone accompanying it was a higher pitch than the one before Calisthenics, and reedier. More like an oboe. Lona's visioneers showed rust, then peach, then the pure color of a ripe tangerine as it faded into Path.

Julian was waking up, getting ready for swim practice, putting in his earbuds as he hunted under piles of laundry for his practice suit.

Ew, not this song, Lona thought. It was one of those songs where a guy who sounded like a girl sang about how sensitive he was. *I hate this song. Why don't you ever listen to better music, Julian?*

Wasn't it odd that they'd never had a power outage before? Nick's family lived out of town, off the regular power grid, and they had a backup generator, just in case. Shouldn't there be a backup generator?

When it happened – the power outage, if that's what they were calling it – the bay erupted in complete chaos.

Something bothered her about that memory. She went over it again in her head. *We were screaming. The Path broke and We were all screaming.* Except that wasn't exactly true, was it? Something about that statement was false. *I wasn't screaming. Everyone was screaming but me. I wasn't screaming because even though I was scared, I liked it.*

I.

Not We.

In Path, Julian ate a banana, brushed his teeth with a depleted, gummy tube of Crest. Lona barely noticed any of it. She was too thrown by her own thoughts to register anything happening in Path.

Until something happened in Path that didn't belong in Path at all.

For a split moment, so quickly she would have missed it if she had blinked, a face filled Lona's screen. He looked like he was trying to say something, but there was no sound and Lona couldn't read lips.

His face was thinner. His hair was longer than it had been when she saw him last, or at least longer than she remembered it being, but still the same curls and the same dark color. Still the same green eyes. Still the same serious look in them.

Fenn.

4

"What did you tell them?"

"The situation has been contained, Architect."

"I didn't ask whether it was 'contained,' Greevey. It's not an oil spill. I asked how you explained it."

"We told them what you said to tell them. It was a power outage."

"Did they believe it?"

"Who?"

"The children. Of course."

"The children are turnips, sir."

"Careful."

"I'm sorry, Architect."

"I'm going to come down tomorrow."

"You don't have to worry. I told you the situation is—"

"It is not contained, Greevey. Nothing about what happened yesterday even remotely resembles 'contained.' Please don't use words that you don't understand. Someone got in."

"Do you think it was *them*?"

"Nobody else would understand what effect it would have had to interrupt the Path. It was them."

"Our system says it looks like they were trying to target one pod."

"Did they reach that one pod?"

"Eventually they reached all the pods."

"Figure out who they want. I'll be there tomorrow."

"You don't need to come down, sir. I'll take care of it. If something else happens, I'll figure out what made it happen."

"I do have the other mess to deal with."

"And I can handle this here."

"You will tell me about anything – and I mean *anything*. If a fruit fly wanders into a pod and goes Off Path, I want to hear about it. What has happened here is infinitely bigger than your job, as difficult as that may be to understand."

"I understand."

"Fine. That's all, then."

"Sir?"

"Yes?"

"One more thing?"

"I'm waiting."

"Do you think they'll try again?"

"I think they are trying right now."

5

Don't panic.

There were explanations. Like, maybe it hadn't been Fenn on her screen. Maybe she was just thinking about him because of what happened earlier, and then when Julian's face appeared in the bathroom mirror, she thought it was Fenn.

That was unfeasible, too. She wasn't supposed to be able to think about other things when she was in Path. She wasn't supposed to be able, for example, to ignore what the coach was saying about the meet tomorrow, and instead remember what shape Fenn's lips made, what word he might have been trying to say, and why his eyes looked so terrified when he said it.

Doing that would have been impossible. But she was doing it right now. While she'd been thinking about Fenn, Julian had somehow made it to swim practice and was sitting next to Dan on the slippery tile floor.

So one of two things had happened, both of which were impossible. The first was that her brain had fallen Off Path and was now running behind, trying to catch up. The second was that Fenn was in her machine.

He had looked into her eyes. He had opened his mouth, and he had started to tell her something. *What was it?*

Unlike the earlier interruption, this time the interference had been in her pod alone. No one had screamed. No Coping Technicians had stroked arms. Only Lona had seen Fenn, and she didn't know why.

He would come again, she told herself. If she waited long enough, he would come again. She just needed to focus. *Focus*.

Coach Armand was saying that the relays for the district meet would be chosen based on the splits from this one. He wanted everyone at the van by four. Was Fenn in some kind of trouble? What did he think she could do from her pod?

"Are you having problems focusing, Lona?"

The voice wasn't in her pod, it was coming from Off Path. Her visioneers lifted again, for the second unscheduled time in twenty-four hours.

It was a Monitor, standing to Lona's left. Lona knew her name was Talia, but she didn't know how she knew.

"Were you having trouble focusing on Coach Armand?" Talia asked again.

Saying no would have been lying. Saying yes would mean admitting there was something wrong with her. In one way or another.

"Yes. I was. We were. We couldn't hear him."

There. That felt like a reasonable excuse, especially after what happened earlier. They would be expecting technical glitches. There was no need to explain that she couldn't hear him because she was seeing people who were not supposed to be there. Saying that out loud seemed like a bad idea.

A look flickered across Talia's face. Her skin was tan and drawn tight across her cheekbones in a way that reminded Lona of a hazelnut or round pebble. Not in an unpleasant way – she would be pretty if she were smiling.

Lona remembered why she knew Talia's name. This was the Monitor from before – the one who made the whispers stop about her and Fenn.

"Your sound levels are reading as normal," Talia said cautiously. "But it *is* possible that our equipment is faulty."

She didn't sound like she exactly believed Lona. Then again, Lona was lying. Maybe Lona was a bad liar. Maybe lying was something that required a lot of practice. Julian was a bad liar. His mom could always tell; now he barely ever tried.

"Why don't you come with me? There's a spare pod in the back of the bay you can use until yours is repaired."

If she went to a new pod, Fenn would never be able to find her. If she acted like she didn't want to follow Talia, then the Monitors would know something was wrong. "What about . . . will it just keep . . . if We go to a new pod . . . We don't want to miss anything."

"Your Path will stop until we set you up in the new pod. Then it will start again, just where you left off."

The bay was quiet. She'd never thought about how quiet it would be outside of her pod, or how claustrophobic, like a snowglobe. Talia led her down a dim aisle, surrounded on either side by pods close enough to touch. The Pathers' faces were placid and inexpressive: mouths slack, limbs loose and limp. As they rounded the corner out of Quadrant 1, Lona accidentally brushed the toe of

30

a tiny Pather. He giggled. Lona looked at the screen in front of his pod, which displayed what he was seeing to the Monitors. Julian was petting a baby chick on a field trip to a farm. That's what the giggling had been about. Nothing to do with Lona.

If she listened closely, she could hear that the bay had its own sound, a rising and falling, like ocean waves set to a timer.

"How did you know that our sound was malfunctioning?"

"I was alerted. Your brain scan said you were Off Path for a pretty long time." Talia peered sideways at Lona and waited, giving her a chance to explain what had happened. As if Lona had any idea what had happened. As if she didn't also want to know.

Talia's spare pod was in the corner of Quadrant 6. If Lona was permanently reassigned here, she would become Lonf. This pod looked too big. Lona started to climb in anyway, until a sharp voice from above broke her concentration.

"Bring her here," it said.

Her eyes adjusted to the dark as she searched for the source. First she saw the rickety metal stairway, running adjacent to the back wall. *Fire escape*, she thought, remembering a trip to New York that Julian went on last year. The stairs looked like a fire escape. The stairway led to a door; the door led to an office of some kind separated from the rest of the bay with a sheet of glass.

"Bring her up," the man said. If Lona hadn't known he was talking about her, she would have thought he was talking about a feral cat.

31

Talia hesitated, as if she'd been hoping she could slide Lona into the pod unobtrusively. Lona wondered if she would say something to the man, but she just gestured to the steps. Lona took them slowly, her soft footwear cludding dully against each metal riser.

"Don't be afraid," Talia muttered, as she reached around Lona to open the door at the top.

She hadn't been. Until Talia told her not to be. Funny that the only time people told you everything was fine was when nothing was.

Inside, the control room was dark, lit only by a few computers. One chair was empty. The only other one was occupied by the man with furry eyebrows, the one who had detained Ernd. He wore a brown suit. His hair was gelled to his head, like a plastic bobble-head doll.

"Do you know why you're here?" he asked.

Lona looked to Talia for guidance. Talia nodded.

"Our sound—"

"Was fine. Your sound was fine. I checked it myself. What wasn't fine were your brain rhythms, which should have been synced with Julian's, but were instead off picking flowers. I need to know how this happened."

He would have had better luck getting an answer if he hadn't interrupted her. Not that she had many answers.

"You," he continued, "are not supposed to be here. Do you understand that?"

"Mr. Greevey, I was taking her to another pod," Talia said. "While she's there I'm sure we can figure out what went wrong with hers and fix it."

Mr. Greevey continued as if Talia hadn't spoken at all.

32

He stood, folding his arms across his chest, bending down to her eye level. "You don't belong here, standing in my control room and consorting with my Monitors. But here you are, and here we're talking with each other, and neither of us is going to leave this room until we figure out how this happened. This morning you were Off Path for ten minutes. Until yesterday, no one had ever been Off Path in Sector 14 for even sixty seconds. You saw what sixty seconds did to everyone in the room."

She had. She had seen the panic.

"We were scared," she said, but he waved her off.

She disliked him, disliked the way he leaned over her and breathed. His hair gel smelled like coconut, tropical and cloying.

"I should say," he continued, "what sixty seconds did to everyone but *you*. Today when we got back on Path, everyone else's brains synced even faster than usual. They were happy to be back on Path. But yours didn't. Yours didn't settle down at all. At first we thought your mind was just wandering around, damaged from the shock of going Off Path. But that wasn't what happened, was it?"

"It might have been what happened."

She wasn't lying. It *might* have been what happened. Instead of calming her, the thought worried her. She didn't want that to be the solution – a technicality, a brain bump. If Fenn hadn't been in her visioneers, she didn't know where he was at all.

"But after one minute, your brain rhythms weren't wandering. They were more active than brain rhythms are ever supposed to be on Path. Do you know what I think?

I think your brain rhythms were active because someone was trying to tell you something."

"Something? What?"

"You tell me. You're the one the rebels told it to."

"The rebels?" She almost laughed. They thought some rebel group was trying to contact her. They had no idea it was just Fenn.

Unless they thought that Fenn was part of some guerilla uprising. In which case they would be looking for him. Whatever relief she felt was replaced with terror. If they found him, she didn't trust whatever this coconut-scented man would do.

"We don't know anything," she insisted again, her voice cracking. "We don't know why We went Off Path, but We bet it was just what you said – our brain was reacting to what happened yesterday. We swear. That's it. We didn't see anything."

The man was silent. It was a purposeful quiet, designed to make her get nervous and start talking to fill the space. It wouldn't work. No one was more accustomed to staying silent than a Pather. Lona used the time to look around the room. Let him think she was bored. Let him think she was stupid. Better than him thinking Fenn was a criminal.

The Monitor desks were neat, each with a few personal effects. On one desk, a picture of two young Asian children climbing a tree, another of a Middle Eastern family celebrating a holiday. Of course – the Monitors must share desks, for multiple shifts. Just because the Pathers lived here didn't mean the workers would. In the center was a pamphlet for some sort of expo. *New levels in comfort technology*, it said, over a photo of a pod that looked sleeker than the ones in Sector 14. *You'll want to take one home for yourself!*

Eventually Greevey spoke again, louder than before. As she suspected, he was the one who couldn't handle silence. "Before I came here, I managed a computer factory. When computers are broken, you run a diagnostic and it tells you exactly what's wrong, and you fix it. It doesn't *lie* to you."

"We're not *lying*."

"If one of the pieces is broken, you find out which one it is, and you throw it out."

To Lona's right, Talia's jaw was clenched.

"Of course, we don't throw out Pathers here." A bead of sweat or coconut oil trickled from his head. It was wrong for him to smell like a luau.

He crossed his arms again. When he spoke the next time, it was to Talia. "Take her to be remmersed," he said.

That word again.

"Sir, what?" Talia sounded shocked.

"The remmerser. I – we – can't afford to take any chances."

"Are you sure you have the authority to—"

"To make decisions for the sector I have been hired to run?"

"Mr. Greevey, there's no evidence that she's lying. Even if someone was trying to contact her, how could she have known it was going to happen? How could she be part of some conspiracy? She's been in this room every day of her life."

He was already shuffling papers on a desk, though, and neatly placing them into a briefcase.

"All the more reason. It will make her a less desirable target for anyone who may be trying to reach her. Her mind is broken. It needs to be fixed. So we take her to be remmersed."

He said it like it was a mathematical formula – after carrying all of the ones, there was only a single remaining solution. "There's a transport van available outside. You can take her yourself. Unless, of course, you feel it's a job more suited to a Coping Technician."

"I can take her," Talia turned to Lona. "I can take you." She gestured for Lona to follow her out of a door near the rear of the control room. Lona looked back toward the window overlooking the bay, the only home her physical body had ever known, but all she saw were Mr. Greevey's eyes, disappearing into jolly slits as he smiled. He waved in farewell.

"Goodbye, Lona. Don't be afraid. It won't hurt a bit."

6

The van Talia led her to had a logo on it – the back of a small child's head, facing a sun that was either rising or setting. It was long and white, parked in the far corner of a small garage attached to the building. Talia unlocked it with her key fob, opening the passenger door by hand, watching Lona as she climbed inside.

"Don't forget to buckle—"

"What is 'remmersed'?"

Talia raised one eyebrow, gave her a level stare.

"Your seatbelt."

"But what is—"

"It might be too loose. The last person in that seat was a Monitor who's a lot bigger than you."

Talia adjusted the rearview mirror and turned the keys in the ignition. For a moment Lona was distracted by the sensations of being inside the van. The leather seat was too hot. It was never too hot in Path. Even when Julian said, "Mommm, why can't we let the air run before getting in the car, it's like a freaking oven in here?" the seat had never been too hot for Lona. The Path must have regulated it.

As they backed out of their parking spot, Lona craned her neck to see through the windshield. All she saw was darkness. The windshield was blacked out – all of her windows were. She couldn't see anything beyond the interior of the van.

"We can't see out the windows over here," she said.

"No. You can't."

"But you can."

"Or I'm driving blind."

"Is your half of the window tinted differently than this half? Is it something you did to our eyes or something you did to the van?"

She used Path speak deliberately. She'd already slipped once in front of Talia, back in the bay. Talia sighed, debating whether to answer the question.

"It's the van. The light refracts differently on the driver's side. It's for your protection."

It must not be a perfect system. Talia drove with her nose inches from the windshield so she could see through the limited viewing space.

"Our protection? Or *all* of our protection? Have other Pathers ridden in this car?"

Talia engaged a turn signal and Lona felt her body swoop to the side of the van. Movements felt so much bigger Off Path. She clutched the side of the door.

"I supposed it doesn't matter," Talia muttered.

"What?"

"I was talking to myself."

"What were you saying?"

"If I tell you things, I suppose it doesn't matter at this point. Other Pathers have ridden in this van, but not while they're Off Path."

"How are We on Path in here?"

"Sometimes even Pathers get sick and need to go to the doctor. We mix a sedative in with their nutrient tube, and take them in the van." She nodded toward the rear compartment, which was separated from the front by a black curtain. "There's a pod in the back."

Talia paused then, deciding whether to say something, waiting to see if Lona said something first.

"Lona. *You* have been in this car before."

Whatever Lona expected her to say, it wasn't that.

"When?"

"You were little. Your eyes were weak – nearsighted. They fixed them. I drove you to the hospital and back."

Lona searched her memory for car trips, hospital visits, eye drops, Jello on a paper tray – anything that sounded like part of that narrative. Once she thought she had something, or at least a wisp of something. She was sitting in a hospital bed. She was drinking something neon yellow. The door to her room opened. Julian's mom walked in and said he could have sherbet, if he wanted, for his throat. So it wasn't Lona's memory after all.

"Did We drink Gatorade?" she asked anyway.

"Gator—" Talia wrinkled her forehead. "No, you wouldn't have had Gatorade."

"Did We talk about all of this then? Did We ask the same questions?"

"You were supposed to be asleep," Talia non-answered.

"But . . . We weren't?"

"The sedative wasn't heavy enough. On the way back from your surgery, I heard you through the curtain, talking in your sleep. Crying, actually. You were crying for your mom. I had a picture of Julian's mom in the van. Just in case a Pather woke up and got scared. It's all planned – you were five, so she was the right age for five. There are appropriate pictures of Julian's parents for every age. But when I showed it to you, you started crying harder. You said, 'Not that one.'"

"Not that picture?"

"That must have been what you meant. Later I realized that must have been it. But at the time . . . at the time I thought you meant something else." Talia shook her head. "Anyway. It *did* help us realize that we didn't have the right cocktail for you. If you woke up in the van, you could have woken up in Path. We adjusted your dosages and everything has been fine since."

Until today, Lona mentally inserted. "For the eye surgery? For the eye surgery, you used the pod in the back?"

"Yes. When I took you for your eye surgery, I transported you in the pod."

"Why didn't you use it today?

"Because. It doesn't matter for you today. You are going to be remmersed." Remmersed. Remmersed. It was a nonsense word that controlled Lona's fate.

"Talia," she said softly. It was the first time she had used Talia's name. She saw Talia stiffen at the sound. "What is 'remmersed'? I need to know what is going to happen to me." Talia had risked something to answer Lona's questions, and Lona would risk something in return. Unprotected by the plural 'We,' she felt vulnerable, exposing a piece of herself that no one had seen since Fenn left almost a year ago. "What is 'remmersed'?" she asked again. "Please."

40

"It's . . ." Talia took in a deep breath and exhaled, slowly, but when she spoke again, it was with the same brusqueness that she'd used for everything else.

"The most crucial thing to know is that you'll still have everything important. Your family. Your school, and friends, and swimming. All of that will still be there."

"What won't be there?"

"The unimportant stuff. The stuff that happens Off Path."

"Oh." The air whooshed out of her lungs. The car dashboard was swimming. She blinked. "Oh," she said again.

Julian's mom was a surgeon, and sometimes she came home with horrible stories. There were these conjoined twins once, toddlers, who had their own hearts but shared other vital organs – a liver, maybe, or part of an intestine. Doctors decided when they were born that separating them would be too dangerous. The twins learned to do things together; they could pedal a tricycle, each with one leg. But when they got older, it turned out that leaving them together was also dangerous. The way the blood flowed through their shared body meant one twin wasn't getting enough of the blood to her heart, while the other twin's kidney was failing. The family chose the operation. One of the twins died. It was always a possibility. They had to choose what they chose anyway. If they hadn't, both twins would have died. The weaker twin was sacrificed.

Being remmersed meant killing the weaker twin. It meant no longer having anything to do with being Lona. So that's why Talia was telling her things. It didn't matter. She wouldn't remember any of it later.

"Do you have to do it a lot? Remmerse?" She managed

41

to stop the dashboard from swimming by staring at the air-conditioning button. Her voice sounded like a scream to her, but maybe that was only in her head. Talia responded as if she didn't notice.

"Not a total remmersion. For babies sometimes, but not often when you're this old. Usually it's adjustments. Smaller modifications, like what we did after your eye surgery. This is special. It re-immerses your mind. In cases like this, if you've gone too far off-track, it helps the Path work better for you."

"The Path is in you," Lona said automatically.

"What?"

"It's something they say to us. You know. The Path is for you. The Path is in you. You are the Path. The Path is you. Because the more We can dedicate ourselves to the Path, the better our lives will be."

In response, Talia reached over and turned on the radio, flipping channels until she reached a guy with a tender, emo voice. It was the same singer Julian had been listening to as he got dressed earlier that morning.

"You like this, right?" Before Lona could respond, Talia turned up the volume. "Julian's favorite in the early 6000s. Let's listen to music until we get there."

Lona still couldn't see out the windows, but she could feel the van slow to a stop. Talia turned off the ignition.

"Is this the hospital?"

"It's the remmersion center. It's just for Pathers – when you need readjustments. It's in a strip mall. Next to a Chinese restaurant."

42

This was something that the Monitors and CTs probably joked about. A strip mall.

The older kids in Julian's high school, the ones who had off-campus privileges, they liked to hang out at a strip mall. It had a Chinese restaurant, too. Plus a nail salon, a sandwich place and a bowling alley. Two-for-one deal: Pedicure and Mind Erasing.

Talia peered through the windshield. "There's supposed to be someone waiting here. They usually come to the van."

She scanned the car interior, looking for something – a phone? – and then patted the pockets of her shirt. Empty.

"Shit," she said.

This was not a word used often in Path.

"Wait here," Talia decided. "And I'll bring out someone to escort you in."

"Is it too far to walk?"

"It's against protocol."

"Protocol?" *The protocol before you remmerse my brain?*

"I'm going to take the keys. I'm going to find someone. You cannot move. You must wait for me, okay? Okay?"

Lona could hear her footsteps walking away for a few seconds, and then she could hear nothing.

She thought about screaming. She thought about calling for help. She thought about all of the times that Julian had played Karate Houdini in the back yard, a game where the famous magician got a black belt so that he could be an escape artist *and* a crime fighter. *You have to hold me tighter,* he would say to Dad or Melissa or whoever was playing the game with him. *You have to hold me as tight as you can so I can chop free.* She thought about chopping Talia in the

43

head and running . . . running where? Into the Chinese restaurant and ordering some lo mein?

Where would she go? She didn't know how to get back to the bay, and she couldn't go there even if she did. She might be able to find a telephone, but she wouldn't have known who to call. Nick? Mr. Orlando? Was she even in the right city? If she called them, what would she say? "Hi, Nick? You don't know me, but you are my best friend. Can you come and pick me up?"

Why would she even want to run?

She thought of the boy in the dog cage. Foster care. Maybe foster care was right outside. Maybe that's why Talia had told her to stay there.

But what if there was nothing outside but the sun? What if she could get out of this van and run? Lona looked at her feet. Her shoes were thin-soled and flexible, made for sitting, but looked capable of running. What if, after they remmersed her, she went back to Path and she thought that basketball was a good day, and that it was funny when other people teased Curtis?

There had been no power outage. There had been no electrical failure. They could be lying about other things, too.

Lona heard traffic behind the van. That's where the road was – a busy street, judging by the short intervals between cars. That's where she would run. She would get to the street, and she would keep going. She unbuckled her seatbelt. She reached for the door. Just as her fingers were centimeters from the lock, it popped up on its own.

The door exploded open and two hands reached in.

"Hold her—" A male voice. "If you don't hold her still then you're not going to get the needle – don't let her hurt herself!"

She tried to shake herself free, but only managed to flip herself around. The grip tightened. Now one arm was across her chest like a metal brace, pressing her against a person who was tall and broad. She reached up with her left arm, which was a little less trapped than the right, and felt something soft. Hair. She pulled down, hard, and the mouth on the face below the hair said, "Ow," so she pulled harder. The mouth grunted. A spray of spit flew from the mouth, and landed on her eyebrow. She bucked her head back, aiming for the person's chin, and making contact with something in the general face area that was hard enough to make her own head hurt.

"Don't let go."

"She *headbutted me*."

She was probably the first Pather to ever headbutt a remmersing technician. Talia was going to get in trouble. She reared her head back again, but this time the mouth moved out of the way and she hit nothing but air. She needed to aim higher. If she could just move up a little bit, slide through the arms closer to the chin, then maybe she could—

Pain.

There was a pinch in her upper arm, then a sensation that was both acutely sharp and throbbing. She tried to slam her head back again, but instead it rolled back onto her captor's shoulder.

The idea of running was beginning to seem impossible.

It felt like all of the blood in her body had rushed to her toes. They must have swollen to the size of watermelons. They were going to burst open any minute. She still had the hair, but she wasn't pulling it anymore. Just holding. Holding the hair of the person who was holding her, and thinking that it felt very soft.

When she woke up again, she wouldn't remember any of this. She wouldn't remember soft hair. She wouldn't remember Fenn. After all of this, she would finally break her promise to Fenn.

She wouldn't remember anything but whether Mr. Orlando had postponed the Chemistry test and how she needed to get a more reliable ride from swim practice.

The arms holding her loosened, and she collapsed gently against the back of the seat. She could still get away. She dragged herself toward the door on the driver's side. The hands didn't try to stop her. Too pathetic to hold down a girl who was slipping into unconsciousness anyway. The van was extremely wide. How had she not noticed how wide it was? She inched over the console that separated the driver's side from the passenger's, which had grown to the height of a large mountain.

Her captors stared at her, their faces woozy and shimmering. The person who'd been holding her had a square jaw and thin lips, and a nose as straight and even as if it had been measured out by a ruler.

The person who had been talking to him was Fenn.

Her heart sputtered. Was she dreaming him? Was this the last image her brain was going to conjure up before it disappeared? As Lona slipped into darkness, she willed her eyes to focus on his face. If she tried, she could hold it in focus, like a microscope training in on a slide.

"What were you saying to me?" she asked. Her mouth was filled with wool socks and marbles. "When you broke into my Path, you were saying a word but I couldn't understand it. What were you saying?"

Fenn looked at her and smiled, but the smile was sad and ghostly. "Run," he said. "I was saying, 'Run.'"

7

Orange.

Scratchy.

Cool.

Lona was awake. She didn't know how long she had been that way. She was the fuzzy, clotted kind of awake that could have been drifting in and out of asleep for a couple minutes or a couple hours. *Open your eyes,* she instructed herself. She could. But her eyes were the only things she could move.

Where am I? Where have they taken me? Why can't I move?

Orange. Was she back in Path? Was she about to wake up with Julian again? No, that wasn't right. She wasn't looking at an orange light but an orange striped cloth. When she blinked – see? – her eyelashes brushed against it. The left side of her face was pressed against something. Sheets. She was lying in a bed, flat on her back, and the orange-striped sheets were tangled around her face.

Is this what it feels like to be remmersed? But she couldn't have been remmersed. If she had been, she wouldn't even know what the word was.

If she raised her chin, she could see over the covers. A

48

bedroom. A big window that looked over a forest. Old wood on the floors, nicked and scratched and smelling of lemons. A chair. In that chair, the boy with the straight nose and the thin lips.

"You're awake," he said.

Fenn slept on the floor next to him, his head against the windowsill.

He was here. She hadn't imagined him or conjured him up in her visioneers. He was here, unscarred, uninjured, which meant that, in spite of everything that had happened, one small corner of the world was okay.

"Fenn," she whispered. *Open your eyes and look at me.*

"Fenn, she's awake." The boy tipped his chair to the side, nudging Fenn with his foot.

As he tilted it back toward its original position, his arms flung out toward Lona. She flinched, before realizing that he was just steadying himself. The chair rocked uneasily before settling on all four legs.

Don't come closer. For all she knew, he'd kidnapped both of them. For all she knew, he'd forced Fenn to help bring her here, only to knock out Fenn and tie Lona to the bed. If he came closer she would do something. Like bite his ear. Or scream. Or continue to lie there, completely vulnerable, because she couldn't move. So maybe she wouldn't do anything. Except hope he didn't come closer.

"You're awake." Fenn opened his eyes and scrambled to his feet.

"Said that already." The boy yawned. "Twice."

"How are you feeling? Your head."

"I'm fine. I'm fine," She said. *I'm fine*. After months of not seeing him? *I'm fine*. She'd stored up so many sentences since the last time they were together, hoarding them like a squirrel, and what she finally came up with was, 'I'm fine.'

"Are *you* okay?" Lona started to stand, before remembering her leaden body. She turned to the boy. "Did you tie my legs?"

He snorted. "Do you see any ropes?"

"*Gamb*." Fenn's voice was a warning.

"Well, *do* you see any ropes?"

"You're not tied down," Fenn told her. "The anesthesia hasn't worn off yet. We overdid it on the sedative."

"We? *I* don't recall mixing any sedatives," said the boy named Gamb.

"No, you just stabbed it in my arm."

Gamb seemed unfazed by her comment, stretching his arms above his head, working out a kink in his back. "You okay here?" he asked Fenn. "I think I should go help Ilyf with surveillance. If they don't know what's happened already, they will soon, and she doesn't have another implant ready."

"How's she doing?" Fenn asked.

"Scared. But what did you expect?"

"What else were we supposed to do, Gamb?"

"I know. It's just . . . do you think the Monitor saw anything?"

"I don't know."

"And you're sure that Lona is better off here?"

"I don't know." His voice had acquired an edge.

"I mean, just – what are we going to do with her *now*?"

"I don't *know*."

Fenn slammed his fist against the wall. A hairline fracture appeared in the plaster, spidery and crawling.

"I don't know *everything*!" Fenn hissed. "I'm trying to figure it out!" He punched it again, this time dislodging a chunk of drywall.

Lona cried out before she could stop herself, shrinking back against her pillow.

When he faced her, she barely recognized him.

When she'd seen Fenn in her visioneers, she'd thought his face looked thinner. It didn't just look thinner. It was stonier, too, with anger that looked permanently chiseled into it. Hairline fractures, like this wall.

"Fenn, stop it!"

He should have listened to her. He should be calming down. He wasn't. She could see his shoulders rise up and down in violent, heaving pants.

The Fenn she knew wouldn't have yelled like that, wouldn't have lost control. The Fenn she knew also wouldn't have mixed a sedative to knock her out. He wouldn't have worked with Gamb to kidnap her. She felt bile rising in the back of her throat.

Gamb casually kicked the piece of fallen drywall across the room, then continued speaking as if Fenn hadn't done anything unusual. The fact that this might be Fenn's usual behavior scared her more than anything.

"Do you think she will be up by Thursday?" Gamb said, nodding toward Lona.

"I don't know," Fenn said again, more calmly this time. "Because. Well. You know."

"Just have Ilyf work on the implant. That's the best we can do right now."

The implant. It was the second time he had mentioned it. The Fenn she knew wouldn't implant her with something.

"Is that why you kidnapped me? You're going to implant me with some message?" She managed to use her left forearm, the only part of her body that didn't hurt, to prop herself to a half-seated position. "They were going to erase my brain anyway."

"Kidnap?" Gamb scoffed. "Pickle, we were your rescue mission."

"Rescue?"

"If we were going to kidnap someone, would we really go for a Pather orphan with no money?"

"I thought . . ."

Her brain was foggy. Her tongue still felt swollen. "I don't understand."

Fenn opened and closed his mouth a few times before speaking. It was a Fenn-like habit – that thoughtful precision, the careful considering of words. It should have calmed her, but she couldn't stop thinking about the grotesque, gaping hole in the wall next to her. It looked like a wound.

"I won't tell you everything," Fenn said. "Do you understand?"

He waited for her to nod.

"Nothing that will put you in even more danger."

A vague way of acknowledging that she was in a lot of danger already. At least he wasn't shouting. She tried to ignore the shattered hollowness in his voice.

"We were just going to monitor everything for a while," Fenn began. "Figure out patterns and rhythms and things before we tried to get you out. When Greevey ordered the remmersion yesterday, we had to act a lot sooner than we'd planned. We didn't want them to know how far we were in, but—"

"But now they know." This was a new voice, belonging to a wiry girl with springy dreadlocks, coming through the door. She stood on her toes, quickly inspecting a bruise Lona hadn't noticed before on Gamb's cheekbone. His bruise and the screaming spot on Lona's head must have been two halves of the same collision.

"Lona, Ilyf," Gamb drawled, as if introducing two friends at a party.

"They found the Monitor," Ilyf said. "She woke up after a couple hours and drove back to the Path. They know we have Lona. We rescued her like you wanted, and now they know."

"Eh," Gamb scoffed. "I needed some hand-to-hand combat training, and I got some. With Lona's freakishly pointy head. Ilyf, I get worse from you every time I forget to do the dishes."

"That implies there's a time when you remember to do the dishes."

"I remember before I met you, Ilyf. It was nice. I was in a pod. No one ever hassled me about—"

"But how do *you* know they found Talia?" Lona interrupted. "If they found out about the surveillance, then wouldn't they just turn it off, not leave it on for you to listen in?"

There was a long moment of silence, and then a reaction

she hadn't expected: Gamb coughed, then smiled, and then – of all the bizarre things he could have done – he started laughing.

His whole face changed when he laughed. It made the room feel smoother, like a hot iron working out wrinkles.

"That," Gamb said, "is one of Ilyf's more brilliant ideas."

"We wanted to have a bug in there, to know what was going on," said Ilyf.

"But security around Path is insane," Gamb said. "They would have caught us in a millisecond. Security at the homes of Path workers, though – that's nothing."

Now Ilyf was smiling too, revealing beautiful teeth. Her smile became a giggle, which Gamb caught and turned into a wheezing high-pitched guffaw. Desperate laughing. The kind of laughing that breaks out at funerals or in church.

"It's very easy, actually, to slip into someone's house while they're out, and implant an itsy-bitsy little recording implant into something that that person is going to take to work every day."

"Like a security badge," Ilyf said.

"A security badge!" Gamb bellowed. "Every day this week, Greevey has been coming to work paranoid that the rebels were getting in. Meanwhile, he is carrying the breach *into the system himself* every time he swipes his freaking badge. *He* is the security breach!" Gamb gave the absent Mr. Greevey a salute that involved both hands, but only one finger from each.

Their laughter became deep breaths, then gasps, then trickled off. Gamb coughed.

"Effing Greevey," he said, after a couple minutes.

"Effing Greevey," Ilyf said.

"Effing Path," said Fenn.

Gamb's and Ilyf's voices had been jokey, but Fenn's was all bitterness; he spat out 'Path' like the word was laced with cyanide.

Fenn, who had always been so patient, believing in whatever was said to him as well as in the people who said it. If Fenn had become like this, then it – *whatever it was* – was worse than she thought.

8

"We should let you rest," Ilyf said. "I'm sure this day didn't end up much like you thought it would."

"Do I just stay here?" Lona asked. "Does this room belong to someone else?"

The others exchanged a three-way stare, which Gamb interrupted first. "Not anymo—"

Before he could finish, Lona heard the sound of another door, further away in the house. A front door. There was a key turning in the lock, a door handle grinding, then hinges squeaking and a female voice calling, "Hello? Fenn? Hello?"

"Neve," Ilyf whispered. "I thought she wasn't coming back until Thursday,"

"I suppose she came back early," Fenn said.

But Lona thought she detected concern, and her detection was confirmed when Gamb said, "Crap."

The unseen girl was getting louder. "Gamb? Ilyf?"

"This house belongs to Neve's family," Ilyf rushed. "She didn't know you were coming. She also – well, you'll see."

Lona saw. A few minutes later, a disconcertingly pretty girl, a few years older than Lona, swooshed into the room and to Fenn, oblivious to the fact that Gamb and Ilyf were arranged in a stiff tableau around a stranger.

"I decided to take the other train," she said. "I got a new ticket, and almost missed the shuttle, but then it was delayed anyway, so . . ." She shrugged and started unwinding a silky scarf from around her neck. "Wait," she finally laughed. "What are you all doing in *here*?"

Neve's eyes backtracked, until they landed on Lona. *Pounced.* Lona thought incongruously. Her eyes pounced on Lona.

"Genevieve," Fenn said. "This is Lona. Lona, this is Genevieve."

"Genevieve. Nice to meet you, Genevieve."

As soon as Lona said the name, she wanted to say it again. First, because it was as pretty as the person it referred to, which was extremely. Genevieve reminded Lona of a panther, sleek and graceful, flat muscles with energy coiled beneath the surface. Her eyes were green like Fenn's, but lighter – a celery color somewhere between interesting and otherworldly. The second reason Lona wanted to keep saying the name was because she hadn't had many occasions to say a name like Genevieve. It spilled out of her mouth like a waterfall – it was long, yet every letter was exactly in place. This was a name that had been chosen by someone, not assigned.

Which meant, Lona realized with wonder, that Genevieve had never lived in Path.

"You said you wouldn't," Genevieve said. "You promised you wouldn't without talking to me."

"They were going to remmerse her, Genevieve," Fenn said. "We had to."

"Had to?" Genevieve was tall enough that she and Fenn

57

were exactly eye level. "Don't you think there are enough other things you *had to* worry about?"

"No one saw us," Gamb jumped in. "There was only one Monitor with her, and we snuck up from behind. No one could have traced us back here."

"It's not the *house* I'm worried about."

"I know," said Fenn. "But it could have been any of us. If it was me in there, or Gamb, or Ilyf, or . . ." He dropped off the sentence. "You would have done this for any of us."

"Would I?"

"Of course you would."

No. She wouldn't have. Even Lona could tell that. Something in the way Genevieve's eyes darted away. She wouldn't have 'done this' for Gamb or Ilyf or whomever else was at the end of that dropped sentence. But she would have done it for Fenn.

"There's not enough *time*, Fenn."

The way Genevieve said Fenn's name. It sounded – what was the right word? – familiar. It sounded like she had used it a million times. Different from when Gamb used it. Like the name had been invented for her to say. Like she owned it. Lona didn't know why this bothered her. She should have been happy Fenn had other friends.

"They were going to remmerse her," Fenn said again. "You don't understand what that means."

A muscle in Genevieve's jaw twitched. "I *understand*. You act like because I'm not a pod person, I couldn't possibly understand you." Pod person. It obviously meant something mean. A phrase designed to hurt in a very specific and precise way.

"Then you understand. Remmersion. Genevieve, there is more than one way to die."

Genevieve's jaw muscle stopped twitching. She sighed. "Neve. You know I don't like Genevieve."

"Neve." The shortened name was a peace offering. Fenn lifted his hand and delicately traced the air between Genevieve's cheekbone and chin. It was a small, quick gesture. But it was intensely personal. Lona knew that she was witnessing something private. She knew that she should turn her head away, but she couldn't make herself. Instead, she stared at Fenn's hand and tried to measure, in millimeters, how close it was to Genevieve's actual skin. Two, maybe? Three?

It pleased her that it wasn't actually touching. Path had ingrained in her the sanctity and strangeness and vague distastefulness of touching. To touch was to break rules. To break rules was to have an allegiance to someone worth the disobedience.

I am the one he touched, she reminded herself. Twice, on his own, on her hand that recorded the memory like an ink etching. *I am the one who knows Fenn*.

But then Genevieve moved her hand, too. She closed it over Fenn's and brought his palm to her cheek, brushing it over her lips and chin. Even when Genevieve removed her hand, Fenn left his there, stroking her face with his thumb, their green eyes boring into each other's like a matched set.

Now Lona looked away.

He was supposed to move on. She had expected that – he even prepared her for that. She said goodbye to him when he left for Eighteens with the understanding that she wouldn't see him again, that this was all part of the plan of Path. But she didn't expect to have to confront evidence of this moving on.

She hadn't thought, if she saw him again, that she'd still feel alone.

When she turned back, the moment had passed. Genevieve scanned the room, looking for something. Her scarf. It had fallen on the bed when she unwound it from her neck. Lona picked it up. It was soft and slippery, and smelled like gardenias. Without making eye contact, Genevieve snatched it away and stalked out the door.

After everyone was gone but Fenn, Lona wanted to close her eyes and sleep for a hundred years. Her throat ached. The bed was too flat. The only thing she'd learned in the past twenty minutes was that Gamb was not trying to kill her, but that she was living in the house of Genevieve, who clearly wouldn't mind if he did.

"Would you like some ice for your head?" Fenn asked. She kept waiting for him to come closer, lean in, do something familiar that would make things okay, but he was oddly formal.

"No. I'll be fine."

"You should sleep, then. We'll talk more once you're rested." He flicked off the wall light. The room didn't go completely dark. It was an in-between time. Twilight or dawn. "Good night," he said stiffly.

"Julian got team captain last week," she blurted out. One of the hundreds of things she'd imagined discussing with Fenn.

"What?"

"Team captain. Instead of any of the seniors. You told me to look forward to the week when he became team captain."

"Did I?" he said dully. "I probably told you to look forward to a lot of things." He put his hand on the door knob.

"What's going on, Fenn?"

"I know you probably have some questions."

"Some?" she sputtered. "I have *no* idea what's going on. You haven't told me why we're here, or even where here is. You haven't told me why none of you are at Eighteens, or why Sector 14 thinks you're a rebel army."

"Well, Lona, we've been a little *busy* around here."

There it was again. That caustic, icicle tone, which hurt no matter how many times she heard it.

"You're different," she said finally.

"What?"

"You're different. You're rougher. You're meaner than when we knew each other before."

"You didn't know me before," he snapped.

She flinched. *The meanest things feel that way because they're true*, Lona thought. It was something Julian's dad used to say – his way of telling Julian never to prey on other people's weaknesses, never to lash out in anger. Fenn could not have said anything meaner if he'd tried.

Lona had spent the past year keeping her promise. She didn't forget him. Now he was telling her that the person she fought to remember didn't exist. Maybe never had.

"I didn't mean to yell." He slumped down on the floor. He didn't look mad anymore. Just lost. Like he was a little boy, holding on to a paper he wasn't supposed to have, containing information he wasn't supposed to know.

"Fenn," she asked again, more quietly this time. "What is going on?"

He shook his head.

"I know you can't tell me everything."

"I can barely tell you anything."

"Just tell me *something*." *Just tell me something that makes me feel like I'm glad to be here instead of back in Talia's van with my mind erased, not having to feel any of this.*

Fenn looked vacantly over her shoulder, out the window with the trees. A bird feeder swung from one branch. It was empty, but a gray starling perched there anyway, poking its head into the feeding tray and ruffling its feathers.

"This is a big house," Fenn said. "It has five bedrooms – it was built as a bed and breakfast. Genevieve's dad used to have parties out here on weekends, until he bought more houses and forgot about this one. We liked it because it was big and private. We thought it would be a good space for us."

"For you and Gamb and Ilyf."

"The reason that we needed all the bedrooms is that there used to be three more people who lived here. Byde, Cadr, Czin. We all met at the Eighteens center. Genevieve – we met Genevieve too, and she said her parents were rich and had lots of houses, that they never used this one and wouldn't even know if we were here. And we did live here. All seven of us. But then . . ."

Fenn's hands shook, even though they were pressed down hard against his knees.

"Then Byde was killed. A couple days before his nineteenth birthday. And then Cadr. And then Czin. Freakish deaths. Things that could have looked like accidents."

"What kind of—"

"Don't make me tell you the details." He closed his eyes, just for a moment. "When we saw Cadr on the news, half of her face was still perfect."

Half of her face.

Lona's insides lurched.

Whatever else Fenn told her, she never wanted to know what had happened to the other half of Cadr's face.

"All of them. Everyone died. Everyone was murdered. Do you understand? Everyone who leaves Path dies before they are nineteen."

For a split second she missed her pod. She wanted to close her eyes and open them again in Julian's bedroom. She wanted this to be a nightmare.

"You're trying to break into Path," she said slowly. She would start with simple information. She would move point by point, to help everything make sense. "You are trying to figure out what happened with these murders. You are the rebels."

"Yes. We are the mighty rebel army."

Yesterday it seemed so ridiculous. But Mr. Greevey was right, and now it wasn't silly at all. The rebel movement was four scared kids hiding in a farmhouse in the middle of the country. Lona felt sick.

And then she thought of something else.

"Fenn, what is today's date? Today, what is it?" In her Path it had been September. Back to school season. Organized lockers and fresh starts.

"Today is May 11," Fenn said.

May 11. It was the first good news she'd heard.

"But, we still have time, if it's only May 11. It's six months until October."

Fenn's responding smile was patient and acidic. "You're still thinking in Path, Lona," he said. "It's Julian whose birthday is October. My birthday is June 5."

Her face surely betrayed her understanding, but Fenn went ahead and said the horrible thing anyway: "I turn nineteen in twenty-four days."

9

"Is this Talia Nechayev?

"Yes, Architect. From Sector 14. I heard you wanted to speak with me?"

"You were the Monitor escorting Lona Sixteen Always to the remmersion center."

"I was, but I can't tell you anything. The attack happened from behind – I felt something sharp going into my arm, and I woke up on the pavement a couple of hours later."

"That's what's in the report."

"Yes, sir. I put everything in the report."

"Did you?"

"That's what the report is for. I'm not sure I understand what you're asking."

"Did anything unusual happen on the way to the center?"

"What does unusual mean?"

"I trust you're not asking me to define a remedial word. You have been monitoring this girl for sixteen years. You'd be as able as anyone to assess whether her behavior was unusual."

"She asked about remmersing. I don't think that was unusual. Anyone would have been curious after what Mr. Greevey said to her. Sir?"

"Yes?"

"Sir, I don't think that Lona was a part of this. She couldn't have known what was going on. I – I liked her. I liked Lona."

"You have been told by now, that we suspect another of your former Pathers was involved in orchestrating the attack."

"I monitored Fenn. He was one of the gentlest Pathers I've ever met. Responsive, earnest. Passive, even. Everything he was supposed to be. Lona was the mischievous one."

"Mischievous?"

"Come on – not in some kind of malevolent way. She was just quick. Curious. You could see a light in her eyes."

"Fenn Eighteen Beginning had a relationship with Lona Sixteen Always."

"He often sat next to her in the sixty minutes a day they were not in Path. If that's what you call a relationship."

"And you never worried about their interactions?"

"No."

"Never?"

"Are you going to make me answer all of your questions twice?"

"Do you think Fenn is dangerous?"

"I just got done telling you – he was always respectful."

"Was it respectful when he shoved a needle in your arm?"

"My degree is in electrical engineering, Architect. If you want someone who can assess the mental state of a Pather, maybe you should speak with a Toucher. I'm sure I can find one for you."

"Talia. I appreciate how exciting it must be for you to

sass off someone with my title. But let me ask you again: Whoever we are looking for accosted you as you stepped out of your vehicle, stabbed you with a needle though you were unarmed, then left you unconscious in the middle of a parking lot while they kidnapped a Pather that you have just admitted that you 'liked.' So let me repeat the question. Do you think that Fenn Eighteen Beginning is dangerous?"

"Yes, sir. I suppose I believe he is."

10

"Make her try the peanut butter next!" Gamb tried to jockey his jar for a better position in the row of foods sitting on the kitchen table.

"No, she's still in salty now," Ilyf complained, pushing the jar away. "Your peanut butter is going to mess up my average. And I don't even think we can do peanut butter without putting it on bread or something. No one eats it plain. If she doesn't like it, it doesn't count."

"Stop trying to change the rules. I'm not going to take pity on you because you're pathetically losing, you pathetic loser."

Fenn reached for another spoon, scooped out a dollop of peanut butter, and handed it across the table to Lona. She licked it. *Sticky. Thick. Smooth.* Not what she would consider a solid food, though: she didn't need to chew it. She swallowed twice before announcing her verdict.

"Yes."

"HA!" Ilyf made a check mark on the paper in front of her. "So now we're tied, eight and eight."

'What Will Lona Like' was Gamb and Ilyf's favorite game. In Path, Flavor Buds replicated the taste of food, and intravenous tubes provided nutrients. But Lona had never thought about how much texture influenced the experience of food. She loved peaches in Path, but now couldn't stand biting through the fuzzy skin.

"Olives!" Gamb was cheering now. "Give her olives!"

"Gamb." Lona's stomach sloshed. "I don't think I can."

His disgusted look clearly said 'wimp,' but he removed the jar he was wafting under her nose.

"Fine," he said. "But you are going to looove them."

"Leave her alone, Mr. 'The-first-week-I-ate-real-food-I-spent-two-days-on-the-toilet.'"

"That was different. I think there might have been an alien in my stomach. Humans are not meant to eat shrimp. I think they come from space."

"Those came from an organic market and were crazy expensive."

Sometimes when she watched Gamb and Ilyf bicker with each other, close and three-dimensional and real, it was like watching a movie, with the characters sitting in her lap. Sometimes she liked the intensity. Sometimes it felt like an avalanche.

Genevieve glided into the room, plucking her car keys from the hook near the door. "I'm going out for an hour. Ilyf, I'll get the thing you wanted if you write down exactly what it is."

"Lona likes peanut butter," Gamb informed her, while Ilyf made notes on an envelope.

"Eating solid foods now," Genevieve said. "Just like a big girl." She leaned over Fenn's chair and whispered something in his ear that made the right corner of his mouth twitch up. An inside joke.

"Well, *I* thought it was interesting," Gamb grumbled. "None of us liked it at first."

"Maybe we can actually start eating real meals again like we used to, instead of taste-tests," Genevieve shot back. She grabbed Ilyf's envelope. Gamb waited until they could no longer hear the jangling of her keys before speaking.

"Fenn," he said. "Your girlfriend is in an awesome mood. As usual."

Girlfriend. It wasn't the only time someone had used that word about Genevieve. Lona knew what a girlfriend was, and a boyfriend. Friends who spent a lot of time together. Sometimes they went to dances or gave chocolate on Valentine's Day. *Not a bad thing,* a Coping Technician had explained during Calisthenics. *But nothing you need to worry about.*

Fenn had told Lona to give Genevieve time. She was under more pressure than any of them, since she was a fulltime college student, had a houseful of undocumented Pathers, and was trying to feed four extra people with a credit card that her parents paid the bill for. Gamb told her Genevieve thought she was too pretty to bother with manners. Ilyf told Gamb to shut up.

Lona tried to be patient with Genevieve. The Path taught patience. The Path taught kindness. But it was hard when the other girl so transparently had no interest in interacting with her. Genevieve never talked about her parents, Genevieve never talked about school, Genevieve never mentioned any other friends. And when everyone eventually went to bed, Genevieve and Fenn went to the same room.

"Calisthenics," Gamb had answered, when Lona asked, worriedly, if he was sure she hadn't taken Fenn's room and forced him to sleep with Genevieve. "It's their Calisthenics hour in there." Ilyf laughed and punched his arm, and Lona didn't want to admit she didn't understand the joke.

She understood enough, though. If Fenn and Genevieve were turning to each other, and Lona was still trying to turn to Fenn, what did that make her? Extraneous. Unnecessary.

Friendships don't work like that, she told herself. Julian had Nick *and* Dan *and* Sarafina. Fenn should be able to have Lona and Genevieve and Gamb and Ilyf. This was different, though. She didn't know how, but it was, and she wasn't the only one to feel that way.

Sometimes she caught Fenn looking at her with a pained expression and wondered whether he regretted the fact that she was there at all.

Genevieve's car pulled out of the driveway and the activity in the kitchen picked up where it had been before her interruption. Gamb set the olive jar on the table and then, waiting to make sure Ilyf wasn't looking, leaned into Lona's ear. "Olives are nasty as hell. Eyeball texture. I'm just trying to use reverse psychology on Ilyf. Don't tell."

"Gamb?" Ilyf waited expectantly by the pantry for him to help her clean up.

"Ma'am!"

As Gamb and Ilyf harassed each other around the kitchen, Lona and Fenn sat at the table. Like the rest of the furniture in this house, it was made of knotty woods and simple lines, what the home magazines that Julian's dad read would have called 'country casual.' The patchwork quilts on the beds probably cost a fortune. New stuff designed to look old.

Fenn methodically screwed the lids back on the jars they'd opened. Lona helped. Activities that could be done silently were nice.

The strangest thing about being Off Path was the talking – the constant having of ideas and the expressing of them out loud. Someone would ask Lona a question and she would wait for it to be answered, forgetting that she had to answer it, just like she had to actively choose to walk into another room or select what to eat for breakfast.

"Here." She handed Fenn a container of pickles.

"Thanks."

"You're welcome."

Their relationship had changed out here in this house. Back in Path, there had been no subtext, nothing unspoken. Back then, she would have said that she was feeling worried about something, he would have asked what it was, and, in between the pulsing of their machines, he would have disassembled her fears one by one. Out here, everything she wanted to know was something he didn't want to discuss. She wanted to ask about the three dead Pathers, but he deflected her questions even more than Talia had in the van.

He couldn't disassemble her fears when what she worried about was him.

*   *   *

"What should we do today?" Gamb plopped back into the chair next to her. "I could show you the *Godfather* trilogy. Julian never watched any good movies."

"Is that going to be as fun as when you showed me *Citizen Kane?*" She made her voice a deliberate monotone. "Because I'm not actually sure I've woken up from that yet."

Gamb clapped his hands. "Sassy Lona! We have Sassy Lona today! Much better than Timid Lona yesterday."

Had Sassy Lona felt like a natural choice? Did it feel more right or less right than the day before, when she had tried to be deliberately agreeable?

If she were being honest with herself, whatever she did, she was thinking about what Julian would have done and trying to model that. His absence was still a relentless presence.

So she was faking it. When Julian was thirteen or fourteen, he went shopping with Nick and Sarafina before they started high school. Sarafina's mom managed a boutique in the mall and she led them from rack to rack, piling them with clothes and saying things like, "What about nerdy chic? Do you think you'll join the debate team? I could see that working."

Now Lona wasn't trying on clothes. She was trying on personalities. Was she meant to be goofy and cavalier like Gamb? Withering but kind like Ilyf?

What had Mrs. Baker said? Something like, "Sometimes clothes reflect who you are, and sometimes they help shape who you are."

And then Sarafina had responded, "And sometimes that shape is a big, fat—"

Stop it, Lona willed herself. *Stop it*. Remembering what Sarafina said years ago wasn't going to teach her anything about what she should do now.

But they were the only memories she had.

"I have an idea," Fenn said. Fenn almost never offered ideas on what Lona should do out here, so when he spoke, Gamb leaned in on his elbows. "Lona, do you think you're ready to go outside?"

She hadn't been outside yet. Fenn worried about sensory overload – the brightness hurting her light-sensitive eyes, the temperature searing her climate-regulated skin. "I checked the weather – it's supposed to be cloudy today, and not too hot. I thought it would be a good day to try."

"Outside? Really?"

"Just in the yard."

"Now?"

"If you want."

She wanted.

Wanting. That felt like a good emotion to have. It had come from inside her, not in response to anyone else. She made a note of it in her head: *I have a personality that wants things.*

11

It felt like . . .

How could Lona find something to compare the feeling of being outside to, when this is what everyone should compare everything to?

The peanut butter was an attack on her senses. The weather felt like a dance. A wind gust picked up a strand of her hair and whipped it across her cheek, tickling her nose. Even as Julian she would never have felt anything like this. His hair was too short to move with the wind. The sun was warm, but the breeze was cool. If someone asked her if she was too warm or too cold, she would say, both. Neither. Yes.

"Is she going to cry?" Gamb whispered to Ilyf.

"We're not all you."

Lona did feel something bubbling inside her. It wasn't tears. Before she could think more about whether this was a good idea, she spread her arms out like wings and ran down the steps to the grassy yard. Her legs felt like they were made for this. She was smoother and faster than Julian had ever been, and the realization made her erupt in giggles. When she'd run as far as she could, she collapsed into the grass, squeezing it between her fingers, feeling the slick sponginess of the earth.

"Lona!" Fenn dropped to his knees next to her, trying to catch his breath. She wondered if he'd be annoyed with her for ignoring all instructions to take things slowly. But when she looked up, he was laughing. "You're fast."

"I guess I am."

"But are you tired now?"

"No. Not from this, at least."

It was funny, the different ways her muscle groups responded to being Off Path. Her legs felt strong and powerful; it was her air supply that ran out first. And her stomach muscles were weak. This morning she'd had to roll onto her stomach and slide off the bed like a slug.

"It's pretty out here," she said, finally looking up at her surroundings. Gamb and Ilyf went to a tire swing that hung on a tall maple next to the house, taking turns spinning each other around. The house was in the middle of a clearing, with a gravel road on one side and woods on the others. The trees in the back grew on a steep hill that eventually bottomed out, Fenn told her, into a wide creek. They were in Maryland. Several acres of land in the western part of the state.

Funny, Lona thought when she learned that. Julian had never been to Maryland so she always assumed she hadn't either. Really, she was living there the whole time.

"It is pretty," he agreed.

"And quiet."

"In the night you can hear the cicadas. It's stupid, but the first night I was out here I kept thinking they were the sounds of the stars. I knew they weren't – it was just two things I wasn't used to experiencing, happening at the same time. Stars and cicadas."

"Stars could sound like cicadas. I'd rather think they'd sound like wind chimes."

"Wind chimes would be the moon."

This conversation was coming so easily, like conversations between them were supposed to be. The realization made Lona giddy, but once she became aware of the ease, it disappeared. The way Nick could juggle three balls, unless he tried to teach Julian. He could never explain it, and in thinking too hard about how it worked, became unable to do it himself.

"It's also . . . leafy."

Soon she was going to run out of adjectives, and this conversation would be over. She started queuing them up in her head. Leafy. Wooded. Deciduous. *It's so deciduous out here, Fenn.*

The things she really needed to ask him had nothing to do with trees.

He spoke first. "Can I ask you something?"

"Can I ask *you* some things?"

"What does the grass smell like?" His tone was sincere.

"You know what it smells like."

"I don't know what it smells like to *you*."

"It smells like grass, Fenn. We've just been rolling around in it."

"I want you to really concentrate on it. Please."

He looked so expectant. She leaned over, pressing her face into the earth, and inhaled the grass. It smelled sharp and fresh – almost citrusy – and clean. And totally incorrect.

"It's wrong! Or, not wrong, but – something."

Fenn was nodding. "It's different, isn't it? I wondered if you'd notice. It's the only smell I've noticed that Path didn't seem to get right. I wonder why – I guess there's a chemical that's hard to replicate."

She sniffed again, slowly this time. This time she smelled more: layers of earth and rain and soap and – what was that word? Photosynthesis. She would swear she could smell the photosynthesis. "This is better."

"I thought you'd like it."

He wore what Lona had come to think of as his New Fenn smile. One part happiness. One part bitter. One part loss. But he seemed so pleased – as pleased as New Fenn could be.

What was Fenn's personality? It was harder to describe than Gamb's, with his sloppy easygoingness and perpetual glee. If she stripped away Fenn's bitterness – if she believed, as she desperately wanted to, that those qualities were temporary injuries to the boy she knew – then what was left?

Fenn was too serious to be funny. He was too quiet to be loud. He was too familiar in every way to be considered a stranger, and yet for her entire life most of their conversations had been about their experiences being someone else. She'd never had to think hard about who Fenn was, because Fenn's identity was wrapped up in being part of Julian.

She suddenly had a flashback to one of those conversations, three or four years ago. For weeks, Fenn had been asking her what day she was in. He kept trying to bring it up casually, but it was almost starting to worry her. Maybe something terrible was about to happen. Instead, one day she got to

Calisthenics and Fenn's eyes lit up as he motioned her over to the quadriceps machine he'd saved. "Today was 4471, wasn't it?" he'd asked.

When she'd told him it was, he leaned over, as far as he could with his leg trapped in a tube of metal. "Tell us everything – tell us about the horses."

It had been a nice day. Not an extravagant day, but a nice one, on vacation in Colorado, riding horses through a meadow; meeting the farmhand who showed Julian how to calm a pregnant mare; cooking chili in a firepit.

It was Fenn's favorite day, and he'd held onto it for two years – the smallest minute details of it – to talk about with Lona.

"That's an eleven, don't you think?" he asked when she was done re-describing the day for him. "That's got to be an eleven."

There was Fenn. The earnestness. The appreciation of the small things, and the desire to give them to other people. Even in Julian, she could find who Fenn was, inside his perfect Colorado vacation day, inside the experiences that he believed were worth an eleven. Fenn was a person who liked being outside. Fenn was a person who noticed simplicity. Fenn was a person who did not need much to be happy.

It was no wonder Fenn was now a person who was bitter and angry. Off Path he learned that the simple things that he had thought made him happy were just facsimiles of the real thing. Wasn't that worse than expecting the world and not getting it? Fenn had only expected a small piece of the world and it still couldn't be delivered. They hadn't even gotten the smell of grass right.

She wished right now that she could give Fenn back his perfect day, that they could go back to when none of them knew anything, except that after eating campfire chili, the right way to cook a marshmallow was to sear the outside layer quickly, then peel it off, then cook the next layer and peel it off, down and down and down, until everything had been peeled away and everything was goo.

"What are you thinking about?"

"I was thinking about that Colorado trip. The one you once told me was your favorite day. Actually – not really. I guess I was more thinking about talking to you about the Colorado trip. Do you remember?"

"I bet the real Colorado is a lot better. Maybe someday you'll go there. Rope a cow."

"But do you remember that day? You were so excited – you'd been keeping better track of my days than I was."

"Lona . . . Let's take our shoes off and walk in the grass, okay? It's better if you close your eyes."

"I just wanted to remember how we used to be. I thought – I thought it might help me figure out what I should do now."

"Let's not talk about the Path. It's back there. It's behind us. Let's just be here while we can be here. Doesn't the grass feel good?"

He slipped off his shoes and rose to his feet, eyes closed, arms hanging to his sides.

She sighed. It was hard to deny him simple pleasures, when she'd just decided that enjoying them was one of Fenn's defining characteristics. She kicked her shoes off as well, still the soft-soled ones from Path that were going to be in tatters soon, and stood barefoot on the earth. She liked the way the grass rose between her toes.

She liked the way that closing her eyes freed her brain from the rules she was trying to learn about living Off Path.

"I think you've been avoiding me." She hadn't planned on saying it so soon or so bluntly. It was easier to speak her deepest fears out loud with her eyes closed. "I think sometimes you wish I wasn't here."

She waited an eternity for him to answer.

"You're right." She winced. It was both validating and horrible to hear him admit what she'd suspected.

"It's because you know I want to know more about everything that's happened to you. At the Eighteens center."

"It's complicated."

"You've already told me about—"

"Let's not talk about them."

"About Byde and Czin and Cadr. If you told me about them, can't you tell me everything else?"

He sighed. "Telling you about them is something that hurts me. But telling you about everything else is something that will hurt you."

Lona didn't want to peek in order to check, but something about the way he said that sounded like his eyes were wide open.

"It can't be worse than what you already said."

"Yes. It can."

The grass rustled. It sounded at first like wind, but wind didn't rustle in a steady beat. Footsteps.

"What are you doing?" Genevieve was home. Lona's eyes flew open, hoping that she hadn't been watching for long.

81

She handed Fenn a small paper bag. "I got the chip Ilyf wanted. I hope. She'll have to take a look."

"Hi, Genevieve," Lona said.

Genevieve glanced at her, but addressed Fenn.

"What are you doing out here?"

"I thought Lona was ready to go outside."

"We were talking about Colorado." Lona wanted to show Genevieve that she, a younger, useless pod person, could still remember the manners that Genevieve seemed to have forgotten. It's what Julian would have done. Make a point, but indirectly. "A trip that Julian took when he was little. It was Fenn's favorite day."

A flicker of something traveled across Genevieve's face, just as Gamb and Ilyf re-appeared from around the side of the house. "With the horses?" Gamb panted, having caught the end of the conversation. "And that old guy who kept telling us to call him Curly-Q?"

"I loved Curly-Q," Ilyf said. "The blade of straw he was always chewing on."

Genevieve nodded. "Julian was very well traveled. It was a good reason to select him. That, and his high scores on the temperament exams."

She turned to Lona and raised a single eyebrow. "I'm majoring in Path Studies. Or didn't Fenn tell you?"

Fenn had obviously not told her, or Genevieve wouldn't have asked. Here was a giant piece of information that Lona had missed. She was not as observant a Pather as she'd thought she was. Her face burned.

"Is that the chip?" Ilyf asked, either oblivious to the tension, or wanting to break it up. "Let's go see if it's the right one."

The others started for the house, but Lona felt rooted to her spot.

"Fenn," she called. He paused, looking uncertainly between the porch where Genevieve waited and the grass where Lona still stood. "Fenn, come back here," she said more loudly.

Genevieve looked momentarily angry, but then surprised Lona by stepping languidly off the porch. She laced the fingers of both hands between Fenn's, slowly and deliberately, as if she wanted Lona to see.

"Go," she encouraged. "Your little friend is upset." She smiled brightly at Lona before going into the house. "I can always talk to him in our bedroom later."

"What is it, Lona?" Fenn sounded tired.

"You didn't tell me that Genevieve was majoring in Path Studies."

"Does it matter?"

"Of course it does. You know it does."

"I *don't* know that," he said.

"It means she's learning to – to *inspect* us."

"It means she's learning to understand us."

"So everyone in this house gets to understand something but me."

"No. Everyone in this house has to deal with knowing something horrible and sad but you."

"You're a coward."

She could almost see the words fly out of her mouth, a poison dart piercing Fenn's chest. Julian never would have said something like that. Julian would have found a way to be more diplomatic. Julian would not be shouting with

83

his friend. Lona waited for the feelings of disappointment that should accompany veering so far from the Path. Instead she felt like she had just seen a glimpse of herself. Not herself through Julian. But her. Lona.

"I'm a coward? For trying to protect you?"

"You're a coward for using me as an excuse not to find out what happened to your friends. You have Ilyf, this computer genius, who figured out how to hack into a system so that you could rescue me. But ever since I got here, you have me eating peanut butter and watching movies. What are you *doing* here besides waiting to die?"

"It's not that simple, Lona."

"It was simple enough for you to take action to save me."

"Are you saying you wish we hadn't?"

"I'm saying that you're scared, Fenn. You're scared – and that's not cowardly – but it's cowardly not to ask for my help when that's what we have always done." She softened. "Ones and elevens, Fenn."

He didn't need to ask what she meant. They both remembered the first day they became friends, the day Lona read his ones and elevens.

"I'm older than you. I'm supposed to be the one helping you down your Path."

"Not that day, you didn't. That day you were afraid to look. You didn't want to disobey. So I did it for you."

"We're not on Path anymore. You can't just look at a piece of paper and read my fortune."

"No. We're not on Path. Now we're just in life."

"So it's harder than it was when we were just kids in pods."

"Fenn, if you don't want to tell me what's going on, I'm going to find out somewhere else. So let me in, or tell me to go. Your choice."

For a long time, she thought he wasn't going to answer. She'd issued an ultimatum she had no idea how to follow through on.

"Tonight." He sounded resigned. "Meet by the back door. Midnight. I'll tell you everything I know. You'll hate it, but I'll tell you. And then you'll wish you didn't know."

12

Talia waited for the line to click as the Architect hung up the phone. Instead of a dial tone, though, she heard a man's startled grunt. Greevey had been listening in on her conversation.

That didn't seem his style. He was blustery and big-mouthed – the kind of person who would *tell* you that he was listening in on your conversations, who would make sure you knew that he was allowed to do it, and brag that he was paid a lot more money to listen to you doing your work than you were paid to do your work.

So this must mean he was really scared.

New rules were implemented as soon as Lona disappeared. Top-down rules, mandatory for all Path centers run by Pequod, like Sector 14 was. Rule number one: The employees of Sector 14 could not say anything about 'The Incident,' which was such a little word for such a colossal clusterfrack. The public could not know.

Rule number two: Ever since the kidnapping, there were double-staffed Touchers and Monitors. Everyone was issued new IDs, everyone was working overtime. Immediately after Lona's disappearance, Talia didn't go home for three days straight, instead catching naps in an unused pod in the repair room downstairs. All of this extra staffing had to be costing a fortune. They couldn't keep it up forever without blowing one of Path's top reasons for existing – that compared to old systems for raising at-risk children, and especially in an age of inexpensive technology – it was dirt cheap.

"I just got off the call," Talia said to Greevey, after knocking on his office door. She decided to carry on the façade that this would be news to him. Did he know that she knew? Exactly how ridiculous was this charade?

"Good. I would've joined you, of course, but I'm very busy today."

This charade was completely ridiculous.

"I just told him that my report was comprehensive, and that I didn't have anything to add."

"Was that the truth?"

It was close to being true. She really hadn't seen Fenn. She really hadn't expected anything to go wrong. She really had woken up on the pavement, roused by the screaming of the Chinese woman who owned Wok Don't Run next door. She'd accepted a bag of frozen peas to put on her throbbing bicep and then driven herself back to work. The things that were untrue about the report weren't lies as much as they were omissions. She omitted the fact that she'd intended to leave Lona alone in the car. Why should she mention it? She didn't know why she'd done it. It was stupid. She should have honked the horn until a remmersing technician came outside.

"Talia, I don't think I need to tell you that you are at a very important crossroads."

"I am?"

"I could easily fire you, of course. The Incident happened on your watch. Or, we could recognize that sometimes mistakes happen that are . . . beyond our control. If you see what I mean."

What he meant was that he didn't want Talia blabbing to everyone how quickly he'd made the decision to send Lona to the remmersion center. That's what he meant. That would look bad for everyone.

"Because," Greevey continued, "I really think your career could advance. Perhaps you're interested in completing more education. Maybe—"

Talia didn't get to hear what else he planned on bribing her with, because instead she felt someone tap her arm. The newcomer cleared her throat.

"Excuse me?"

There was a Toucher behind Talia, a short one who first tried standing on her tiptoes to see over Talia's shoulder and then resorted to peering under Talia's armpit. Sanjeeta – she was one of the new ones.

"Yes?" Greevey fumed. He was just getting into the lecture.

"We have a new arrival. Male. In his 1500s."

"Really!?" Talia didn't mean to sound so effusive. But the Julian Path rarely got anyone so old. Too many background checks. Too many pre-parenting personality tests. The system was supposed to prevent this. In the eighteen years she'd worked there, there had been maybe seven.

"He's in the CT lounge. He needs to be measured for his pod, and all the other Monitors are on rounds."

Greevey looked like he wanted to have a good reason for Talia to stay, but lacked the imagination. "Talia," he said. "I'd like you to go assist Sanjeeta."

"Of course." As if that wasn't exactly what Sanjeeta had asked, and what she was already heading to do.

The Coping Technicians' lounge was a small room with a tile floor, down the hall from the bay. Monitors were allowed, too, but they had less need for a lounge since they got their own workstations in the control room. Every time Talia visited, she felt like she was sitting at the wrong table in the cafeteria.

The new boy was thin, gangly, with a spiky haircut. He wore a blue T-shirt with a fish on it and sat on a faded sofa, blowing bubbles through the straw of a juicebox. Talia pulled her measuring tape out from her pocket and gently measured his leg from his knee to his ankle, the circumference of his head. While she did this, Sanjeeta knelt down to the boy's level and asked him jovial, kindergarten teacher questions.

"Hello, little boy. Do you remember me? I brought you the juice before? I'm just going to ask you a few things. If you want, we can play with some toys while we talk. I have a box over here with dinosaurs in it – and a castle!"

Talia wasn't sure if it was developmentally appropriate for four-year-olds to roll their eyes, but that's what this kid was doing. Rolling his eyes at Sanjeeta's suggestion, and refusing to look in her direction.

"Cool shirt," Talia said to the boy, deliberately avoiding eye contact, casually jotting down that his left arm was half a centimeter longer than his right. "What is that, a goldfish?"

"Rainbowfish."

"Neat."

"I'm Gabriel." He allowed Talia to shake his hand, then puffed out his lower lip at Sanjeeta. "Not Little Boy."

Sanjeeta giggled. "That was going to be my first question for you – What's your name? – and you already got it right!"

"Do you like fish?" Gabriel asked Talia, continuing his ignoring campaign against Sanjeeta.

"I don't know much about fish." Talia deftly lifted Gabriel's arm and measured from armpit to his waist, then from his waist to hip bone.

"I like fish. I have a guppy."

"What's your guppy's name?"

"Puppy."

Over Gabriel's head, Sanjeeta was biting the inside of her cheek to keep from laughing.

"Can you answer a question for *me* now?" Sanjeeta asked. "Do you know when your birthday is?" Sanjeeta already knew his birthday, just like she already knew the answers to all of the questions she would ask him. It was all part of the assessment.

"April," he said wearily. "Tenth."

He'll go in Lona's space, Talia thought. It was the spot most logical for him to fill – central location, working outlets. *So his new name will be Djna.*

"Do you remember what you did for your birthday?"

"Quarium."

Sanjeeta smiled at Talia. "His mother took him to the aquarium. Then she brought him home and tried to drown him in the bathtub. The housekeeper walked in."

Gabriel was back to blowing bubbles in his juice. Or pretending to.

"So if he remembers the aquarium," Sanjeeta continued, "then he remembers what happened after that, and lots of other things, too."

Gabriel – Djna – was at a cusp age. Children aged two or younger could be assimilated into Path fairly easily with the right mixture of prescription drugs. But Gabriel – Djna – was over three. He would either need dangerously intense drug therapy, or—

"I think we should remmerse him, don't you?"

Remmersion was the other option. It wasn't ideal – Path infrastructure tended to work better if it was layered over existing brain cell activity. The woman who trained Talia for this job had explained it in architectural terms: Sometimes old houses have better bones than new houses. When you're building a new structure, work with what's there if you can.

"You're the expert," Talia said. Sanjeeta was the one qualified to make this assessment, not her. Sanjeeta's approval, and Mr. Greevey's, would only be the final yeses in a long line of permission-gathering. There would have been a trial. A social worker. An investigation as to why the father or grandparents were not fit guardians. This was a serious matter.

"He showed signs of reactive attachment disorder earlier. He screamed when we tried to bathe him. I'm afraid that trying to cope with this on a pharmacological level isn't going to be enough. Better to have a clean slate, I think."

Sanjeeta grinned at Gabriel and ruffled his hair. "Feel like coming for a ride?" When he nodded, she held out her hand and Gabriel hopped off the sofa to take it. Sanjeeta looked at Talia. "Feel like coming for a ride?"

The new rules required at least two adults – one Monitor and one Coping Technician – to accompany all Pathers on any off-site transport. But when Talia thought about another car ride back to the remmersion place, her skin felt like it was crawling with lice.

"Paige or Sam should be free now," she said. "Take one of them – I need to customize a pod for him, anyway."

She squatted on her knees, down to Gabriel's level. "It was nice to meet you. Thanks for telling me about your fish." She started to affectionately clasp her hand on his shoulder, but as soon as her palm made contact, Gabriel let out a panicked shriek and twisted his head. Talia felt a sharp pain in her hand. There was now a mark. A perfect indentation of four small teeth.

"Sorry," Sanjeeta said. "I should have warned you. That's where his mom held him when she pushed him underwater."

Now that Talia looked closer, she could see – a burst blood vessel near his neck.

"Oh well," Sanjeeta sighed. "We won't have to worry about this in a couple of hours, will we?" Gabriel's left hand was clutching hers; his right held the juice box, which was now empty and deflated. "Bucko, you're going to be good as new!"

After they left, Talia went back to her desk to check the inventory for available pods. She typed in a few measurements, and the search function spat back three possible matches, all in storage. She took the stairs instead of the elevator. They would be deserted, and she didn't feel like talking to anyone. Her hand hurt.

She started this job not knowing what this job would be. Path was so new then. The recruiter told her she could use her engineering degree and she could help children. It sounded like a good idea. She knew something about kids who needed help. She remembered moving into dorms her first semester of college and how horrified her roommate's parents looked when she told them she had no parents – that she'd been on her own since she was fourteen, and that being on her own was better than when she had had parents, anyway. She tried to say it in a joking voice. They didn't laugh.

The dorms were fine, though. Her roommate found a boyfriend their second month, and slept at his apartment almost every night. Better to be alone in a dorm room than to lie paralyzed in a bedroom waiting for the door to open, to decide whether to cry or just pretend to be asleep.

When she started the job, there were still people who didn't get it. Who didn't get it technologically – "They can do that with virtual reality now?" they'd say, not understanding how much bigger this was than virtual reality. Some of them got the technology but didn't agree with the concept. But Talia believed in the Path. Not like Greevey, because it was a paycheck, but because she needed to believe that society was looking for ways to make things better for children.

The storage room was cold, not toasty and temperature-regulated like the bay, and Talia remembered too late her hoodie hanging on the back of her chair upstairs. She shivered, then consulted the grid she'd printed off to help locate the potential pods for Gabriel. Djna.

The first one had a service tag hanging on it – faulty sensors – but the second appeared to be in good working order and fit the required specifications. With a slender wrench and screwdriver, she adjusted the arm cradles so they would fit Gabriel's skinny forearms, then lowered the footrest to accommodate his long legs. She was done with all of the adjustments after thirty minutes, and when she checked her watch, she saw that it was almost time for Quadrant 1 to have a restroom break. Perfect time to swap out Lona's old pod for the new one. It wheeled onto the elevator making only the tiniest squeak. The squeak she could fix with a little bit of WD40 upstairs.

After finishing the installation, Talia realized she hadn't been outside all day. The weather was supposed to be beautiful. Maybe she would drive somewhere for lunch. She didn't do that often. But it would be good to get away. If she took the back exit, she wouldn't have to walk past Greevey's office again. She checked her pockets, relieved to feel the bulge of her car keys and a wad of cash, then slid out the rear entrance into the parking garage.

"Playing hookie?" Marvin, the security guard, waved at her from the entrance. He was nice. She should talk more to him.

"Just getting some fresh air."

Before she could reach her truck, though, she was distracted by the cheerful sound of a car honking. The Path van. It had an irritatingly pleasant honk. *Meep-meep*, like a cartoon caricature of what a honk should sound like. Sanjeeta was driving, and Sam was in the passenger seat. Since they'd both waved, Talia had no choice but to wait for the van to pull around, coming to a neat stop directly in front of her.

"No, it was mouse poop," Sam said as he swung his legs out the door. "I know what a bean looks like, and it was mouse poop."

"If there was a mouse dropping in your burrito the last time you went to Café Olé, then *why* would you suggest eating there today?"

"Because it has the best enchiladas."

As he slammed his door shut, he called to Talia. "Hey! Weird – I thought that was Paige's voice on the phone when I called. Thanks for coming help unload."

Before Talia could explain that it had been Paige – that she was just trying to get a sandwich – Sam was gesturing to the rear of the van. "Can you?"

Talia held the back door of the van open while Sanjeeta engaged the ramp and Sam slowly rolled down the portable chair with the small boy in it.

He wasn't sleeping. Sometimes they were sleeping when they came back, but he wasn't. He wasn't crying, either. He wasn't moving. What he was doing was sitting. If it could be described like that – even sitting implied some kind of intentional act. Slumping, maybe. His eyes were glassy. They passed over Talia's face the way they might have passed over a pair of drapes or a picture of a cow or a bowl of fruit. His mind was scrubbed clean. A thin thread of drool spooled from the corner of his mouth and down his chin. When Talia reached out to touch his face, his head lolled to the side like a rag doll, grazing off the padded headrest.

His blue fish T-shirt had twisted itself around his small body, revealing a patch of skin that was milky white and unbearably soft-looking. She resisted the urge to fix the shirt. *He's getting new clothes*, she reminded herself. One of his shoelaces was untied. *He's getting new shoes. They'll need to take these off anyway.* Around his ankle was the tracking bracelet that all Pathers were now required to wear. Part of the new rules. Too bad they hadn't been part of the old rules. Lona and the others would have easily been found.

Talia couldn't see the mark at the base of the boy's skull, but she knew it was there – a round indentation made by the prod that the remmersing techs would have used to send the right pulses into his brain.

"There we go!" Sanjeeta said. She folded the ramp back into the van and brushed her hands together. Pleasure in a job well done. "I should go fill out the paperwork right away, shouldn't I? Mr. Greevey seems to be a stickler for protocol."

Sanjeeta continued to stand there – waiting for a response from Talia.

"The pod is all ready," Talia said. "I'll go back up to the control room and make sure that the feeds are working, if Sam wants to take Djna down to the bay now."

"Fantastic!"

It was only after she watched Sam and Sanjeeta disappear that Talia realized how easily the name "Djna" had come to her. Gabriel was totally gone.

13

Midnight was cold. Cold and damp, and the trees that looked green earlier were now just shadows. It was almost silent, but not quite. The cicadas hummed, and underneath that drone something sounded like rushing water. Sounded, irrationally, like the noise of the pods in the bay.

"Ready?"

Fenn brusquely closed the back door behind him, pausing once to look up at a dark window on the second floor. He was wearing thick-soled shoes.

"Does everyone else know where we're going?"

"No."

"Do you think they should? Ilyf or Genevieve?"

"No."

He slipped in front of her, heading toward the clearing. Lona scrambled after. She might be faster than him, but his shoes were better, he knew the area, and he'd obviously built up lung capacity Lona didn't have. She sensed he was trying to go so fast that she would decide to turn back. She refused. She focused on his footprints in the mud and made her shoes land in each one. After a hundred yards, Fenn roughly pushed aside a branch to clear a trail, and it flew back, slicing Lona across the cheek.

"Ow." She raised her hand to the scratch.

Fenn whirled around. When he realized he was the one responsible for Lona's cry, he slowed down. He still didn't talk to her, but he slowed down.

"Where are we going?" she asked when the house had disappeared and the woods had grown blacker.

"The creek."

"Why are we going there?"

"Because I don't want to leave them in the house – it's safer down here."

Who was them? Why were they at the creek? Did Fenn have a whole colony of Coping Technicians who were living on lilypads? She was panting too hard to make the joke.

They moved together through the forest, leaves crushing under feet. After ten minutes, she fell into a rhythm. When she could let go of her worries and ignore the reason for this midnight trek, she could almost enjoy it. It felt good to do something so physical – to hike through the damp, focusing on tangible problems that had solutions: where to put her feet so they wouldn't slip. Which branch would support her weight if she grabbed it. How she would find the house again if she lost sight of Fenn.

The rushing sound from the top of the hill grew louder. She could smell the creek before she could see it, earthy and cold and muddy. The water was high, rippling swiftly over rocks and branches. The moon peeked through one of the oak trees, forming a yellow pool of light on the water.

"Oh!" Her brain stopped before her feet and she stumbled. "Look at that."

Two river otters splashed in the water, their fur sleek

and their noses black and shiny. One chased the other, through the current and between flat stones. Fenn was watching the otters, too, as one of them reached a dam made of logs, then flipped on its back and swam in the opposite direction. Lona knew about swimming, and these were lovely swimmers.

"The first time I saw one, I wondered if I could get one somewhere," Fenn said.

"An otter? You wanted an otter?"

"I thought I could live in a house on the water, and I could have an otter named Otto. Dumb name, I know."

"When was that?" Julian had never seen otters in real life. He always went to the big cats at the zoo, though Lona had a vague memory of walruses. "Does it happen in 6000s?"

Fenn glanced at her quickly. "It happened five months ago. At Eighteens."

One of the otters climbed out of the water and found a patch of soft needles, flattening itself to the ground. It was adorable, but also creepy, like an otter-skin rug. She didn't like how vulnerable the otter was out of its element.

"I haven't meant to shut you out," Fenn said. "It wasn't about me trying to act like I knew what was best for you. Maybe it was partly cowardice – I didn't want to see it that way, but maybe it was. But it's also that if something happens to us, it's better for you to be able to say you knew nothing, and have it be the truth. I shouldn't even have told you about . . ."

The sentence hung in the air, trailed into nothing. If he wouldn't finish it, she would. "About how they're all dead?"

He nodded.

It felt strange to be standing here, staring at each other face to face. In Path, their conversations were always side by side, each of them exercising on adjacent machines. "Can we sit down?" she asked.

He gestured toward a flat, moss-covered rock on the river bank. She sank onto it, stroked the cool moss with her hand. They both looked at the river.

"You're the rebel army."

"The mighty rebel army."

"How did you become rebels? How did you . . . escape?"

He laughed, though Lona didn't think her question was particularly funny. "I didn't escape. I was a perfect graduate of the Eighteens Training Center for Post-Path Integration. ETCPPI. I expect they'll shorten that, though. It's not the sort of inspirational acronym that gets a lot of funding. But then, they were still figuring that out with their first class."

"I think I'm going to need you to start earlier. At the beginning."

"From when I left Path?"

"From then. From the beginning after the end."

Fenn wordlessly walked to the creek and rinsed his hands in the water. He patted them dry on the grass, then walked back to the rock, and felt around underneath. When he pulled his hand out again, he was holding a plastic bag, zipped shut, wrapped around something about the size of a deck of cards. He opened it, and handed the contents to Lona.

A stack of photographs, creased around the edges.

"I don't want to keep them in the house," he said. "In case something happens to me. I just want these to be safe.

Everyone else thought I should get rid of them but I couldn't."

With the reflection off the water and the light of the moon, Lona could just make out the images on the photograph. It was a group shot. Gamb and Ilyf stood on one side, and Fenn was at the other end of the line. Next to Ilyf was a petite girl with wavy black hair, and then a curvy girl with an overbite that made her look like a rabbit, and a boy with knobby elbows and knees. They were all standing in front of what looked like a retirement home, with a circle driveway and ramps instead of stairs, and landscaped bushes planted in gravel.

"What is this?"

Fenn picked up a small branch and started pulling off its leaves. "Seven weeks."

"Seven weeks?"

"Seven weeks is the beginning after the end. That's how much time you get. For post-Path integration. To learn to be like everyone else." He shook his head. "Correction. To learn to be not like Julian."

"I don't understand." She touched the faces in the photograph. All six of them were smiling.

"We can't stay in Path forever, Lona. It wouldn't be legal to keep us there. Once we turn eighteen, we're technically adults. They can't keep paying for us – there's no funding. We have to go Off Path. Post-Path integration is supposed to prepare you for that."

"To live . . . alone."

"Off Path. On our own, Outside."

"But what happens to Julian?"

"Yes, Julian. What *happens* to precious Julian?" He hurled his branch into the water, watching the current take it away. "That's what we all wanted to know. Funny, no? We'd all been told that in a couple weeks we were going to be shoved out on our own, and we were all just worried about what happened to Julian. How does the story *end*?"

He scoured the ground looking for another stick to rip apart. "Julian's fine. We got the highlights reel, through college. He went to Northwestern. Started as a Chemistry major, switched to History. Dated a girl named Lucy but they broke up because she was Pre-Med and didn't have time. Sarafina has cancer, by the way. Ovarian. She couldn't make it to Julian's college graduation because she was too sick. I'm surprised they showed us that, actually. They must have figured it taught us important things about compassion or bedside manner, or how to act when your friend is dying. Actually, now that I think about it, those are very useful lessons. For our current situation."

Her heart stung, abruptly, like a staccato note in Julian's choral music. To have Sarafina's life, Julian's life – *her* life – reduced to a sardonic monologue. To have Fenn make jokes about it.

"That was cruel," she spat out.

"What was?"

"Everything you just said."

"You wanted to know."

"You didn't have to tell it like it was some ironic story."

"It's not a fairy tale."

"You know what I mean."

"It doesn't matter, Lona. That's what I'm trying to tell

103

you. You can learn it in a pod set to nice music, like I did, or you can learn it like a ripped off Band-Aid. In the end, it doesn't matter." He sounded pleading, not angry. "Do you still want me to go on?"

"Tell me."

He raised his eyebrows, giving her one last out.

"I *am* the one who wanted to know," she said. "I still do."

"They didn't talk about any of that at first – about college or anything. At first it just looked like the bay – a little smaller, but the pods were the same. It started with the night before Julian's birthday. Some swimming guys had this whole thing planned – the Legal Debauchery Tour. Getting a lottery ticket. Buying cigarettes. All the stuff you can't do until you're eighteen. Julian didn't really seem that into it, but I don't know for sure because I never saw the Legal Debauchery Tour."

"What happened?"

"I woke up. I woke up and there was a man in my visioneers – an older guy, in a suit. He congratulated me on 'Completing the Path,' and said that it was now time to begin the next phase of my journey."

"What was the next phase of your journey?" In the picture, far behind the smiling six, a guy on a riding lawn mower cut the grass.

"There are more pictures."

The top photo made a moist, ripping sound as she tore it off the stack. In the one underneath, Fenn, Ilyf and the dark-haired girl sat at a table, studiously reading what at first looked like books, but were, upon closer inspection, fashion magazines. A middle-aged woman stood at the head of the table, pointing to one of the pages. In the second, Gamb, the buck-toothed girl and the knobbly-kneed boy were in a kitchen. The boy proudly held a loaf of some kind of bread, which Gamb was pretending to lick. In this one they weren't wearing their loose Path uniforms anymore. Under the cooking aprons, there were T-shirts and pants.

"Byde was the best cook," Fenn said. "He always got textures right on the first try."

"Who's this?" Lona pointed to the older woman in the magazine picture.

"That's Celine. She was one of our Advanced Coping Technicians. ACTors. Cadr called them Super Touchers." Seeing Fenn smile, a real smile, made her ache. It reminded her of all the real smiles they shared in Path, and of all the time passed since then.

"So this is where you learned to be Off Path."

"It was gradual. The apartments were there so we could practice living in them. We started to get some vocational training so we could find jobs or apply to colleges or whatever. I was learning to work in a pharmacy. Ilyf was good with computers. They'd be unhappy to realize how good she got. After a couple of weeks, we got field trips. Into town, mostly, but sometimes nature ones."

"Where you saw otters," Lona pictured all of the people in the pictures sitting on a yellow school bus with pack lunches.

"Otter babies. In one of the rivers that feeds into the Chesapeake."

"And then they made you leave?"

"The week after the otters was graduation. They had

caps for us. Caps and gowns. We all had to walk across the stage and collect Path diplomas. Some of us had to walk across twice, because a video camera wasn't working. We didn't get our diplomas again, though. They said it was just the walking and smiling that was important."

"Oh."

"The ceremony wouldn't have been so bad, except for the caps and gowns. They said we couldn't take them off all day. Didn't we want everyone to know that we were unique Path graduates? That we had avoided tragedy in our childhoods and were now ready to be productive members of society?"

It sounded like something they would have said, like some greeting that would have been played in Lona's pod. She could almost hear the oboe tone. "But that didn't happen?"

"No one *wanted* us, Lona. Genevieve was the only person. She came to the graduation. She said she was looking to rent out rooms. When Cadr was killed—"

He cut himself off, as he had before.

"What do you think happened to them?" she asked. "Who do you think – do you have theories?"

He sneered. "All I do is theories, Lona. That's all I do, every day. Who would want us dead? Why near our birthdays? If it is people from Path, then why would they raise us to eighteen just to kill us? If it's not people from Path, then why would they care about us at all? If it's Path, then we obviously shouldn't contact any authorities, right?"

"But if it's not Path, then you *should* contact them because you want all of the help you can get."

"Right. You understand. All I do is theories and waiting to die."

"And saving me."

"Or dooming you."

"Saving."

"And doing situps to strengthen my abs, and trying to keep Gamb and Ilyf from killing each other, and hating this angry person I've become."

"You're still you," she said before she could help it. Why should she presume to know who he still was? She didn't know if she said it to reassure him, or to reassure herself – that all of this was reversible.

"Do you think so?" His voice broke.

The pictures were still in Lona's hands. There was one of the rabbit-toothed girl holding up a jar of honey triumphantly – she must have just discovered what an unusual, sticky texture it had. In another, all six of them wore new pajamas – you could still see the creases in the flannel legs – looking excited at having sleeping clothes that were different from waking clothes.

"This is about me, too, Fenn," she said quietly.

"Because I've dragged you into it."

"No. Because if something happens to the three of you, I'll be on my own. And because now that I'm Off Path, too, how do we know that I won't become as angry as you? Or that someone won't try to kill me?"

"I didn't even think of that."

He was looking at her in an odd way, too hard and too long. Lona was remembering that day in Path when he had stroked her arm with his soft fingertips.

"See? I was right to make you bring me here."

"You were right about so many things, Lona," he said quietly. He hadn't moved his eyes from her face.

"What are you talking about?"

"About this. Me needing to tell you. But also about other things. You were right that We should have gone to Grandpa's hospital room before he died, instead of getting scared. You were right that the best season is fall."

He was remembering minute conversations that had happened years ago, as if all of their interactions had been eleven-rated days that he had committed to memory. "Mostly you were right to question it. I was always looking for reasons to trust the Path. You knew to question it when I believed."

"Maybe now it's good to believe in something," she said. "Maybe we all need to believe together. In whatever."

"Do you believe in me? Do you really think – do you think I'm still me?"

"I do. I know it." For a second she wanted to reach for his hand, the way he had once reached for her. She had almost worked up the nerve – his fingers were long and lovely, splayed on the rock. She moved her hand, tentatively, keeping her eyes on his. He wanted this, too, she told herself, this kind of comfort. She could touch him and everything would go back to how it was supposed to be.

A splash jerked her back to the present. An otter, sliding into the water. She pulled her hand back onto her own lap; whatever boldness she'd felt disappeared.

"You know what you helping means, though?" Fenn asked. "It means that we're going to all have to go Outside."

Outside. A place Lona had always been taught to fear. A place that was supposed to be dangerous for people like her.

She looked down at the photographs still in her hand.

"Fenn, the girls in the pictures . . . the one with the big teeth, is that one Cadr?"

"Yes." He sounded surprised. "How did you guess?"

"No reason."

But really it was this: Czin had the prettier face – so delicate she looked like a doll. Cadr's features were less perfect, which made her seem more friendly. When she smiled, her top teeth bit her bottom lip, like she was literally biting back a laugh. Her face was open and honest in a disarming way.

Her face was the one that was hardest to imagine blasted in half. And so somehow Lona knew that must've been what happened.

14

"You're still squinting."

"I'm not. I'm looking right at you."

Genevieve frowned. "You're looking right at me with squinting eyes."

Lona tried opening her eyes wider. The light hurt – maybe she *was* squinting – but she made herself keep them open until they watered. "Better?"

"Worse. Now you look like someone taped your eyelids to your forehead. Are you watching me?"

Lona was watching. Lona had been watching Genevieve for an hour now, as they stood side by side in front of the mirror in Genevieve's room.

The assimilation lessons were Lona's idea, but it was Fenn's that Genevieve be the teacher. "If you all learned it, why can't you all teach me?" she asked, but Fenn insisted that none of them were natural enough, that she needed to learn from someone natively raised Off Path. What Lona was receiving was a condensed version, then, of what the others received at Eighteens, which was in turn a condensed version of life. It did not inspire large amounts of confidence.

"Do you see the difference?" Genevieve asked. "When

you look at my face and your face, do you see the difference?"

Yes, Lona wanted to say. You look like the poster of the beach volleyball player that Nick kept in his locker, and I look like an elf. Her chin was pointy. Her nose was pointy. Even her ears were a little pointy. She'd never spent so much time thinking about what she looked like, and all of the acute angles that poked out of her body.

"And your voice. Do you hear it? It's still wrong."

"*What's* wrong with it?"

They'd had the same conversation a dozen times, but Genevieve couldn't describe it in a way Lona could fix. Something to do with Lona's jaw being too tight, and speaking in a register that was too low. Lona couldn't hear what was wrong with her voice, but theoretically understood it. Sometimes when Julian stayed home sick, he would lie on the couch and watch old black-and-white movies with his mom on public television, the ones with detectives in fedoras and women in dark lipstick. Everyone spoke English in them, but it was a strange kind of English. Not accented, exactly, just different. That must be what was happening. There was something that made her sound foreign – not like she was coming from another country, but like she was coming from another time.

"I can't hear it."

Genevieve rolled her eyes.

"I can't *hear* it. I'm trying. Can I just promise not to talk?"

111

"*You're* trying? *I'm* trying."

When she and Fenn first told everyone what they'd discussed, Gamb immediately agreed and Ilyf didn't require much convincing either. *I just want to do something,* she'd said. *Anything is better than sitting here waiting.*

Genevieve was harder. Genevieve was just . . . harder. She hated that they all had to travel together, but Fenn thought Genevieve's knowledge was necessary; Gamb wanted to go with Fenn; Ilyf wouldn't let Gamb go alone; everybody agreed that Lona couldn't be left by herself either in the house or Outside. It was like one of those logic puzzles: you're having a dinner party and certain people will only sit next to certain other people, so what does the seating chart look like? Genevieve, Lona bet, would find this a lot more enjoyable if Lona hadn't been invited to the dinner party at all.

This was their third day. Lona had gone from barely seeing Genevieve at all to spending hours a day with her. It wasn't all unpleasant. Genevieve was smart. Unrelenting, yes. But definitely smart. She anticipated the problems that Lona would have, and she knew the Path references that could help her fix them. She was never warm, but she was insightful. "Julian swims, correct?" she'd said yesterday. "It would help your voice if you breathed deeper – like he would when he was diving in the pool."

"Maybe we should take a break," Lona said now.

"*I'm* not tired."

Genevieve was right. Time was limited. If they were taking breaks when they could have been doing something that would help the others, Lona never would have forgiven herself, and she knew Genevieve wouldn't either. Genevieve worked unbelievably hard.

Only instead of acknowledging this to each other – that the long hours were a symbol of concern, that they shared things in common and were both on the same side – they'd somehow turned the work into a match of wills. Lona didn't even understand how this had happened. It wasn't anything she'd experienced in Path. Under different circumstances, it might have been a good question – Why don't we get along? – to ask Genevieve.

"I know it must be hard – to have another person in your house. I appreciate you doing this for me." Lona tried to smooth over the tension.

"I'm not doing this for you."

"I appreciate you doing this anyway. All of this."

Genevieve sighed. "I guess we could work on your wardrobe. Sit." She turned and began to rummage through her closet, throwing occasional pieces of clothing onto the chair. Now the only place left to sit was the bed, and Lona felt wrong about sitting there. Instead she leaned awkwardly against the bedpost and watched as Genevieve tossed out a sheer red top, a slim skirt, a pair of silky pants, all with labels that even Julian, who rarely wore anything but T-shirts, would have recognized as designer.

"Genevieve?"

"Hmm?"

"Why did you decide to study Path?"

"Why not?"

"It just doesn't seem something someone like you would be interested in."

"You mean, why did such a spoiled princess choose a helping profession?" Genevieve asked sharply.

"No – I mean – no."

Although, in fact, yes. That's exactly what she wondered.

"Put these on." Genevieve handed her a pair of jeans and a flowery blue top with complicated buttons. Lona slid her arms into the sleeves but couldn't figure out how to fasten the back.

"Here." Genevieve brusquely grabbed Lona's waist. Lona involuntarily stiffened at the feeling of hands on her body. She relaxed when she realized Genevieve was just pivoting her around to fix the buttons, but not before Genevieve noticed her discomfort.

"The touching," Genevieve said. "Pathers and touching."

"We're just not used to it. Not unexpected like that."

"You're like turtles in a shell."

"Fenn lets you touch him."

"Yes. He lets me."

"Doesn't he want you to?"

Genevieve hesitated. "Of course he does."

"Did it take a long time?"

She had to know the answer. It had taken him years to stroke her wrist. How much more quickly had he bonded with Genevieve?

Genevieve ignored her question, suddenly engrossed in searching through her vanity. "Makeup now."

She produced a tube of something peachy and iridescent. "Put this on your face. Dots on your forehead, nose and cheeks, then blend them in." The cream smelled like baby powder and gardenias. It made Lona's lips feel greasy and her face feel smothered, what glue felt like in that kindergarten game of spreading it on your fingers, letting it dry and then peeling it off.

Genevieve continued to rummage through her drawer, lining up mascara and eyeshadow, holding up different shades to Lona's face.

"My parents," she said abruptly, without raising her eyes.

"What?"

"Everyone thought I'd pick something useless. Communications. English. Live off Daddy's money, spoiled rich girl that I am. I knew they'd like it if I chose this."

"That's . . . admirable."

"I don't talk about it a lot."

"Oh." Lona was confused. "You don't have to now."

"I know I don't have to," she smirked. "But I'm trying to be *nice*. Besides. You're oddly easy to talk to. Your face hasn't learned to express judgment. Or disgust."

Lona kept her face unexpressive as Genevieve applied her lipstick, careful not to show surprise at this divulgence of personal information.

"Why don't your parents ever come over?"

Genevieve raised one eyebrow. "We don't really talk. They think that I'm living in a dorm on campus."

"So you don't have any brothers or sisters or anything?"

"Well, now I have all of *you* lovely people. And of course, I have everybody who is in Path."

The weirdest thing about Genevieve saying that sentence was that, under the layers of dripping sarcasm, Lona had the unshakable sense that she actually meant it. Exposure made Genevieve more likable. This must be the version of her that Fenn saw behind closed doors, when they came upstairs to sleep. But then, just as soon as the shield had lowered, it was back up again.

"Turn around," Genevieve ordered now, inspecting Lona's full ensemble. "Your butt looks weird. Are you sticking it out on purpose?"

"Can I come in?" Fenn was standing in the doorway. "Ilyf wanted to look something up in one of your textbooks."

"We're done, I think," Genevieve said. "As done as we can be."

It made Lona uncomfortable whenever Fenn interrupted their work. It was a reminder that he slept here, that he belonged here, and that Lona was the odd person out. She was the thing that was not like the other, like in that old children's show.

Fenn looked at Lona. She thought he'd be pleased – she knew she'd gotten better at some things, like maintaining eye contact and making her posture less rigid. Instead he looked disappointed.

"That bad?"

"You just don't look like you anymore. You look like everyone else." There was a tiny, tiny birthmark under his right ear, shaped a little like the state of Ohio. How had she never noticed that before? Did he always have it? Of course he did. Birthmarks were things you were born with.

"I'm still me just like you're still you," she said.

"I'm glad."

Behind him, Genevieve slammed her makeup case shut. Fenn jumped at the noise.

"Neve," he said, looking so quickly away from Lona that it felt like ripping off a Band-Aid. "Thank you."

It was one of those 'thank you's that had a lot of meaning behind it. Fenn and Genevieve were never affectionately teasing, like Gamb and Ilyf. But sometimes, like now, they seemed to have a bond that was built deep below the surface where Lona couldn't see or understand it.

"You're welcome," said Genevieve, just as intensely. She crossed the room and smoothed back a piece of Fenn's hair where it had fallen across his forehead. He barely flinched. "I did the best I could."

"You did amazingly."

She didn't have to witness the moment any longer. Gamb burst through the doorway, carrying a sandwich. "Lona, dahling! You look so civilized! Is everyone ready for tomorrow?"

She wasn't ready in the least.

15

The station wasn't far – fifteen minutes using the shortcut through the woods. It was just a plain wooden platform: no ticket agent, no kiosk.

The train was cylindrical with a pointed nose. It arrived on time, silently. The entrance was blocked with a gate, which opened every time Genevieve tapped her OneCard – five times, once for each of them. Lona had a OneCard, too, but just a decoy. The real ones contained medical information and managed banking.

"The first couple passenger cars will be full," Genevieve said, when all of them were crowded in the tiny vestibule. "Just keep heading toward the back." Lona let Genevieve go first through the car's doors, which opened automatically. Then she gasped.

"Fenn," she whispered. "Visioneers."

The train cars were filled, as Genevieve had predicted, with morning commuters wearing suits and skirts. On their bodies, at least. On their eyes, they wore black goggles like the ones from Path. Sleeker, though. Less chunky. And some, now that she looked closer, weren't black at all, but dark purple, or tortoiseshell. Fashion visioneers?

"Shhh," Genevieve hissed. Lona clamped her mouth shut until they reached an empty car at the rear of the train.

"Visioneers!" she whispered again, as soon as the door to their compartment closed, giving them some privacy. "Why are they wearing them?"

"They're not on Path," Genevieve said. "Some of them are just braincationing, going to Paris for a little while. Some of them are celebritrekking."

"What's that?"

"Renting a celebrity's life for a couple days. Mildly entertaining, but usually it's only C-listers who need the publicity, and even they redline out the personal stuff you'd really want to see. But you can ride with them in a limo to the Golden Globes, or whatever."

Lona watched as a male passenger crossing through the car paused to press a few buttons along the earpiece. Changing the channel? Fixing the volume?

"You look wonderful in blue," he purred, his face turned toward Lona's. She looked down. The shirt she had borrowed was a deep aquamarine. "You should wear it more often."

"Ah. Thank you?" Genevieve kicked her seat. The man continued the conversation as if Lona wasn't there at all. "No, I think I'll stay on the beach for a while, Cathy. Go ahead. No, *you* go ahead. No, you. No, *you*." He giggled hysterically. "No, youuuuuu." The giggling man drifted down the aisle without looking back. As soon as the far door closed behind him, Lona felt a tickle in her ear. Gamb.

"No," he said, wispy and falsetto. "*You*."

The landscape was rural in the beginning – trees and fields of young soybean crops – but soon houses appeared, grew closer together, and became industrial buildings. Then everything disappeared as the train went under a tunnel, crawling deeper into the earth, before climbing again toward a light.

"One more time," Fenn said. "I want to go over the plan one more time."

Fenn had made them drill it over and over again. They would get off the train. They would go to Genevieve's university, where she had an appointment to meet with a professor who taught criminal justice, to discuss a made-up paper she wanted to write about crimes in the city. He would give Genevieve a pass that would allow her student access to police department files. They would go to the police station and Genevieve would present the pass. They would say that they wanted to read about the Georgetown Sweetheart, a big-name case from last year, featuring an impeccably dressed man who had killed three women and was later discovered to be a cardiologist. They would instead read about Czin, Cadr and Byde. Then they would go home.

When Lona thought about the gaping flaws in their precarious plan, she felt sick.

Students in criminology classes could get access to police files, but only closed cases to learn about investigative techniques. If the deaths were still under investigation, Genevieve wouldn't be able to learn anything at all. It was no news or good news.

"No more drills," Genevieve said. Her face was rigid. "No more dry runs. We're here."

* * *

The station they pulled into was nothing like the platform in Maryland. It was cathedral-ornate, all marble and brass – solid old-fashioned materials that would need to be polished and tended to. The roof was big plates of glass. It looked cloudy outside.

Beyond the train platforms, there was a long, open area lined with restaurants and stores: a kiosk for visioneer repair, a fancy lotion stand. There was a gift shop, a pharmacy, and a storefront that looked, as far as Lona could tell, completely empty except for a smiling woman holding a scanner.

"What's that?" she asked Genevieve.

"A library."

And there were people. So many people – talking, shouting, buzzing. The trains whistled and an intercom spat out static-electricity announcements with too many consonants and too much crackling. A waiter dropped a tray of plates; they slid to the ground in a crescendo. All of it was too much. Nothing here was calibrated. Everything completely unfiltered. Lona's pulse galloped away from her. She couldn't rein it in and—

"*Fenn,*" Genevieve said. "Stop her."

Lona had paused in the middle of the train station and put her hands over her ears, curling herself into a ball on her haunches to drown out the noise.

"Lona." His face appeared a few inches away, his green eyes digging into hers. "Lona, I know," he said.

"It's too much."

"I know it's too much. But you can do this. You have to pick something to look at. Just find one thing in here

121

that you can focus on, and focus on that thing. You can do this."

She couldn't do it. Everything was swimming. There were strangers rubbing against her. They were going to peel her skin off. It was hard to breathe.

"Breathe like a tree," Fenn whispered.

Like a tree? Why would she breathe like a— then she remembered. A willowy blond Coping Technician, giving a presentation about self-soothing. "Learn to breathe like a tree," she said, and Lona had leaned over to Fenn and said, "Does she know trees don't breathe?" Fenn had said, "shhhh," dutifully concentrating on the exercise, but Lona wouldn't stop. "Breathe like a visioneer. Breathe like a pod. Breathe like a Coping Technician."

"Breathe like a tree," she repeated.

"Slowly."

"In and out."

"Now focus on something in the station. Pick something to latch onto."

A tall woman swung past and bumped Lona's arm with her tote bag.

Focus on the tote bag. She could do this. *Read the tote bag.*

The bag was tan and canvas. It had a symbol on it. The symbol showed the back of a child's head as he watched a yellow sun that was either rising or setting. She had seen it before.

"Fenn. We have to follow that bag."

Gamb laughed. "He told you to focus on something, Lona, not stalk it."

122

"No," she said. "Read it."

Just below the sun symbol were words. The name of a conference.

Nineteen Years of Brighter Futures, it said.

Path Expo.

"It's this week. I saw the pamphlet when I was in Mr. Greevey's office but I didn't know what it was or that it was this week, and we have to go because if we don't—"

"Are you insane?" Genevieve asked. It was a fair point. They were here with a relentlessly specific plan, and now Lona wanted to scrap it to tour newly improved pods built by the people who wanted to wipe her brain, and possibly kill her friends.

"Genevieve's right," Fenn said. "We're totally unprepared for that. Maybe if we'd had some more time."

"But we don't have any time. That's the one thing we don't have. Time. We have fifteen days until your birthday. And the Expo is today. It's not coming back. I don't know what we'll find there that will help us, but we might find something. Are we trying to save your lives or not?"

Gamb cleared his throat.

"Personally," he said. "I vote for life saving."

Ilyf nodded.

Fenn looked between Lona and Genevieve's two sets of unyielding eyes.

"All right," he said, mentally taking their plan apart and gluing it back together. "I'll go with Lona to this Expo. You three go meet with Genevieve's professor. We meet in one hour at the police station."

Genevieve looked furious. "Why don't Gamb and Ilyf go with Lona? Why do we have to split up at all?"

"What happens if one of us gets—" Gamb began.

"We don't have time to argue. One hour."

16

The square structure took up a full city block. Other buildings around this one were taller, but this one looked low and mean. Although maybe Lona just imagined that, because of what she knew was inside. The front of the building said CENTENNIAL CONVENTION CENTER. Banners announcing the Path Expo hung outside.

Someone with a spray can had added the letters 'S' and 'T' to the word 'Expo' on one of the banners, and 'ological' to the word preceding it. Pathological Sexpot. This reassured her. To someone, the Path didn't represent anything but a chance to make a dumb joke.

Under 'Convention Center' and 'Sexpot,' people with nametags walked through a row of revolving doors, carrying paraphernalia marked with the rising sun symbol.

"Do you think we need badges?" Fenn asked. The woman with the tote bag had already gone inside, disappearing into the crowd.

The front entrance led to an atrium, several storeys high, containing skylights and fake potted plants and waxy, slippery floors. Inside, groups of conference-goers bought coffee from a stand and pored over their itineraries. The Julian Path wasn't the only event in the convention center today. In addition to Teen Crusaders, a floor plan advertised a big meeting for something called Women With Values, and something with the acronym MEBAP, though she didn't see any signs explaining what MEBAP stood for. Path took up the most space, though – all of Hall B, the largest meeting space on the third floor.

On the escalator, Lona tried to prepare herself for all of the things that could happen inside. She could fall apart. Fenn could fall apart. She and Fenn could both fall apart. She could walk in and immediately be spotted as an escapee, put in handcuffs and dragged back to Path. She could see Mr. Greevey and drag her fingernails across his greasy, coconut-scented skull.

None of these things happened. When they walked into the Path Expo, a cavernous, open space with rows of booths and tables, what she mostly felt was a wave of longing.

Everywhere she looked, Julian's face. There he was on a T-shirt, on a screensaver, at booths set up by some company called Pequod, and other businesses that were involved in the Path. There was Julian at four, at twelve, at fourteen. Footage on a large screen played bits of his life, the good bits, the greatest hits. Julian's dad, leading a Trick-or-Treating expedition through a clear Halloween night. Julian's first swimming coach, screeching because Julian had broken the pool record in the twenty-five-yard breastroke.

There was her whole life.

"What do you think we should be looking at?" Right now Fenn was looking at her, and she bet that it was so he didn't have to look at Julian.

"I'm not sure," she admitted. "I guess just anything that

mentions Pathers dying? If it's happened to Pathers from other sectors?"

"Right."

The room was loud, but not like the train station. The train station made her want to cover her ears and hide. This room was full of things that were familiar, just put together in odd ways, the way characters from reality might show up in a dream – the dead mingling with the living and the real with the imaginary.

Focus on something. When her eyes couldn't find anything to focus on, she picked something she couldn't see. *Focus on Byde and Cadr. Focus on Czin.*

She didn't see anything about dead Pathers. What she saw was booth after booth explaining the backstage workings of her existence for the past sixteen years. Visioneer cleaning wipes. Flavor Buds with extra vitamins. A couple of universities advertised their Path Studies departments, and a woman circulated a petition to have Julian's ninth grade Shakespeare unit become a part of mainstream curriculum.

Julian was, it seemed, a lucrative industry.

Off in one corner, a few rows of chairs were set up in front of a projection screen that announced:

A More Perfect Path
Next Showing Begins In 2 Minutes.

The '2' flipped to '1,' and a cluster of people filled the front rows. When the '1' became a '0,' the screen went dark. A man's voice projected from a speaker.

"What could the world be, if every childhood was perfect?" The music playing underneath was a mellow string ensemble. "How far could we go, if that perfection could be replicated?"

Beside her, Fenn stopped moving. "That's the voice," he said. "That's the man who was in my visioneers at Eighteens."

It was a nice voice, low and smooth. It sounded a little familiar even to Lona. Maybe it was used for announcements in Path. She could imagine this voice being responsible for writing what she'd listened to for sixteen years.

The Path is in you.

"We spent a year seeking out perfection, in all of the obvious places," the voice continued. A series of faces appeared on the screen. Smiling children, all of them. A few seemed familiar – one looked like a scientist that Julian learned about in History, another appeared to be a violin prodigy. "But with LifeCapture Technology spreading even to the average public, we soon found that sometimes perfection can actually be found . . . in the ordinary."

The faces began to blur and rearrange themselves, combining into one large image of a smiling Julian. The audience clapped.

"Let's go," Fenn whispered.

"Don't you want to hear?" Lona shook him off, straining to hear what came next in the video. "Don't you want to know how they chose Julian and how they made us?"

Fenn jabbed his index finger toward the screen. "Do you think that what they're showing looks like the Path you lived in? Is that where We were?"

On screen, a small boy in a workout facility that barely

resembled a proper Calisthenics room was swept up in a bear hug by a Coping Technician who was as pretty as Genevieve. If Lona was ever hugged that way, she didn't remember it. If Lona ever laughed the way that the boy was laughing – Off Path, not because of something in Julian's world – she didn't remember that, either.

"But—"

"We're almost at the end of the aisle," Fenn said. "Let's just keep going."

Lona dragged herself from the video presentation, trying to ignore the man's voice as they made their way toward the rear of the hall. There, another small crowd of people was gathered. Not around a screen, but around a pod.

The pod. The main event of the convention, displayed like a third-grade diorama: a glittery platform. An oily salesman. The pod. It was the one from the brochure on Talia's desk – the very latest in comfort technology. Lona slipped in between two older women for a closer view.

The Pro-Tech revolved slowly, lit by footlights, sprouting cords and wires and equipment that Lona didn't recognize.

"You see, the Pod Pro-Tech has all the necessary muscle-builders built right in," the salesman crowed to his audience. "Also, a catheter and advanced heart-rate monitors. There is really no need to ever leave it!"

"We're due for a replacement in Sector 25." A man with giant ears and a pronounced Adam's apple craned his neck to see the undercarriage of the contraption. "Are you saying that Pathers wouldn't ever get out of their pods? Not even for Calisthenics, or to meet other Pathers?"

"There's really no need! There wouldn't be a need for Pathers to have Off Path identities at all. Think of the staffing reductions you could accomplish."

A machine that effectively performed the conjoined twin surgery. A machine that effectively killed them all.

Sector 25. That would have been Ilyf's sector.

"Would you like to try the Pod Pro-Tech?"

The salesman was talking to her. Out of all of the people in the crowd, the salesman had made eye contact with her. Her muscles tensed. Did she just look like she belonged in a pod? "It's the future!" He stretched out his arm, offering to help her on the stage.

Behind Lona, a younger boy was mesmerized by the Pro-Tech. "Cool," he whispered to his mother, a powder-caked woman whose badge said she was at the convention center for Women With Values. "If I had this, I wouldn't ever have to get up for anything."

"Don't say that," the woman snapped. "Pathers deserve your pity, not your envy. They are not normal. They will never really be normal."

"Oh, you're so right." One of the women next to Lona simpered in agreement. "My church took up a collection to donate toward their assimilation. It's such a good cause, but when the pastor asked if any of us wanted to be a temporary host family for the new graduates – well, we have *children* at home. I just worried it would be a little . . . *odd*."

"Pod people," the boy snickered.

Lona stumbled away from the Pro-Tech and the oily man. He called after her. "Don't want to give it a try? It's size-adjustable!"

She walked blindly; her only destination was away. Everything in the hall was the same as when she'd walked in fifteen minutes ago, but now instead of comforting it looked twisted. Grotesque.

"Would you like a Julian?" a chipper woman held out a paper mask of Julian's face with the eyes missing. Gouged out, like in a cautionary bedtime story.

"*Chocolate Flavor Bud?*"

"*Julianbase is now illustrated for easier searching—*"

"*Lona.*" The last voice was Fenn. She wanted so badly to get away from the horribleness of the Pod Pro-Tech that she forgot he was even here. He jogged behind her, dodging a man carrying a tray of visioneers. "What's wrong?"

"It's awful in here." She fought to keep from screaming. "We need to go now."

Fenn didn't ask her to explain. He didn't ask anything. He did exactly what she needed him to do. "Exit's over here." He pivoted in the opposite direction. "Not too fast or people will look at us."

Every part of her wanted to break into a run.

"Would you like to learn about Monitor Car—"

"No," Fenn said. The smiling woman shrank back. The crowd was stifling. Everyone in the enormous hall seemed to have crushed around them, ravenous and sweaty. "We're almost there. Do you see the exit?"

She could see the exit. It was less than twenty-five yards away. The only thing keeping them from the exit was one more person passing out fliers. Probably fliers that advocated for pre-emptively remmersing all Pathers, or for finding a way to surgically attach them to their pods.

131

The woman passing out these pamphlets was small and strong-looking, even in her loose black pants and top. She wasn't as smiley as the others; she thrust sheets of paper at people whether they wanted them or not.

"Fenn," Lona couldn't stop looking at the woman even though she knew it was bad. "That's Talia."

"It's – what?"

"At the entry. Passing out fliers." Lona bent over and picked up a discarded pamphlet from the ground. 'An Endangered Missing Child,' it said. She turned the glossy paper over.

Her fingers went numb.

They'd used the only photo option they had, the one that was taken for files and records every year against a plain gray wall in the Calisthenics room. She was smiling. Somebody had said 'Cheese.'

"We'll go back and find that woman passing out Julian masks." Fenn said. "We're going to put them on, and then we're going to walk out the door. Okay? Okay?"

She wished it would be okay. But twenty-five yards away, Talia dropped her armful of papers and started in Lona's direction.

"No." Lona found her voice, and it was surprisingly strong. "We're going to run."

"Stop!" shouted Talia.

"Go!" screamed Lona. "The emergency exit! In the back!" She scrambled under the table behind them – souvenir visioneers – and Fenn slid over it, upturning it behind them to block Talia's path. The booth attendant cursed behind them, as Lona whipped past a snack stand. Fenn was just to her side but then a thick hand thudded on her shoulder. Security.

Fenn's blockade had delayed Talia, but it had also made them into vandals instead of just runaways. Now the whole room knew something was wrong.

The guard's fingernails dug into her shoulder. He smelled like a hot dog.

The last time she'd been in this situation, she pulled Gamb's hair. She reached desperately to the head behind her, but her palm slid over oily skin. The guard was bald. Lona bucked her head back, trying to jam her head into his skull, but felt only the doughy wall of his chest.

"Honey," he said incongruously. "I have a daughter your age at home. I don't want to hurt you."

He had a daughter. Lona let herself go limp, as if acquiescing, and the second his grip loosened, she made her elbow into a spear and jabbed it backward as hard as she could into the guard's fleshy stomach. He wheezed and sank to the ground, clutching his gut.

Acute angles. That's what she'd seen in the mirror next to Genevieve. She'd seen only underdeveloped weakness, but it was a strength.

"Move!" she shouted at Fenn, who stared, horrified, at the writhing guard. The guard reached toward his pocket, toward an aerosol can. Lona kicked him again. "*Move!*"

She shoved Fenn to the exit, smashing into a woman who was carrying a tray of Julian buttons. They made a clangy tinkle as they rose into the air and crashed to the ground. It's raining, she thought, one of those disjointed thoughts that your mind has when you're focusing most of it on other things. *It's raining Julians.*

They were going to make it, though. They were almost at the exit. Fenn's hand was inches from the door.

And then everything went dark.

The whole hall, all of it. Everything in the room was an inky black. The other conference-goers issued muffled protests; there was the sound of feet crunching on feet, cries of panic and annoyance. Under those noises, there was something else. An oboe. A sweet, clear oboe, and then the whole hall went orange. The screens that earlier projected scenes of Julian's life disappeared. Now the whole hall was a screen. A 360-degree screen, playing a movie Lona already knew by heart.

"Don't go." The voice belonged to Julian's mother.

The hall hadn't become a screen. It had become a visioneer. Lona and Fenn and everyone else in the convention center were trapped in the equivalent of a giant pod.

"Don't just walk out on everyone," Julian's mother said. She wore the beat-up jeans and scruffy Illinois State sweatshirt she wore on weekends when she wasn't on call.

It was a scene from the 4,500s. Julian had just gotten the cast off of his broken leg. He went back to swim practice, but was out of shape and frustrated. He told his parents he wanted to quit, and his mother tried to talk him out of it.

To Lona it felt like the words were being directed just to her. Julian's mother didn't want her to give up on the Path. She wanted her to stay. She wanted her to come home. Lona wanted to come home, too. Why was she fighting so hard to stay in a world she didn't belong in?

134

Think of everything you've accomplished," Julian's mom said. "I love you, and I'm so proud of you – but I really think that if you walk out on this now you are going to regret it."

A stillness overtook the room as everyone looked up to the ceilings and the walls, transformed into Julian's familiar kitchen, with the island in the middle and the overstuffed mail rack. The conference hall seemed unimportant now. Lona's real life was the one on the screens.

To Lona's left, Fenn clamped his hands over his ears and was screaming something to himself, trying to drown out Julian and the scene.

Lona's heart ripped in half, down the middle, in shredded, pulpy pieces. "Mom," she heard herself whimpering. "Mom."

"*Lona.*" Fenn mouthed her name. Shouted it, from the looks of how his mouth was contorted, and told her to keep following him. He seemed very far away. He seemed like he was on other plane entirely.

Did she really have to follow him? Couldn't she stay here instead? Seeing Julian's mom again felt like being wrapped in a blanket when she hadn't even realized she was cold.

On the periphery of Lona's consciousness, Talia picked through the wreckage Lona had left in her wake, and slowly approached Lona's right side. The security guard scuttled toward her left, the fatherly kindness erased from his face. Scuttling. Like a scorpion.

Another memory was trying to claw its way to the surface.

The Colorado trip. At the end of Fenn's perfect day, Julian's mom found a scorpion in her shoe. She'd screamed, but Julian grabbed a pot and captured the thing. When Fenn remembered that day, he forgot about the scorpion. Lona didn't. Fenn was the one who remembered the beauty. Lona remembered the fight.

This recording of Julian's mom? That was wrong. The point of Mom's lecture wasn't to get Julian to do what seemed easy. It was to get him to do something that seemed too hard, because it would make him stronger in the end.

Lona took a lurching step toward Fenn, and then another. Each time she planted her foot, it felt like it was landing in a pool of lead. On her third step Fenn's hand closed on her sleeve and pulled her through the emergency exit.

"Lona, please!" Talia yelled as a piercing alarm went off.

The audience on the other side of the door burst into applause: a brilliant show put on by the Expo. Lona ran her tongue across her lips and tasted salt. When she reached up to her face, it was wet with tears.

17

"Are you okay?" Fenn was frantic. "Lona, are you okay?"

The back stairwell had concrete steps and a metal railing. Fenn wedged something under the door leading to the hall, but there was banging on the other side; it would only be a matter of seconds before it gave out.

"Are you okay?" he asked again.

"Let's go!" she wiped her face with the back of her hand. "I'm fine."

The banging was getting louder. "I'm *fine.*" She started down the stairs. Voices echoed above.

"There's a Metro across the street," Fenn panted. "I can distract them – they'll want me more than you. Use your OneCard, go to Foggy Bottom on the Blue Line, then—"

"I can't go without you!" Was he insane? Why would he think she would leave him behind?

"They can't catch you!"

"They can't catch *either* of us."

They burst out of the exit into disorienting sunlight and an unfamiliar street. "The arch!" Lona pointed to a decorative arch they'd passed just before reaching the convention center – the fire exit placed them just around the corner from the front entrance. Underneath it, a capital 'M' for Metro.

Let us be lucky, just once, she begged as they sprinted into the subway entrance and down the escalator to the platform. She knew that the guards behind them were close.

The train was coming. The doors were opening. If the platform had been more crowded, if the train had been delayed, if the doors had opened further down the platform, they would have been caught.

But they were lucky. Lona and Fenn got on the Blue Line train just before the doors closed. Two security guards stood on the other side of the glass window, looking angry. As the train pulled away, Talia joined them, looking not angry but sad.

Lona collapsed onto a seat, and wished for the train to take them away, as fast as it could.

For the first two stops they said nothing. The car was nearly empty, and Lona's mind was still in the convention center with those horrible people and their souvenirs, like Path was some kind of amusement park. With the chic mother, and the way she said 'pity,' with a mixture of actual pity and revulsion.

Her mind felt wrung out, like a damp sponge. It felt almost like she had left a piece of herself back in Hall B, with the recording of Julian's mother. *I'm still here*, she reminded herself. *All of me.* She hadn't left any of herself behind.

After the subway left its second stop, her thoughts were interrupted by laughter – loud giggles that seemed vulgar, considering what she and Fenn had just been through. *It's not rude to laugh*, she reminded herself. Not everyone had been through what she had. Not everyone was on her Path.

It was group of teenagers, six of them. They'd just come out of a movie theater, still carrying bags of popcorn and sodas. Two kept saying, "I'll see you in Hell!" which Lona gathered was a line from the movie. One of them, a boy, snuck up behind another, a girl, and stuck an ice cube down the back of her shirt.

"Jackson, you're so ANNOYING." The girl shook the ice cube out of her shirt, jumping up and down in a pantomime that was more elaborate than it needed to be. She swatted her hand out toward the Jackson boy who, cackling, dodged away and weaved down the length of the subway car. The girl wore a tight skirt and tall, tottering shoes that made her stumble on the moving train. Jackson slowed down to make it easier for her to catch him, and when the girl got close enough, he grabbed her around the legs, throwing her over his shoulder.

"Put me down!" she shrieked, but she was laughing. When her feet touched the ground she flung her arms around his neck.

Should that girl be me? Lona wondered. *Is that what sixteen is supposed to look like?* What Jackson and the girl were doing made them seem really old but also really young. Totally carefree. Imprecise. Uncalibrated.

But normal.

Lona looked at her reflection, and Fenn's, in the glass window of the subway car. How had she not noticed before how incorrect they looked? They had pinched eyes, like they needed glasses. Their posture was stooped; they

139

naturally cringed away from other bodies, avoiding the physical touch. This is what Genevieve tried to show her, but she couldn't see it before. *Freaks*. They were freaks.

"Fenn," she said. "In the Expo, it was—"

"We don't have to talk about it," he interrupted. "I'm so sorry for letting us go there. I knew it wouldn't end well. I think – I think that some part of me wanted you to understand how awful it was. But I shouldn't have let us go. It was selfish."

"It was horrible."

The Metro car pulled into a stop. Fenn waited to respond until the swell of people leaving was replaced with another coming in.

"Do you remember when you asked what I thought happened? If I had any theories?"

Lona nodded. "At the creek."

"The people at the Expo is what I think happened sometimes. Some crazy who has decided that we're unnatural – I think someone like that thinks it's his mission to wipe us out."

Lona couldn't imagine anyone else caring enough about their existence that they would do something like that. But then, every minute she learned something new that people cared about Outside. Four rows ahead of them, the movie theater boy was pretending to bite at the girl's ear while the girl was pretending to think it was annoying.

"I think I understand about Genevieve," Lona said. "What it meant that she gave you guys a place to stay." It could have been so much worse for them. They could have ended up with that woman from the convention center, who would have invited her friends over and paraded the Pathers around to show off what a do-gooder she was.

"Genevieve is . . . complicated," Fenn sighed. "She knows what it's like to feel like she doesn't belong. She had an older brother who died before she was born. She was supposed to be a replacement."

"Oh. I didn't know." How horrible. That explained some of Genevieve's unpleasantness. "I guess I'm glad she has you, then. And that you have her."

"She has me." At first Lona thought he was just repeating her sentence, but something had been inserted in Fenn's version of the sentence that wasn't in hers. "I think in the beginning she thought of us as a good deed. Like inviting us to live with her would be proving something. But then – she's good, Lona. She is a good person, underneath. She used to call Czin 'Cynthia,' and Cadr 'Cadence,' saying they deserved real names. It just all changed. After."

After Cadr's face was gone.

"She doesn't like me, though," Lona said.

For some reason, Lona expected Fenn would deny this, or explain it, or tell her again that Genevieve had reasons for being the way she was. Instead he just said, "She doesn't like you. But she has given us everything. And when I told her how important it was, she even gave me you."

"Guys. GUYS. Jackson and Caroline." Another member of the movie theater group was calling to the couple. "Jackson," the exasperated girl said loudly. "Would you and your girlfriend get out of your bubble long enough to acknowledge that we are the next stop?"

The next stop. That sentence reminded Lona of something

else. Another memory, from way back, in another place. "Fenn," she asked. "Do you remember when Nick wanted to run away from home on the bus? He said his family didn't appreciate him, and he packed us this backpack full of supplies?" It was late one October when Julian was seven or eight, just after Nick's younger sister was born.

Fenn nodded. "He had this idea that We would go to Arizona to live with his grandparents. We don't think he knew that it was just a city bus and it only went to the mall."

"So We keep riding it to the mall and back and around that circle thing, and Nick is looking really bad, and We think that he's just homesick or worried about Arizona or something, but then that lady realizes We've been on the bus for a really long time and comes over to ask if We're okay."

"And Nick opens his mouth—"

"And throws up all over her coat—"

"And We can't stop laughing."

We.

Somewhere in that conversation they'd slid back into Path dialect. It was so easy. The past nine days, she'd been holding up an enormous weight of individuality and it felt good to fall into something familiar.

"Do you ever miss it?" she asked Fenn. "Path?" Why was she even bothering to ask? Fenn didn't miss it. He'd made that perfectly clear.

"Of course." He sounded surprised.

"But you hate it."

"Part of why We hate it is because of how much We

142

miss it," he said. He was still using Path speak. She didn't know whether he noticed. "Because it's still our past. Because We can't get away from it, and We can never have it back. We miss Nick. We miss Mom. We miss how flat the land was there, and how We could see the horizon on all sides."

"We miss . . ." Lona said. "We miss Julian." Fenn didn't say anything, so she continued. "Where do you think he is? Married now? Do you think he has kids?"

"He's probably dead, Lona. It was a long time ago."

"How long?"

Julian would have been at least eighteen when the Path launched. Waiting until he was an adult would have been the only way for them to know that his childhood was happy. But he could have also been much older.

"Fifty years, maybe?" Fenn said. "I've never tried to figure it out. Getting sucked back into Path isn't good."

"Why do you think they chose him, though? That video said that they found perfection in the ordinary? Do you think that was it? That he was ordinary? Do you think we had an ordinary life experience?"

Fenn chewed on his lip. Like Fenn. Like Julian. "It had to be better than average, right? A happier family? Or more friends? Or . . . There had to be reasons why they picked him that were good enough that they thought we would all be happy in Path. Because sometimes, if I can forget about everything I know now, I think that I was. Happy."

Lona's left hand felt warm. She looked down. It felt warm because Fenn was holding it. His palm was under the back of her hand, and his thumb was in her palm,

143

making small circles and leaving little trails of fire that crawled up Lona's arm, then spread through her body.

Startled, she looked up. Fenn slowly lifted his other hand. His fingertips landed lightly on her collarbone, and then he traced it from right to left, pausing at the hollow of her throat and letting his cool fingertips rest against the heat of her skin. No one had ever touched her like this. She waited to feel panic, but felt only something she didn't quite have words for. *Excitement?* No.

"I thought I was happy with you," Fenn said.

Wanting.

His hand traveled up her throat, brushed against her earlobe. He started to touch her face. Lona was afraid to breathe.

"I think I need to tell you something," he whispered.

The train lurched to a stop.

"Give it a *rest!*" At first Lona thought the older woman was talking to her and Fenn, but they weren't the target of the woman's complaints. Four rows ahead of them, Jackson and the girl were doing something Lona had never seen before. His arms were clasped around her waist; her hips leaned into his. Their eyes were closed and their lips, hungry and searching, were pressed together.

"Fenn. What are they doing?" She nodded to the two figures, still locked together.

"Making out," Fenn said. She didn't think anything could have distracted her from the way Fenn was touching her, but now she was desperate to understand what she saw. "Kissing. Hooking up. They all do it Off Path."

"Why didn't Julian ever do it?"

144

"I'm sure he did, Lona, and they just edited it out. Who knows what else they did to us on Path."

Kissing. She could kiss Fenn. Fenn could kiss her. She could feel his lips on hers. Could she even bear what that would feel like, when his fingers on her collarbone were almost more than she could handle?

The vision was replaced by a new image, though. One that made her stomach feel choppy. She was going to be sick. She leaned over, putting her head in her hands, trying to erase what she saw in her mind.

"Lona?" Fenn asked. His hand was on her shoulder, but instead of touching her tenderly, he was roughly shaking her, trying to get her attention. "Is everything all right?"

"That's what you and Genevieve do," she finally whispered.

"What?"

"Kissing." The unfamiliar word was sharp and bitter on her lips. "That's what Gamb meant."

"Why are you asking this?"

"That's what you do when I'm not around. Kissing. Making out. Hooking up."

Fenn's silence was its own response.

"It's true. Just say it."

"Lona—"

"*Say* it, Fenn. Or is this something else you think I can't know? Are there pictures down by the creek?"

"Please don't."

"*Say* it."

He paused. "Yes."

How stupid she'd been. Gloating that Fenn touched her

face without prompting, when every night he went into Genevieve's bedroom and did *this* with her. How idiotic to think she and Fenn had anything at all.

"Lona, I'll try to explain," he begged.

"You did explain. You thought you were happy with me. Then you left and you found out what happiness really was."

"That's not what I was going to say."

"I don't want to hear what you were going to say."

"I'm trying to apologize."

"You were my *only friend.*"

"Is *friends* what you think we were?" He looked shocked, and she realized she'd misread the situation again. They weren't even friends.

"Not anymore. You don't ever have to worry about that anymore."

The word 'friend' – that also tasted bitter on her tongue. Because it was so wrong. This whole time, she'd thought that's what they were. Friends. That was the only word the Julian Path had given her to describe what they meant to each other. This whole time, that's what she thought she'd been upset about. That she was losing a friend.

It had never been the right word. She didn't know the right one, and now she didn't need it either. Now she just needed to be angry. At Fenn, and at herself, for the way she could still feel his fingerprints burned into her skin.

18

"We're here."

"Fine."

The first words they'd spoken since getting off the train.

Fenn had tried, half a dozen times, but she felt too broken to respond. Her legs moved mechanically up the escalator and down the two city blocks to the police station. She hated feeling this way, bruised and exposed. How did people ever bear being Off Path? How did they withstand feeling?

There's beauty, too. She reminded herself of the grass. Of the breeze. Of the chills spreading through her collarbone. *Don't*, she admonished herself. She couldn't afford to feel this way right now.

The police station was drab, with ugly pebbled walls. Gamb and Ilyf were already standing outside, in front of an abstract sculpture. "Justice," the placard said. It looked like a clothes peg holding a barbell.

"What happened?" Ilyf took in Lona and Fenn's disheveled clothes. Lona reached up. Her hair, which Genevieve had styled into something intentionally messy-looking, was now messy for real. "Were you crying?"

A new wave of embarrassment. Her humiliation, on display for everyone else to see.

"Where's Genevieve?" Fenn asked. Maybe he was trying to change the subject, but the question still stung.

"She just went in," Ilyf explained, still looking at Lona. "Her student pass is only good for her, so we have to wait outside."

Just as Ilyf finished that sentence, Genevieve appeared on the steps of the police station, standing next to an egg-shaped officer with big ears. "*There* she is!" Genevieve said in an uncommonly bright and cheerful voice. "There is my sister!"

Lona almost turned around to figure out who Genevieve was talking about – Gamb actually did – before realizing that Genevieve was talking about her, for the benefit of the pot-bellied policeman. Ilyf's shoe nudged her heel, telling her that she had to say something.

"Here I am," Lona stepped awkwardly toward the entrance. "I am right here."

"Officer Moretz was telling me how he was going to *sit with me* and help me find the files that I needed for my school project," Genevieve said. "Which was *so nice*. But I told him that before we started, we had to come and get my *underage sister* because she really shouldn't be sitting out here *alone*."

"You're right." The lie came surprisingly easy to Lona's lips. Pretend they were sisters. She could do that. It was easier to pretend they were sisters than think about Genevieve's mouth pressed against Fenn's. "Mom would have killed you. Sis."

Officer Moretz beamed. "It's nice to see two sisters who care about each other so much."

Lona forced her lips into a twisted smile. "We are very close."

The file room was a jumble of old desks, dust, the scent of something burning. A coffee maker stood on top of a stack of papers – someone had used it and forgotten to turn it off. Now it was just an empty pot with a brown crust and a scorched smell.

Officer Moretz installed Lona next to his desk and Genevieve at a computer on the conference table in the middle of the room.

"See, here's where you put in the file number." He leaned over Genevieve to type with his right hand. "And your password is going to be the temporary one your professor gave you. See? So for the Georgetown Sweetheart, we would type in—"

Over the computer, Genevieve glared pointedly at Lona. *Do something,* she mouthed.

"Officer Moretz?" Lona said. "Have you been a police officer for a long time?"

He didn't look up. "Four years? Three?"

"Um, how did you decide to be a police officer?"

"What?" he asked, distracted, typing something else on Genevieve's computer. "Oh. My mom was."

"What did your dad do?"

"Died."

Genevieve scowled, in a way that clearly meant, *Something better than that.*

Lona scanned his messy desk for ideas of anything to talk about. Bubble gum? A receipt from a sushi restaurant?

149

His overdue cable bill? A picture of Officer Moretz in a bright neon vest with a dog that was also wearing a bright neon vest?

"Officer Moretz, is this your dog?"

Now he looked up. "Officer Boo-Boo? Officer Boo-Boo was the best tracking dog in the state."

"That's . . . amazing."

"Now let me tell you why. See, most sniffers do their best work in the first four hours."

He walked around the table, lovingly picking up the picture of the deceased Officer Boo-Boo. Out of the corner of her eye, Lona saw Genevieve move her hand almost imperceptibly, clicking open a new window. She was totally calm. Totally unflappable.

If Lona could have chosen anyone for this task – anyone to be in here with her, it would have been Genevieve. The bizareness of the realization almost made her laugh. Almost.

"But Boo-Boo – Officer Boo-Boo – could go longer?"

"Oh, you bet. His nose could pick up a scent after two weeks. I think it was in the breeding. Most people like a hound for this sort of work, but Boo-Boo had some shepherd in him, which made him better at staying focused."

He droned on. Behind Officer Moretz, Genevieve wrinkled her forehead in concentration, oblivious to the comprehensive education that Lona was receiving about the merits of various dog breeds' scent receptors.

"Did you ever have a dog?" Officer Moretz asked.

"No, I'm allergic." He looked so put off that she had to refrain from saying, "Actually, the boy whose brain I have

150

been living in for sixteen years is allergic. I have no idea if I can have dogs."

"We were thinking about getting a Portuguese Water Dog," she said instead. "They're better for allergies." This was true. Julian's mom brought it up over the summer.

"Portuguese Water Dog is no kind of tracker," he said dismissively. He briefly looked back at Genevieve. Lona was afraid she'd lost him, but he turned back and lowered his voice. "Your sister's not allergic, is she?"

"No?" Lona said. "I mean, no. She's not."

"Do you think she'd ever be interested in an older guy? I mean, not a lot older. But someone a little more mature?"

Officer Moretz had a young face, but the hair above his forehead was prematurely thinning and patchy. She tried to picture him throwing Genevieve over his shoulder or sticking an ice cube down her shirt. She tried to think about him kissing her.

"I think she has a boyfriend."

The meanest things feel that way because they're true, she thought. For both herself and Officer Moretz.

"Right. I should have guessed."

This conversation was excruciating. When was Genevieve going to finish with the files? What was she finding in them?

As soon as she started thinking about Genevieve's progress, she realized the sound from the conference table had gone silent. There was no tapping keyboard, no scratching sound of a pen.

When she looked over, Genevieve was still looking at the computer. Her hand was still holding a pen. But her face had gone completely white. Her eyes traveled up to

151

Lona's and then, expressionless, deliberately shifted to the right.

Lona followed her gaze, until her own eyes landed on the computer on top of Officer Moretz's desk. An alert, blinking in the center of his screen: a photograph of a smiling girl standing in front of a gray background.

Talia had been busy.

Beep.

The computer was announcing the alert. It might as well have just said it: The girl you are looking for is in this room.

Officer Moretz noticed the sound, too. He hadn't registered where it was coming from yet, but he shook his head, like there was a mosquito in his ear.

"Officer Moretz." Her voice was strangled. "Are you going to get a new dog?"

"Um, maybe," he said. "The thing about dogs is that they all have their own personalities. You have to really . . . find one . . . that you click with . . ."

He'd figured out where the beep was coming from. She saw in his liquid, limpid eyes that he knew the sound was coming from his own computer. "Hold on a second, now. This thing is a piece of – let me just make sure that—" He leaned back in his chair, blindly feeling behind him for some switch or button. When he couldn't find it by touch, he began to spin toward the computer. Thirty degrees. Forty-five. Sixty.

"OFFICER MORETZ," she yelled, and he almost fell onto the floor. "Officer Moretz, I need to tell you something right away." She crooked her finger and leaned in toward him. When he didn't do the same, she wildly waved both hands until he finally abandoned the computer and faced her.

"I think my sister would definitely date older guys," she whispered. "Maybe you should give me your card so I can tell her later how nice you were."

"Really?" His smile was elated and surprisingly vulnerable.

"I think it would be good for her to be with someone . . . who, um . . . likes dogs."

He fumbled around in his desk drawer, looking for a card. Behind him, Genevieve signaled manically toward the exit. Whatever she was going to get, she already had. When Lona didn't move, Genevieve came to the desk and grabbed her arm, wrenching her out of her seat and dragging her toward the door. By the time Officer Peter Moretz finally produced a business card, both of the girls were gone.

"What did it say?" Fenn asked as they spilled out of the building. "Did you find out anything?"

"I found out that they're sending her picture around." Genevieve broke into a jog.

"I would have *told* you," Lona said.

"Before or after we were sitting in a cop's office?"

"You turned me into your sister before I could say anything."

"Neve," Fenn began.

"Not now. On the train."

Lona turned toward the Metro station again, but stopped when Genevieve put two fingers between her lips, signaling a cab with an earsplitting whistle.

They were only a few minutes from the same station

they'd pulled into a few hours before. Lona waited for the cab driver to recognize her, or for Genevieve to yell at her for the stupid trip to the Expo.

But the ride was silent. On the other side of Ilyf, Genevieve barely paid attention to anyone at all. Which meant that she was either so upset that she was bottling everything for an eruption when they got on the train, or that whatever she had found in the files of Cadr, Czin and Byde had overshadowed anything she felt toward Lona.

The frost continued as the cab pulled up to the station. Ilyf helped Lona buy a pair of toy visioneers – from more than a foot, they looked just like the real ones – to wear as a disguise. Genevieve swiped her card to put them all on the next train. As soon as they entered the first empty car, Fenn stationed himself at the entrance and blocked the door with his body.

"Full," he said to a woman who poked her head in. "Sorry."

When another passenger tried to enter, he produced a sheet of paper, scrawled "OUT OF ORDER" in all capital letters, and creased it into the window pane.

"What did the files say?" He knelt by Genevieve's feet. Ilyf leaned over from across the aisle, and Gamb was draped over Genevieve's seatback. "Do they have a suspect?"

"With an address?" Gamb broke in. "Let's go there right now. I'm ready – my adrenaline's still going."

An address. If there was a suspect and an address, then this could all be over tonight.

Genevieve shook her head from side to side, a small, tight movement.

"What does that mean?" Gamb asked. "No address? No suspect? Have they linked the murders together yet?"

"Genevieve, did they have the files?" Fenn was getting impatient. "You said you found something. What did you find?"

"The cases have been closed," Genevieve's voice was smaller than usual, folded in on itself.

"Closed? That means they found someone, right?" Ilyf's voice was bigger than usual, elated, light like a balloon. "That means they caught someone?"

"I only had time to skim the details. Then Lona's picture flashed up and we had to run."

"But what did the details say?"

Everyone was staring at Genevieve. Everyone had inhaled lungfuls of oxygen, and everyone was waiting for a sign that it was okay to let them out again. For the briefest of seconds, Lona thought she saw something in Genevieve's expression – hesitation, a dark shadow – but it faded.

"It was . . . it was a lunatic. Some religious whackjob who thinks that Jesus told him that the Path is unnatural. He's been stalking you since the graduation ceremony. It wasn't in the papers because they don't want to give other nuts any ideas. So it's good news. It's terrible but it's good. I'm sorry I don't know any more."

It was almost exactly what Fenn had predicted, back in the Metro. A madman who thought he was on a mission, who thought he was doing someone else's important work. How astute, for the crimes to be nearly exactly what he'd predicted to Lona. And what he'd probably predicted at some point to Genevieve.

Gamb and Ilyf were talking over each other, bouncing on the seats.

"Thank you." Fenn leaned over and – in a way that seemed intentional and deliberate – kissed her softly on the cheek.

The kiss was a choice. *He must have been waiting to do that in front of me*, Lona thought. *Now he doesn't have to. Now he can do it all the time.* He was choosing Genevieve. Making it obvious that she was the one he preferred. She swallowed back the lump rising in her throat, willing herself to make it home before she cried. *Something you don't have cannot be taken away*, she told herself. And it turned out that she'd never had Fenn.

Her eyes caught Genevieve's in the glass window pane. She expected to see triumph on her face. Instead Genevieve looked away quickly, tilting her head against the window.

"I'm really tired now," Genevieve said. "It must be the endorphins. I think I'm just going to sleep until we get home, okay?"

She didn't sleep. She looked out the window as the city turned back into suburbs turned back into country, and every few minutes, when Gamb or Ilyf would laugh particularly loudly, she would flinch like she was in pain.

Lona wondered why no one else had noticed that Genevieve wasn't sleeping, and why no one had noticed what now seemed perfectly clear to her. She didn't blame them. They needed it so badly, much more than she did. But she was still surprised no one else realized what she did. Genevieve was lying.

19

"I'm sorry to bother you, Architect."

"It's fine.

"I know it's late, and I really wouldn't have called if I didn't think—"

"It's *fine.*"

"It's just that you told me to contact you if anyone came in looking for those case files."

"Who was it?"

"That's the thing – it was before my shift. That's why I couldn't call you right away, or find a way to detain them. I would have, otherwise – I would have called you the very second—"

"Who *was* it?"

"The on-duty document supervisor just said it was a girl. A pretty girl."

"Lona or Ilyf?"

"I'm sorry, sir?"

"White or black?"

"White, sir. I think."

"Mmm."

"Can I ask, sir, why she's so important?"

"Lona?"

"Yes, this Lona person. Why it matters so much that you find her?"

"She's creating the calf path."

"The what?"

"It's a poem."

"I'm not a big reader."

"The Calf Path. By Sam Walter Foss. One cow goes astray on its way home, and the new trail that it leaves behind is picked up by a dog, then a flock of sheep, etcetera, until the path that the calf has created is the new, well-traveled road."

"Oh."

"It's a metaphor, officer. If this girl has gone Off Path, she can lead the rest of them behind her. She is their symbolic leader."

"*Oh.*"

"Correct."

"Sir? If she read the files – should we have stopped her? They weren't classified, but – does this mean someone knows something they're not supposed to know?"

"She read all three?"

"Yes, Architect."

"She doesn't know everything. She doesn't even know what she knows."

20

"We are having," Gamb informed all of them, "a party."

"A five-person party?" Ilyf asked.

"I could have a party if the four of you went to bed right now."

Ilyf looked dubious. Lona agreed. She was having trouble reconciling Julian's raucous swim team parties with the idea of the five of them holed up in an isolated farmhouse. A setting for a horror movie, yes. A party, no.

She didn't want to celebrate, anyway. "I think I will go to bed right now, actually. I don't feel all that well."

"Everyone parties."

"You just said—"

"Everyone parties." He herded Fenn and Genevieve into the kitchen to assemble some food, leaving Lona and Ilyf behind with instructions to choose music.

"Did something happen?" Ilyf asked carefully, once they were alone and scrolling through songs. "At the convention? You've seemed off ever since."

She thought she'd done so well at holding everything in. Ilyf's words were almost enough to make her spill around the edges. It would be selfish, though, to pour out her confusing problems right now. Not when they were so happy.

"I'm just so tired," she said finally, focusing her eyes on the song titles in front of her.

"We all are. Genevieve looked wrecked on the train."

"Did you notice that? Did you notice that something seemed wrong with her?"

"More wrong than usual?"

"Not just tired. I felt there was something she wasn't saying."

"Lona," Ilyf's voice was teasing while still being gentle. "In this house I think we all have things we aren't saying. Don't worry about it tonight."

"But—"

"Don't worry. Besides. Won't it feel good not to feel so sad?"

"STROBE LIGHT!" Gamb flicked the light switch on and off, making the pulsing in Lona's head feel like it was just a part of the pulsing of the whole house. The sofa cushions had been flung from the floor and there was peanut butter on the lamp. Fenn was in the corner, spinning and jumping around in circles, his sweaty hair stuck to his forehead and his skin glistening.

It did feel good not to feel so sad. It felt good not to feel much at all, and the pounding music seemed like it had emptied Lona's brain, at least momentarily, from thinking about anything but jumping to the beat. It reminded her of being back in Calisthenics, when her job was very simple: move your muscles.

Don't grieve for Fenn, she told herself, making it a mantra set in time to the music. *Don't grieve for Julian. Don't grieve for your past. Don't grieve, don't grieve, don't grieve.*

Sometimes when the light was on, she thought she saw Fenn looking at her. She tried not to look back. She could talk to him tomorrow. Tonight was for living.

"You know what I think?" Gamb stopped jumping. "I think . . . it's . . . BEDTIME!"

When Julian was in his 4,900s, he went on an overnight field trip to Chicago that his dad volunteered to chaperone. He and his roommates ate three large pizzas, drank four bottles of Dr. Pepper, and jumped up and down on the bed to annoy the girls next door. Around midnight, Julian's dad appeared in the doorway of the hotel room in his boxer shorts and, in one of his few instances of voice-raising, roared: "Boys. I THINK . . . IT'S . . . BEDTIME!!"

At that moment, Julian and Andrew Holt landed on the bed at precisely the same time. It collapsed to the floor with first a crash and then a sad little sigh.

Now the four of them ran to Gamb's bedroom, jumping like lunatics. Genevieve didn't follow, heading instead in the direction of her bedroom. Let her. Lona wasn't going to think about her now.

"You know who I am?" Ilyf waved her arms like tree limbs. "I'm the GOD OF INTERPRETIVE DANCE."

"No," Gamb said. "I am the LORD of interpretive dance."

"No, that's not it either," Lona said. What was it? Her thoughts came rhythmically as she bounced on the bed, her chest bursting and sweat running between her shoulder blades. "I am . . . the DARK LORD . . . of interpretive dance!"

It was all inside jokes, memories Lona hadn't thought of in years, brought back by three people with exactly the same memories. By 3 a.m. Ilyf slumped so low into a couch that even Gamb was forced to admit that she no longer could be classified as awake. Following his voice, which was doing an impression of an air traffic controller landing a plane, she zombie-walked to her room.

Then it was only Lona and Fenn, standing in the wreckage of the living room. He stood with his hands at his side, looking cautious, contrite.

"I was waiting until everyone went to bed. I was hoping we could—"

"What? Talk?"

"Yes."

"I don't want to talk to you now, Fenn." She couldn't bear the platitudes he would offer. The excuses. The fact that he might touch her again, as an apology, as a consolation prize. That, above all else, she couldn't bear. "I want to go to bed." He didn't move, though, standing directly in the path to her bedroom.

"Can I get by, please?" she asked. When he still didn't step aside, Lona slid past him, holding her breath, careful that not even the fabric of their clothing brushed against each other's.

"Please don't leave," he whispered as she passed, but his plea only strengthened her resolve. He was the one who left her, a long time ago.

She couldn't sleep, though. She wasn't tired, no matter how much she convinced herself she should be. Her brain felt tangled again, too busy to rest, replaying all the scenes of the day whether she wanted to re-watch them or not. After tossing for half an hour, she padded through the dark house toward the kitchen for a cup of tea, for something to do as much as for hope that it would truly help her sleep. When she got there, Genevieve was already sitting at the table. Her hands were wrapped around a mug, eyes fixed on a random point in middle distance.

It looked like she'd been here for hours, with a half-empty kettle. The second-to-last person Lona wanted to see right now, and she'd just said good night to the first.

"I thought you were asleep," she said.

"A little hard to with the noise."

"I was just going to get some tea." Lona filled her mug and pocketed a handful of random tea bags. She would sort out what she'd grabbed in her bedroom.

Halfway to the door, she debated something. "You were impressive today," she said finally to Genevieve. It deserved to be said. It wasn't Genevieve's fault that Fenn wanted her.

"I saved the day," Genevieve said sardonically.

"Well. You did."

"We *both* did." The saccharine way Genevieve lumped the two of them together was meant as a mockery, not a compliment.

"Fenn seemed especially grateful to you." She couldn't resist that small amount of savageness.

"The princess gets the kiss."

And Fenn had said this wasn't a fairy tale.

"I'm going to take my tea to bed," she said, starting for the door. There were markings on the doorframe that she noticed for the first time. Pencil markings labeled 'Liam,' tracking the progress of a happy family that had lived here in another time. She got almost all the way to the stairs before Genevieve stopped her again.

"I was the one who found Czin," she called suddenly. "Did you know that?"

The water sloshed over the side of Lona's mug, trickling down and burning her finger. She turned back around.

Genevieve's voice was strangely passive; she might as well have said, *I was the one who found the expired milk.* "I was on my way home from school." For the first time in their interaction, Genevieve looked straight at her, unblinking.

"I didn't know."

"We heard about Byde and Cadr through the news. Byde had gone into the city to see a movie that no one else wanted to see. Cadr kept teasing him about it – like, didn't he want to do something that didn't involve looking at a screen? – but he went alone. Sometimes it was better if they didn't travel together, anyway. They looked out of place. He hadn't come home by the time we all went to bed. We didn't think it was a big deal. The next morning he still wasn't back. On television we saw that a body had been found in the river. We still just thought – we just thought that he'd fallen in. That it was a freak accident. Cadr wouldn't have left that afternoon if we'd known. See, we were going to have a birthday dinner for Byde. A big deal, to celebrate his birthday instead of Julian's. After we saw the news, we decided to have the birthday anyway. To remember him. Cadr wanted to go to a gourmet food store in the city. She was only gone for an hour before we learned something was wrong. Czin heard about Cadr through one of her feeds. There were pictures. The gunshot wound only destroyed part of her face."

Lona realized her mug was still dripping. Boiling liquid, seeping on her fingers – she was holding the cup at a slant and she hadn't even noticed it. The things Genevieve was saying were too horrible. Neve, Fenn, and everyone else would have been trapped in the house with the growing realization that Byde hadn't been an accident. They wouldn't have been able to claim either of the bodies because they feared being discovered. No wonder Ilyf worried. No wonder Fenn's face was hard.

She didn't know why Genevieve was telling her all of this, except that it seemed to be spilling out of her, the way Lona had almost let her secrets spill out to Ilyf earlier.

"What about Czin?" she asked.

"I was on the train," Genevieve restarted her story. "We'd just left school. We went over a bump. I didn't feel it, but that's what the conductor said. A bump. And that there would be a delay. I didn't want to wait, because I was worried about Fenn and everyone, so I decided to get off and walk to the next stop. It was only half a mile away and I thought it would be faster than waiting. I had to go around the train to cross the tracks. The thing was, she didn't look dead at all. Her face even looked like she was smiling a little. It was just that her body was under the train."

"The case wasn't closed, was it?" Lona asked.

Genevieve shook her head. "No. It was closed. I didn't lie about that. I lied about something else." She reached down to a vinyl messenger bag sitting near her feet and pulled out a manila envelope, which she slid across the table to Lona.

Lona unfolded the flap and pulled out a pile of photocopied papers. She flipped past the first page, which was blank, looked at the second page, and froze:

CASE FILE 541112. DEATH OF UNIDENTIFIED MALE, AGE 18-20.

"You stole the files."

"Just one. You only need to read one."

Lona slowly turned over the title page, aware of every fluttering sound the papers made, and began to read. The top page was a signed deposition from the dogwalker who discovered Byde's body, washed up on a bank along the Potomac. Next were statements from the officers who arrived at the scene. These pages were followed by the coroner's report, which determined that, despite contusions on Byde's head and body, the cause of death was drowning.

The twelfth page was labeled WITNESS TESTIMONY.

Brian Holtzinger [1150 Columbia Rd.] was jogging on the Wilson Bridge at approximately 10:45 p.m. on February 25. Mr. Holtzinger asserts that he is confident of the time, as he is training for a marathon and regularly takes the same route. As Mr. Holtzinger approached the center of the bridge, he noticed a young Asian male, aged approximately eighteen, standing on the pedestrian path holding a large rock. Mr. Holtzinger believed the boy might be a vandal, planning to throw the rock at a boat passing under the bridge. Concerned for his safety, Mr. Holtzinger crossed to the sidewalk on the other side of the bridge at this time. As he approached the portion of the bridge where the male stood, he saw that the male was not throwing the rock over the bridge, but placing it in the pocket of his coat. Mr. Holtzinger stated that the male "had a big pile of [the rocks]" and was placing all of them in various pockets on his person, as well as in a cloth pillowcase that appeared to be tied to his left ankle.

Lona read all the way to the end of the report, the remaining two pages of Brian Holtzinger's testimony and his repeated apologies that he'd never learned to swim.

"So you see I wasn't lying." Genevieve took another sip of her tea. "The cases really have been closed. The cases have been closed because Byde jumped off of a bridge and Cadr shot herself in the face and—"

"And Czin threw herself in front of a train," Lona said.

"Correct. The cases have been closed because police don't need to investigate suicides."

A sheet of paper drifted off the pile and onto the floor. Neither of them bothered to pick it up. Genevieve set down her cup and leaned in very close to Lona.

"You can never," she said, "tell Fenn. Not any of them. Do you understand?"

She nodded. As horrific as it was for them to think that their friends had been murdered, it would be a hundred times worse to know that they hadn't. She did not want to think about what it might lead to.

"Why did you tell me?" The knowledge was a burden, but it still seemed surprising that Genevieve wouldn't keep it a secret, if the alternative was sharing it with Lona.

Genevieve appeared to think it through. "Now we're the ones in charge," she said. "Now we have to be on the same team. If this is what happens when Pathers turn nineteen, we're the only ones in this house who aren't trying to destroy ourselves."

An alliance, then. The same girl she couldn't bear to think about kissing Fenn was the person with whom she shared the most horrible secret.

Genevieve scraped her chair back and stood up, leaving Lona sitting alone at the table. She paused at the doorway, her hand on the light switch.

"He needs me, you know." Genevieve didn't have to spell out who she was talking about. "He doesn't even know how much. You have no idea what I would do to preserve that."

Lona waited until she heard the door to Genevieve's bedroom click shut before standing. She needed to get out of the house, to have time to process everything. The air in here felt heavy and thick. She needed to take a walk, just a short one, to clear her head. She left her tea.

As soon as she slipped out the back door, she knew she had made the right decision. It was crisp out here, a night as sharp as a knife. Out here it was easy to think clearly about what she needed to do.

Her short walk grew longer. The air cycling in and out of her lungs was regenerating, as if each unit of oxygen recycled different parts of her body. There was still time to figure all of this out. They still had fifteen more days. Fourteen. She and Genevieve could tie the rest of them to

168

their beds, if that's what it took, or lock them naked in a padded room – anything to keep them from harming themselves and buy a little more time while they figured out what was going on.

She walked without a plan for fifteen minutes before realizing she'd been subconsciously following the route she and Fenn took the week before. She was probably almost at the creek – and yes, there was the sound of a rushing stream. She'd walked further and faster than she'd planned.

There was also another water-related sound, one that was louder and more erratic. Plopping. Splashing. The otters. They were mostly nocturnal, the Internet had said. They were probably out fishing, or building a nest. Lona used tree trunks to keep herself from slipping as she edged down the incline toward the water. They hadn't seemed afraid of people before – maybe tonight they would let her get close enough to really look at them.

She heard the sound of bushes rustling. It was coming from too high to be made by otters. *Deer*. Not otters after all.

She crouched low beside a large oak, peering under the foliage to see whatever animal was making those sounds.

It wasn't an otter. It wasn't a deer. It was a man.

She froze.

He had gray hair, pulled back in a ponytail, and what looked like a few days of stubble on his face. He was on the opposite side of the creek, and he hadn't yet noticed Lona – focusing instead on trying to find a good place to cross. Every few yards, he took a branch in his hand and poked it out toward the center of the water, testing depth.

Running would make too much noise. His legs were longer than hers, and he would catch up to her long before she reached the house. He was older – the skin around his eyes was crinkly – but still fit. The muscles under his shirt were smooth and flat. And even if he didn't catch her, she couldn't lead him back to the house, where Fenn and Genevieve, Ilyf and Gamb were totally vulnerable. They were probably sleeping already, not knowing that she'd come down here. *Why had she come down here?*

Don't look up, she begged him. Maybe if she was still, he would just cross the river and keep walking. Maybe he wasn't even looking for them – he could just be a random guy, out for a pleasant walk. In the middle of the night. Without a flashlight. Carrying a gun.

It was holstered, tucked through his belt and hanging down by his left hip, but it was still there, glinting black in the moonlight. Winking.

He found a good place to cross the creek – or rather, he decided there was no good place to cross the creek. He crouched and rolled his pantlegs as high as they would go, then waded into the water.

Hurry, she thought to herself. If she was going to run, she had to act quickly. The sound of the splashing would cover her movements, and there was at least a fair chance that the man would slip if he tried to run after her.

It was too late. The first step she took was onto a fallen branch. It cracked like a thunderbolt when she stepped on it, immediately signaling her location. The man stopped in the middle of the creek, water lapping at his thighs, and pulled the gun from his belt. Lona knew when his eyes had found hers because her heart slowed in her chest – heavy, empty thuds that were the sound of giving up.

She couldn't take him back to the house. She wouldn't be shot in the back.

Lona stepped away from the tree she'd been crouching near and walked toward the man, keeping her hands in plain sight to show that she was surrendering. Tomorrow, everyone else could see this on the news. Body discovered. Half of her face intact.

The foliage was less heavy down by the water, and the light from the moon made every feature on the man's face stand out, the shadows and crevices of his eyes and nose almost black and white in contrast.

She looked at his face, and she looked at his gun, and the water gurgled around his legs, doing its best impression of a pleasantly babbling brook.

"Hello, Julian."

21

**Finalist Application for Untitled
Child Welfare Project
(Affiliated with H.R. 29440)**

Applicant Number: 321775
Name: Julian Pierce-McKay
Gender: M
Parents: Holly Pierce / David McKay
Evaluators: N. Singh and Q. Greene

Notes from Nora Singh (psychologist)

I wholeheartedly recommend Julian as
my primary nominee for the endeavor
colloquially known as 'Path.' Based on
the other prospective applicants I have
been assigned to review, Julian is a
rather atypical candidate. The majority
of hopefuls were equipped with
LifeCapture technology because of their
parents' beliefs in their child's

singularity and importance — what my colleagues in adolescent psychology have come to casually refer to as the 'special snowflake' effect. On the contrary, Julian's parents, a surgeon and a librarian, viewed LifeCapture as a technology of scientific and historic importance, and felt it was their duty to participate in early waves of the experiment. Julian, therefore, maintains a healthy sense of self unencumbered by over-involved parenting. Which is to say, he isn't spoiled.

When I interviewed Julian — now a senior in college — he noted that he was 'really boring' and didn't understand why he was selected. I explained that his life had been carefully reviewed, and that 'interesting' was not an important criterion.

Clearly, even his statements of concern regarding his participation in this project display a level of empathy and self-awareness that would be beneficial in any candidate who is ultimately selected. I therefore recommend that Julian be moved forward to the next level of review.

SIGNED: Nora Singh, PhD / December 21

Notes from Quincy Greene (sociologist)

I see it falls to me yet again to be the voice of reason in this hideous project.

I have been informed that I must support someone's candidacy — that I cannot continue to raise objections, which the committee has deemed 'roadblocks,' but which I view as the desperate warnings of an old man who sees his fellow researchers about to make a deep and despairing decision that changes our understandings of our own humanity.

Therefore, I support the candidacy of Julian Pierce-McKay.

It would be preferable to me not to support anyone at all. You are playing with fire, gentlemen and ladies, and I think you know it.

You insist on stating that your goal is perfection, but you continually ignore the repercussions of stating that one child has experienced the 'perfect' existence. Is 'perfection' not dependent on preference? Is preference not dependent on personality? Is personality not dependent on genetics? Smarter men than I have struggled with these questions, but the fact that Plato and Aristotle weren't able to sufficiently answer them does not mean, I think, that we should preclude ourselves from asking them.

I am reminded of the philosopher Robert Nozick's 'Experience Machine' thought experiment, in which he weighed the potential benefits and pitfalls of a specially equipped tank, which humans could program to give them 'ideal' experiences, and in which they could choose to live for years at a time. Would it matter that those events were not 'real,' Nozick wondered? Would such an existence truly constitute a 'life'? Would the human spirit ultimately be harmed by its lack of harm?

But you want my analysis of Julian. Fine.

Using the rudimentary and abstract standards that you have created, Julian is a very good candidate. I am somewhat bothered by the fact that, in this day and age, our leading applicant for this program is a white male. That being said, I am heartened by the progressive attitudes within the Pierce-McKay household. The fact that Julian's parents elected to hyphenate his name is indicative of an awareness of gender equality, certainly, as is the fact that Holly Pierce, a general surgeon, makes more than twice the salary of her librarian husband.

The Pierce-McKay household and its environs represent what would generally be considered an idyllic living situation — privileged by most standards (see ethnographic charts and summaries in Appendix C), though the fact that his parents both came from working-class backgrounds has tempered the sense of entitlement that might normally be affiliated with such an atmosphere.

At least, as far as I can tell.

Along with Dr. Nora Singh, I have spent approximately one week interviewing and observing Julian at his current age of twenty-two. I have spent a good deal more time reviewing the footage of his LifeCapture. I have seen more of his intimate moments than anyone, including his parents (including some moments that I am sure Julian himself would like to forget and some, I am equally sure, that the committee will excise in the editing process, as part of its mission to maintain 'wholesome' childhoods).

I daresay, however, that I do not

know Julian at all. I know what he has done, I know what he has said, I know how he has behaved. I know your charts, of course — I understand the careful research you have done into the development of children's brains and sense of self. I am entirely aware that Julian's future looks very bright.

But I do not *know* that. What I do know is that we are recommending a personable young man who is still very young. In Dr. Singh's evaluation, she took Julian's bafflement over his selection to be indicative of his modesty, and his appropriateness for this program. I think she is wrong. It think it's indicative of a man who does not yet know who he is. And who, in his later years, could grow up to be a psychopath or a cold-blooded killer, whom we would have recommended as an ideal childhood.

SIGNED: Quincy Greene, PhD / December 23

22

The bullet would tear through the waterproof nylon of her jacket first, and then through her shirt, which was thin as tissues and would shred like a whisper. It would feel like a cross between a stab and a punch. Her blood would feel warm as it pooled around her skin. She would never see Fenn again.

This was not a virtual reality Path experience. This was real – her shoes sinking into the mud as she stared down the barrel of the winking gun in Julian's left hand. *Of course; he's left-handed*, an absurd part of her brain reminded her.

The gun was at Julian's eye level. It had wavered when she said his name, but now it was back up again.

"Who are you?" His voice had deepened since she'd last heard him speak. He sounded like a grownup. He sounded like his dad. "Are you one of them?"

"I'm . . ." She tried to think of the best way to phrase it, not knowing what he meant by 'them' or if being one of them would be a good thing or bad. Julian's eyes were the same. The same light brown, the color of a fawn. His hair wasn't fully gray; she could see that now. Sandy streaks shot through the ponytail gathered at the base of his neck. He seemed tall. Had he always been this tall? She hadn't noticed.

She never saw what he looked like to other people. But she had seen that face, reflected back at her for years. She had seen him practice wiggling his eyebrows, flossing in the bathroom, checking the rearview mirror.

Julian took another step closer, the water shushing around his legs. He bit his lip. His bottom lip. He was still doing that. "Are you one of them?" he asked again, louder this time.

"I'm one of you."

Overhead, in the distance, there was a whirring sound, a metallic grind from a plane flying overhead.

"Prove it." Julian called above the noise. His gun, black and sleek, was still pointed at her skull. The plane passed.

"Prove it?"

"Prove it," he said again. "Where does the Path lead?"

Where does the Path lead? She didn't know what he expected her to say. There was no logical answer to that question.

"The Path . . . the Path is for you. The Path is in you. You are the Path."

Julian's mouth twitched. Whatever answer he'd expected wasn't the one she'd provided. He took another step forward.

"Wait. I can prove it. We were born October 6. We live on Teakwood Lane."

"That's not what I meant."

"*You* are the one with the gun. I am a sixteen-year-old girl. Why am *I* the one proving something to you?"

"It has to be this way."

"For our sixteenth birthday, Dad said We could borrow the old Toyota—"

"That's surface level information," Julian said. "Anyone could have looked that up."

"The first thing We did was drive to Sarafina Baker's house." He'd already told her that this narrative wouldn't convince him, but she didn't know what else to say.

Julian had gotten the keys for the Toyota from his dad. He wore a new shirt, a collared one, the third one he tried on before choosing. In the fall evening, the neighborhood smelled like burning leaves.

"We drove to Sarafina's house, but We don't know what happened next. We remember Sarafina inviting us in and making popcorn and her dad forcing us to play Trivial Pursuit at the dining room table. We remember her walking us to the car. We remember driving home. But there was something else that happened before We drove home, wasn't there? At the time I thought it was a head rush or something – like We stood up too fast and blacked out for a second. But now – I don't think it was a head rush. I think it was bad editing."

Now that the words were coming out of her mouth, it was like they were forming themselves. That night was almost in her grasp. The fragments were there. She just wanted to know if the pieces she was starting to put together would make the puzzle that she thought they did.

After the Trivial Pursuit game, when Mr. Baker loudly commented that it was getting late, Sarafina walked Julian outside. She nudged the dented, rusty bumper with her toe and said, *Nice car* in such a deadpan way that they both burst into giggles. Her lip balm smelled like vanilla.

Then Julian was in the car and he was driving home.

Something was missing. She knew what it was.

"Julian. Did Sarafina kiss you that night? Is that what happened at the car? Our first kiss?"

The gun jerked in Julian's hand. Lona squeezed her eyes shut, waiting for the sound of a bang and the searing pain that would follow it. But the only sound was rustling fabric. When she opened her eyes again she saw that the gun hadn't moved because Julian had shot it, but because he'd decided not to. He lowered the revolver down to his side where it lay, quivering against his thigh. The wetness on his pant legs crept upward, above the water line. The khaki was now dark with moisture all the way to the tops of his thighs.

"I'm sorry," he whispered, though it wasn't clear what he was apologizing for.

"Do you believe me?"

"I'm going to come out of the water now. It's freezing."

"But you're not going to shoot me?"

"Part of me thinks I should—" Lona balled her hands into fists at her side, ready to attack him as he got closer. "If only to spare you what's going to happen to you."

So he knew about the suicides, then.

The moon had come out from behind a cloud and was brighter than it had been ten minutes ago. She could see that the wrinkles around his eyes looked more like bags of exhaustion. Julian wasn't as old as she'd originally thought.

"But maybe you got out at the right time," he said. "Maybe it will all be okay for you."

While he found his footing on the slippery creek bottom, she nonchalantly picked up the sharpest stick she could find, testing the point against her wrist. It would be better than nothing, if it came down to it. He climbed the rest of the way up the bank. Once on dry land, he methodically wrung out his pant-legs, then shook off excess water like a dog after a bath. Lona had seen him do the same thing – felt him do the same thing? Felt *herself* do the same thing? – a hundred times after swim practice. Wring out the suit, shake off the water, towel off the head. She resisted the urge to mirror his movements, to jiggle her own legs. How was it possible for Julian to be wet while she remained dry?

"Julian, why are you here?"

"I followed you." He straightened up from his pants. "From the convention center."

"How did you follow us if no one else could?"

"I'm guessing because no one else has lived inside this brain enough to predict your moves. Or, if not to predict them, at least to keep up with them."

"But why? Why are you here?"

"I think we should get inside for this conversation." He hesitated. "There is an inside nearby, right?"

There was an inside. It was where Fenn and everyone else currently slept, defenseless and unaware.

Julian watched her, pretending to look away, but peering casually through the corner of his eye. "There are more of you," he said. "Where I've come from."

He let the sentence dangle in front her.

"More Eighteens? More Pathers who are going to die?"

"More Pathers who aren't on Path anymore. Strays. Not many of them. None from your sector, but from other places. A few."

182

"You've met them?"

In response, he raised his eyebrows at the forest behind her, up toward the direction of the house.

"Why can't we talk here? Are you afraid someone's watching?"

"When you have had my life, you always think someone is watching you." He paused. "I forgot. You have had my life."

"Part of it."

"You've had the good parts, at least."

"What are the bad parts?"

"Where is your house?"

"Give me the gun."

They retraced the path uphill that she'd cut on her way down, Julian walking ahead, Lona giving directions when needed. Their cadence was the same. She was still performing Julian. As far as she'd come in these past weeks, she was still doing an imitation of an original.

"The others. The other Pathers. How did you find them?"

"They found me. I was a celebrity for a while. I did the interview circuit. Panel discussions at conferences."

"Panel discussions?"

When he answered, he sounded sheepish. "People would pay for my autograph."

Of course. Julian would benefit from the lucrative industry surrounding his face, his past, himself. He could auction off little pieces, a signature at a time. "Is that why you were at the Expo today? Selling your autograph?"

"I don't do that anymore. I was at this one to find you."

Chills ran up the back of her neck. Her hand tightened around the gun. "You said you didn't know who I was."

"I'm sorry," he said quickly. "Not to find *you*. To find others like you. I met the other Pathers when they showed up at an expo out west. We thought others like them might come to this one."

"But I didn't see you there."

"You saw a hundred of me there. A hundred plastic versions of me."

Lona remembered the promotional Julian masks. Julian was at the conference center and he was wearing one. Old Julian dressing up as young Julian. "These other Pathers. Now they're . . . an organization?"

"Not exactly. Maybe you could call them a resistance. A resistance looking for a leader. Though I don't think they know they're a resistance. I'm not sure they know what they are or what they need. You'll see."

"Why don't you lead them?"

"I don't understand what it's like to be in Path. I only understand what it's like to symbolize it."

The wryness in his voice – the fact that it sounded like he thought this was a *joke* – made Lona stop still. "Do you understand that the people who have been following you are killing themselves now? Do you understand that three of them have died?"

"That's why they called me."

"That's why who called you? The resistance?"

"No. That's why Pequod called me. They told me that three kids had died. They wanted me to come in for tests. To see if there was something they missed. To see if the desire to die comes from being me."

"Does it?"

184

"I don't know. The day after Pequod called me, the kids found me, saying they wanted my help. I thought about where my allegiances should lie."

"Just so we're clear, my allegiances are with the Pathers I am living with. And trying to keep alive. They don't know they're killing themselves. They think a madman did it, and that he's been caught."

"It wasn't a madman."

"I know."

"It's the Path. Your friends have to stay away from the Path."

"I *know*."

"There's a signal, you know. A question that they developed to test each other and figure out whether they're a part of it. I tried it on you a few minutes ago."

Their first exchange, when Julian stood in the middle of a river. She'd thought she was negotiating for her life. Really, he was just trying to figure out how much she already knew. "Where does the Path lead?" she whispered. "Is that the question?"

"That's it."

"I said that the Path is in you. But that's not the right answer."

"No."

"What is the right answer?"

Ahead of them, the house appeared through the clearing. The kitchen light was on. Through the curtains, the shadowy outlines of four heads. Fenn, Gamb, Ilyf, Genevieve. They'd discovered she was gone, and now they were waiting for her. One of the heads looked up. She had been spotted.

185

She had thought she and Julian would have hours to plan what they were going to say, but they had less than a minute. "What's the right answer for the resistance, Julian? In case I get thrown out of this house for bringing you inside and I need to go join it?"

"Astray. The correct answer is that the Path will lead you astray."

23

"What did you do?" Genevieve's eyes were scalpels. She flew across the room. "What have you done?"

Behind her, Gamb and Ilyf froze in motion – Gamb with a grape half-raised to his mouth and Ilyf brushing her hair from her face, as if they were an artist's subjects posing for a portrait. Behind them, Fenn was pacing, but he froze, too, when he saw Lona walk in with Julian behind her.

She'd wondered if they would recognize him as quickly as she had. She needn't have worried. Everybody knew.

"No *way.*" Gamb was the first to move, floating over to Julian as if in a trance, not even noticing the stack of mail he knocked off the table. With the grape still between his thumb and forefinger, he poked at Julian's cheek with as little self-consciousness as he would have had touching his own.

"Gamb, leave him alone. Jesus." But Ilyf seemed comforted by the fact that Gamb was touching him, because if Gamb was touching him then it meant that Julian was real.

Fenn said nothing. Fenn watched Gamb's monkey exploration of Julian's face, but when he finally spoke it was to Lona. "Are you all right?"

"Is she all *right?*" Genevieve's face was just a few inches from Lona's. "What did you do?"

"Neve." Fenn said. "Calm down."

"Calm down? Calm *down*? I have spent thousands of dollars creating fake addresses for all of you to keep you hidden, and she comes in here with this . . . this . . . Calm *down*?"

Genevieve raised her hand, open-palmed, but Fenn caught it before it swiped down toward Lona's face. He had a cut on his hand. His knuckles were bloody. Had he punched a wall again?

He turned back to Lona. "What happened?"

What had happened? Or rather, what had happened that she could say here, now?

The others didn't know about the suicides, but they would probably sense that something was wrong soon, when they stopped being relieved about Genevieve's 'good news' and starting thinking about the gaping holes in her story.

"Yes, what *happened*, Lona?" Genevieve's voice had an edge to it, a dare and a plea.

"I . . . was going for a walk. And—"

"Pequod sent me," Julian said.

Gamb took a giant step backward, as if he only just realized that the thing he was prodding was a person, not an inanimate object.

"They contacted me to . . . check on you." Julian went on. "After the deaths?"

After all of these years, Julian was still a bad liar.

"After the murders," Lona guided him. Though she still hadn't completely figured out how this lie was better than the truth.

"But how did they know where we were?" Ilyf looked

188

puzzled. Ilyf and her logical computer brain. "We've been hiding. No one is supposed to know our address."

"I'm sure Pequod has ways," Lona said. "Obviously they have ways. Because Julian is here."

On the other side of the kitchen, Genevieve composed herself, literally and figuratively. She adjusted her shirt, which had gone askew during her frenzied rage at Lona. Her features organized themselves from engraged to placid.

"Julian. Would you like a cup of tea?"

Genevieve's hand trembled as she picked up the kettle, filling a mug for Julian before he could accept or decline. Julian's hands trembled as he picked up the mug with both hands and guided it to his mouth. Lona hoped no one else noticed. Just before it reached his lips, the tea spilled over the side, dribbling onto the table.

"I'm sorry." Julian accepted the napkin Genevieve handed him and mopped up the rust-colored stain.

"No use crying over spilled poo-water!" Gamb jostled Julian. "Who wants to drink poo-water anyway? Right?"

Ilyf grinned in recognition. Julian looked confused.

In Julian's sophomore year of high school, a bunch of girls started having 'afternoon tea.' They brought cups to eighth period English, and Ms. Dwyer, who liked talking about her vacations to London, let them select packets of Earl Gray out of a wooden box and spend the period slurping while discussing *Pride and Prejudice*. The boys called it poo-water.

"Right," Julian said. "Ha ha."

"Do you all do this, Julian? Like Nick and Dan and . . .

189

and Dad? Do all of you come around and do visits?" Gamb was touching Julian again. Patting his ponytail.

Lona was used to seeing Gamb silly or sarcastic, but she had never seen him like this – with big kitten eyes like he was waiting for a pet on the head.

Julian shook his head. "No. This is more of a special mission, just for me. I haven't seen Nick in years. He's a graphic designer in Seattle. And he's in a band. Dad is . . . Wow, look – the sun is coming up."

It was casting shadows on the kitchen table. The sky was pastel instead of inky. The clock on the wall said it was almost six. Lona had been up all night. She had been up since she got up yesterday morning and put on Genevieve's jeans that made her butt look weird. She was still wearing those jeans. She was exhausted. Julian was probably exhausted, too, but Lona had the feeling that he hadn't interrupted himself to comment on the time because the sun was coming up. Dad was dead.

"Are you tired? You can stay here." Gamb quickly looked at Genevieve, and then back away again, before she could say no. "You can have my bed if you want."

"He doesn't want your bed." Ilyf smacked Gamb's arm. "And I'm not letting you sleep with me. You roll around." She turned to Julian, and her voice took on the same hopeful tone. "You are staying, though, aren't you?"

"I'm . . . not sure. I wanted to just meet you tonight. I don't know if I can leave the others alone for that long."

Lona cringed at the slip. Genevieve pinched the bridge of her nose with her slender fingers and closed her eyes.

"Others?" Ilyf asked. "Other Pathers, you mean?"

"There are others. I look after a few of them who couldn't quite adjust to Path. It's sort of another special program."

A special program that Path wasn't aware it was running. The kitchen wall clock ticked. Coming from the living room was the sound of the grandfather clock ticking, too, just a fraction of a second behind. An echo-tick. Listening to the conflicting noise for long enough would make someone want to smash one of those clocks.

"There are more of us." Fenn spoke for the first time since seeing Julian came in. "How many? Can we see them? Where do they live?"

Alaska, Lona thought. *Peru. Lithuania. Be creative, Julian.*

"Not far," Julian said. "An hour. Would you like to meet them?"

"I'm sure there are regulations, right?" Genevieve interjected. "I'm sure everyone is kept separate for a reason, and you can't just break protocol without some evaluation, right?" Genevieve was probably an A student in her Path Studies program. Everything she just said described exactly how Path was supposed to work, if Path hadn't gone so off track as of late.

But Lona noticed something else, too. A feeling in the room. She wouldn't have been able to describe it well for Genevieve, or anyone else who hadn't been raised in Path. She hadn't noticed it herself until Fenn asked if they could meet the other Pathers, and Julian had said yes. When that happened, the tempo of the room slowed down. The mood lightened. Lona's heart, beating inside her chest, became stronger and steadier. It was the soothing rhythm of Path that she was feeling – the sense of serenity and security.

It had arrived with Julian. For all she knew Julian carried it inside him – the entire structure of the Path built around his biorhythms. She didn't want to let that feeling walk out the door. Not when it could help her friends.

"I think they could make an exception," she said. "Don't you?"

"*What?*" Genevieve said.

There was another reason, too. A selfish one – the same thing that made her want to go to the Expo, to escape from the van instead of awaiting her fate. She had to unearth the secrets of the Path.

"We've all been through so much. I think they could make an exception. I think it's time we meet the Strays."

24

The others had gone to bed – for the second time that night, though it was nearly seven and almost pointless. Genevieve sat down at the table across from Julian and Lona, her arms folded stiffly into her lap.

"Are there portions of the truth in the story that you just told them? Or should we start from the beginning and I just assume that everything you've said is a lie?"

"Genevieve, I had to bring him here. When I found him, he had a gun."

"I gave it to Lona," Julian added quickly.

That's right. She still had the gun, cold and heavy in the oversized pocked of her sweatshirt. She took it out and laid it on the table, scooting it to the middle, equidistant from all of them.

She and Julian pieced together the rest of their encounter for Genevieve. When they were finished, Genevieve looked back and forth between the two of them, finally settling on Lona. Her normally perfect posture collapsed as she leaned onto the table.

"I hope you know what you're doing," Genevieve said.

"You're agreeing to do this my way?"

"I don't think we really have a choice. I was going to tell you this tomorrow anyway."

"What?" Lona asked.

"I guess it is tomorrow, technically."

"*What?*"

"When I went to bed a few hours ago, Fenn was thrashing and screaming in his sleep. I couldn't make out any of the words. But the lamp next to the bed – it was broken. He'd knocked it off the nightstand and didn't even notice. Not the lamp, or the blood all over his fist."

"He was having a nightmare?"

"I don't know if it was a nightmare."

"He had something *like* a nightmare?"

"Like I said. I don't know if it was a nightmare. I do know that I've heard it before. It used to wake me up every night, coming from the bedroom below mine. Byde used to do this. Just before he died."

So it was happening. The thing that would take Fenn away, and then Gamb, and then Ilyf, and then, maybe someday, would take Lona, too. It had started tonight with a broken lamp and a bloody fist.

"So we'll go," Lona said. How easy she made it sound. Like going with Julian would automatically provide a solution. "Tomorrow. Today."

"I'm going to go check on Fenn," Genevieve said. She didn't even bother to say it gloatingly. Her footsteps sounded heavy on the stairwell above them.

Julian cleared his throat. "If we're going to go – if we're going to see the others – there are some things I should tell you first."

"Dad's dead, isn't he?"

"No. He's fine."

"Julian, the others you have to protect. You don't have to protect me. You can't protect me. If you try to I can't help them."

He sighed. "Two years ago. Cancer."

She waited for the inevitable wave of pain to roll over her body. Julian's father was a gentle, patient man. She had seen him just two weeks ago. She let herself mourn, tasting the flavor of it like peanut butter. Every new emotion she'd felt in the past two weeks had its own flavor. The old emotions in Path had been like the foods in Path. Flat. She let the texture of this mourning roll over her tongue and mingle with her grief over Fenn.

"You're odd, for a Pather." Julian was watching her.

"Aren't we all odd? Isn't that the point? We're all broken?"

"You're not. You're very strong. I've never seen a Pather so strong. So able to act, to put thinking over feeling."

Funny. Lona felt like she was feeling all the time – confusion, joy, fear, hurt. Her life since leaving Path had been a mess of feelings, of saturated emotions that made her feel raw and exposed.

"What did you expect us all to be like?"

"I don't even know. I was so young when I was chosen. I didn't really understand it. Or I understood the fame, but not the responsibility. Actually, I don't even think I understood the fame."

Lona's eyelids were heavy. The sun was already beginning to stream through the kitchen window.

"I'm sure you did the best you could."

"I still am."

As Lona drifted off to sleep, burrowed under her orange-striped sheets, she dreamed that Fenn was going to pick her up in his Toyota so they could go play Trivial Pursuit. But when they got to the car, Julian was sitting in the driver's seat. Lona wished he wasn't there, but before she could ask him to leave, Julian started the engine.

They drove around the neighborhood in the dark, but every house was Julian's, and out of every house, a new person emerged. Ilyf got in the car, Gamb got in the car, Czin got in the car. Cadr got in the car and she was bleeding from the temple. "There's not enough room," Lona complained, only she wasn't really mad that there wasn't enough room. She was mad because it was supposed to just be her and Fenn.

"We'll make room," said Byde. As Lona watched, Byde made room by pressing his body against Ilyf's until Lona saw it wasn't pressing, it was morphing. Their skin fused together, first sticking like glue and then molding, like two kinds of Play-Doh that could be formed into one ball. It was hypnotizing at first, but then it became grotesque, a revolting science experiment, until the thing sitting in the back seat was a Byde-Ilyf hybrid. Gamb melted next, followed by Czin and Cadr, all of them mushing together as one.

"You don't have to," Lona said to Fenn, who was now alone in the back seat with the thing. "There's enough room for you to stay like you are."

"Is there room for me to come and sit by you?" Fenn said, but when he spoke, the thing – the thing that had Ilyf's hair and Byde's eyes and Gamb's nose – spoke, too. It pressed itself into Fenn's flesh.

"Please don't," Lona begged as Fenn disappeared.

"We have to."

Julian stopped the car in front of his house – this one must be his *real* house, because Lona could see his parents inside – and opened the door for the thing. It got out and climbed in Julian's hand – it was magically small enough for that – and it kept shrinking and shrinking, until it was as small as a capsule of Tylenol. And when it was that small, Julian put it in his mouth and, as Lona banged on the window of the car door, he swallowed.

When Julian had gone inside, Dream Lona picked up her phone and called Genevieve.

"They're all gone," she sobbed into the phone. They all disappeared. I couldn't save them."

"Don't worry," Genevieve told her. "There are plenty more of you. We can always find replacements."

"But why couldn't I save them?"

"Because," Genevieve said – and this was the last thing that happened before Lona woke up, with her sheets twisted around her body and her pillow stained with sweat. "You tried your best but you looked really weird in those jeans."

25

"I don't mean to shout—"

"Obviously you mean to shout, Senator. You are a Princeton graduate, as I know, because I was your freshman year roommate. I'm sure that a man such as you knows how to control his own volume."

"What I want to know is why the hell you're not shouting. Architect? That's your title? Why the hell, Architect, have you not built a better system? Why can't you find those kids? Don't you make them register or something?"

"We do. The address they registered at does not exist."

"Dammit. I am supposed to retire soon. This program was my legacy. Do you get that? My legacy. I pushed hard for it, and I pushed hard for you to be the one to design it."

"In a way, I think it's a testament to the design that it raised these children well enough that they are able to now make plans and decisions themselves, albeit secretive ones. It's very teenage-appropriate, wouldn't you say, Bill?"

"You arrogant bastard."

"There are thousands of children in Path now. We have lost less than twenty, if you count the ones who are missing now, and the ones who are, shall we euphemistically say, gone? You cannot pretend that those statistics aren't eons better than the statistics you were working with for this population before my program started. These children are safer and happier now than they ever would have been before."

"I almost think you care."

"I do care. This is my life's work."

"I can't help but think that if your life had turned out differently, your work would have turned out differently."

"My life is off limits. Do you understand?"

"I'm sorry. I shouldn't have. Christ, though. It's a fucking miracle the media has not learned about this and shut it all down."

"They won't."

"If these kids are as smart as you think they are, I'm sure they can figure out how to get on the Internet and find the number for the front desk of the Washington Post."

"They won't. After the event a couple of years ago, one of the messages we began inserting into the Calisthenics lecture series was a profound distrust of the media."

"Jesus."

"Indeed. Some people say that's exactly who I am."

26

The house looked like a color that used to be another color. Blue, maybe, or green. Now it was dishwater gray. The porch sagged in the middle. Everything looked like it was in the perpetual process of falling down.

There might have been neighborhoods like this in the town Julian grew up in – scraggly, unkempt – but Lona had never seen them. When he rolled the van to a stop now, nobody moved.

"So. This is it?" Lona asked.

"House sweet house." Julian turned off the ignition. His mannerisms had changed so little. The way he held the steering wheel from the bottom, an underhanded grip that annoyed the Drivers Ed teacher until Julian got a perfect score on the exam. The way, this morning, he ate his egg by piercing the yolk and spreading it around the white, making sure there was an even distribution in every bite. All of them did that. It seemed the natural way to eat an egg.

"I should tell you." Julian stopped everyone before they got to the front steps. "These Pathers are . . . different from all of you."

"What do you mean, different?" Gamb asked.

"Well. They didn't graduate. As you know. I guess you might call them . . ." Julian searched for the right word. "I guess you might call them remedial."

Remedial. In second grade, before Nick was diagnosed with dyslexia, he was placed in a remedial reading class. He hated it because, he complained, he had to read an endless series of books about a dog family, and the illustrator had drawn the wrong number of nails on each dog's paw. Lona didn't think Julian was talking about the poor reading skills of these Strays.

"Lona." It was the second time this morning Fenn had tried to talk with her, this time pulling her behind the van while the others finished unloading the groceries Julian had stopped to buy on the way. She held a bakery sack in her arms, a protective bread barrier between the two of them, preventing him from getting too close.

"What is it, Fenn?" The harshness of her voice made him step back, fumble for his words.

"I just wanted to say that I'm sorry. Again. I want to apologize for what happened."

"You don't need to," she managed. "It's not important." Of course it was important. A day later and her throat still swelled when she thought of the teenagers on the train; her face still burned when she thought of how naive she must look to Fenn and Genevieve. But it felt like a luxury, a vapid indulgence, to say that to Fenn now. To cry because he didn't want her when the world of things to cry about was so much vaster.

"It's not important to you?" Fenn looked like he didn't believe her. Her feelings for him must have been devastatingly obvious. She squeezed the grocery bag tighter to her chest and steeled her voice.

"You can kiss whomever you want."

"Lona, that's what I've been trying to tell you."

"And what I'm telling you is that whatever you were trying to tell me doesn't matter." She forced the corners of her mouth into a smile and nodded briskly, hoping to convey a sense of finality. "Okay, then?" *Please just say okay*, she prayed. *Say okay, and we never need to talk about this again.* She would work on burying it. She would learn to numb herself. "Okay, Fenn? Okay?"

He opened his mouth, and for a second Lona wasn't sure which word his lips were about to form – if he was going to finally drop it, or if he was going to tell her that, no, it wasn't all right, that he still had more to say.

"Fenn?" Genevieve appeared around the corner, relieving Lona of having to know what Fenn was going to say next. "Are you ready?"

He looked back at Lona one last time. But when he put his arm around Genevieve, lightly resting it on her shiny hair, the gesture was the answer to any of Lona's lingering doubts.

"Come on, guys." Julian's cheerful voice had a manic quality to it; he clutched his own bag of groceries so tightly he'd ripped a hole through the bag. "Everything is going to melt."

The house was dark inside though the day was sunny. Quiet as a library. It had a sort of sleepy feel to it. Occupied, but not awake.

Julian went inside first; the screen door hissed as he opened it. Ilyf was the last. The door slipped through her fingers before she could properly close it. It slammed shut – one loud slam, then a medium one, then softer and softer until the house was again still. There was furniture in the living room. Grandma furniture, mostly – a couch with a knitted afghan folded over the back, a rocking chair with two broken spindles on one arm. The walls were papered and oily, with empty ovals where pictures used to hang.

"Julian?"

The voice came from upstairs. It was young and high-pitched; Lona couldn't tell what gender it belonged to. "Julian? Julian?"

A figure appeared at the top of the stairway. A . . . boy? It was still hard to tell. The child had fine, blond hair cut short like a boy's, but delicate features like a little girl. It flew down the stairs and wrapped itself around Julian's legs, sinking down like he/she was sliding down a fireman's pole, all the way to Julian's feet. The child remained there, arms wrapped around Julian's knees, rear end resting on his shoes, rocking back and forth and giggling.

More figures began appearing from the corners of the dim house. From around corners and through doorways, they were slinking, each coming to a central point in the living room. Lona heard a low undertone of a hum. It seemed like something to do with the furnace or the plumbing – an old-house electrical kind of noise. But it wasn't that. It was human voices. As each of the children entered the living room, they joined the blond child. They wrapped around Julian's waist and stroked his clothing.

They reached up and touched his hair. And they whispered, "Julian. Julian. Julian."

A girl – this one definitely was a girl; there were the beginnings of a shape underneath her loose shirt – a few years younger than Lona leaned against Julian's sleeve, rubbing her face up and down against it. She reached into her pocket and pulled out something, cupping it carefully in her hand before depositing it into Julian's. A metal washer.

"Thank you, Endl." Julian gingerly patted the girl on her head. She looked up at him and blinked.

"Julian is back." Her voice was airy and sing-songish. "Back, on track, unpacked, shellacked."

Another Stray – a boy, dark skin, narrow, intense eyes – plucked the washer from Julian's hand. "Endl. We're not supposed to go into our things. These are organized by circumference, then by width, then by color, then by year. It's not safe if they're unorganized. It's not safe for anyone. We'll have to start all over now. All over with the whole house."

"Don't get upset." The first child, the blond one on Julian's feet was sobbing. "Endl didn't mean it. We can fix it."

"Fix it, mix it, picks it, licks it." As if to illustrate her rhyme, the girl poked her tongue outside of her mouth touched it to Julian's sleeve, while matter-of-factly pulling a strand of hair out of her own head. She must do that often. She had a bald spot the size of a nickel above her right ear.

Endl smiled.

Lona's insides were churning. She placed her hand flat

against her belly and managed to stop the waves of revulsion. Fenn wasn't as lucky. "I'm going to be sick," He rushed out the door. The screen door slapped behind him, softer and softer and softer.

"What's wrong with them?" Gamb asked.

"It's like they're on drugs," Ilyf pressed in closer to Lona, closing the gap Fenn left, keeping their circle tight and closed. Over by the Julian clump, a small boy climbed on Julian's back and was smelling his hair.

"They are," Genevieve said sharply. "Their drug is Julian. He's been away from them for a day. They were going through withdrawal."

Lona thought back to last night at the table, and Gamb's embarrassing desperation, the way he'd wanted Julian's validation. That was small and inconsequential compared to these Pathers. Not Pathers. Strays.

Was this what happened to Pathers who unplugged before they went through Eighteens? As brief and insufficient as Fenn felt the Eighteens training was, did this represent the alternative? *How long had they all been living like this?*

"It – ahh – gets better after a little while." Julian's face flushed red as he tried to disentangle his feet from the Stray sitting on them, finally hoisting the child up by the armpits and awkwardly patting it on the back.

No wonder he was pleased when Lona said they would come over. Whatever Julian had here, it wasn't a resistance. It wasn't remedial. It was more like a mental institution.

"You'll see. It will be more . . . normal soon. They're usually only like this when I first get back."

When they're getting their first hit.

"Julian. You're back." A new person. This voice sounded older and deeper than the others – someone closer to Lona's age. When its owner stepped through the door into the living room, Ilyf gasped.

This boy was perfection. Not fashion-model beautiful like Genevieve was, but like something that would be painted on the ceiling of a chapel. His skin was white – almost pearly, translucent. His nose was wide and perfectly-shaped; his eyes were glacier-blue. Above his neck, his head was on fire. A redhead, someone might call him, but that was insufficient. His hair really looked like flames, alive and changing in the light.

When he reached Julian, he sank to his knees in one lithe, watery motion. This boy should have been a ballet dancer. He took both of Julian's hands in his, and he pressed them against his forehead. It was an ancient gesture of knights and kings. When he finished, he effortlessly rose to his feet and dropped Julian's hands. Only then did he acknowledge the group of strangers crowded around the tattered sofa in the living room.

"You brought them. Visitors." His Ts were sharp and overly precise. It wasn't how Julian spoke. It must have been a congenital speech pattern, something physical that he was born with that Path technicians never deemed severe enough to correct. The boy nodded at each of them in turn, ending on Lona.

"You are the one like us." He briefly touched her hands with the tips of his fingers. "You left before Eighteens. On purpose, we heard?"

206

"Yes." This boy seemed like he was the most stable of all of the Strays, but she still wanted to pull her hands back when he reached out to them. His fingers were cold. Maybe that was it.

"I am Harm."

This happened sometimes. It was inevitable, with a limited alphabet and a standard naming protocol. There was a boy named Door in Sector 15 once – he was visiting Lona's sector on his way somewhere else – and a girl named Lend. There were always rumors of a Pather born on June 21 in Sector 3. F-U-C. In the rumors, his Monitors arranged to have him transferred to another sector rather than risk him ending up in Quadrant K. It could work the other way, too. In Sector 14, there was a Pather a year older than Lona who was born January 14. Her name was Anna. A real name.

So this boy was Harm. August first birthday. Eighteenth sector.

The others around Julian were noticing the interaction between Lona and Harm and drifting over, clustering in a line behind the fire-headed boy.

"We are Ezbrn." The dark-haired boy who'd taken the washer and tucked it into his shirt pocket. Everything about Ezbrn was tucked in – his shirt was tucked into his pants, his pants were tucked into his socks, his shoelaces were tucked under the tongues of his sneakers. His name meant that he was also eighteenth sector. Born May 28. $Z + B = 26 + 2$.

"Affl." The child sitting on Julian's feet had detached itself, uncoiling like a cat, and presented itself to Lona. "We are Affl. And this is Endl. Endl doesn't always talk. But sometimes does."

Endl was the rhyming one with the vacant eyes, and strawberry blond hair. When she wasn't bracing herself against Julian, Endl swayed gently in place, on her toes, as if her relationship with gravity was negotiable.

There were six Strays in total, enough to outnumber the group of Path graduates that she had come with. All of them looked younger, but it seemed like there were more of them than six. It seemed like they were a swarm of bees.

"We are—" she stopped herself. "I am Lona."

"Lona Seventeen Accelerate?" one of them asked. Affl.

"Lona Sixteen Always."

Affl clapped her hands together in delight. His hands together. "We are Affl Seven Endurance."

"Endl Thirteen Triumph." It was startling to hear Endl speak coherently. Almost as soon as she'd finished, her gaze drifted up to the ceiling.

"See?" Affl said. "Sometimes Endl talks."

"Ezbrn Ten Salvation."

"And I am Harm Fifteen Believe. And I welcome you to this house." Harm pleasantly extended his arm as if he were a formal guide. "Shall we take a tour? If you're tired, we have many places that are quite private. Where you would not be disturbed at all."

She did not particularly want to take a tour with Harm. Before she could reply, though, the screen door banged open again. Fenn looked pale and unsteady, but his face was no longer as green. "What did I miss?" he asked

"You were only gone about forty seconds," Gamb said,

but he didn't sound nearly as carefree as he usually did. "We were just about to take a tour."

The house looked abandoned because it was abandoned. Julian had purchased it at auction when all of the Strays found him.

"Here is where there was a hole in the floor." They were standing in the hallway. Affl pointed to a patch on the ground where the wood didn't match. "We fixed it."

"You fixed it?" Lona asked, confused. The first person plural was more difficult in a situation like this. In Path, 'We' would have meant that all of them would have fixed the floor, at one point or another during Julian's life. But out here, any one of them could have fixed it. They weren't all on the same timeline anymore. Affl, in response to Lona's question, gestured toward Julian.

"Oh, Julian fixed it?"

"Right." Affl was pleased that Lona finally understood. "We fixed it."

There were three bedrooms upstairs, littered with mattresses and bunkbeds, a dim dining room, a small breakfast area and a shabby kitchen, equipped with chipped dishes and overlooking an overgrown yard.

"There's a basement, too, but Harm is using it," Ezbrn said. This explained why Harm had disappeared from the tour, but not what he was doing in the basement.

After the tour, Julian announced it was time for lunch. Plates were removed from cupboards, turkey was placed on bread, an assembly-line production that reminded Lona of the cheerfully working seven dwarfs. Once everyone was settled around the makeshift dining room table – actually a door propped on cinder blocks – Fenn turned to Affl, who was sitting next to him.

"So how did you come here, Affl? Why aren't you on Path?"

He asked conversationally, but the question made Affl stare mournfully at the table, eyes filling with tears.

"Did I say something wrong?" Fenn was dismayed.

Julian shook his head. "Use your words, Affl. I know you can."

"We kept waking up," Affl said softly, eyes still glued to plate. "That's what they said. We were in a car accident with our Monitor on the way back from the dentist. When We got back to the Path, it didn't work anymore. We kept waking up."

Across the table from Lona, Gamb froze mid-bite. A piece of mayonnaise-covered lettuce plopped out of his sandwich and onto the table.

Ezbrn had arranged his breadcrusts in a perfect square pile to the side of his plate. "We didn't wake up. We got bored. Our brain got bored in Path. They tried remmersing us, but We still wanted to go too fast. The crusts are dangerous. It's better not to eat the crusts, for everyone's safety."

"We were remmersed three times," Endl twirled her fork in a loopy pattern over her head. "But We kept calling out for our other Mom. The first two times, at least. Not after the third time. We didn't call out for Mom after the third time. We did call out something, but they said the words We were calling out weren't words anymore. They made sense to us, though."

"And then what happened?" Lona's voice came out strangled. "After it didn't work the third time, then what happened?"

"Remmersed, dispersed."

"I don't understand . . ." Lona looked to Endl for elaboration, but the girl was back in her own world now.

"Endl was declared mentally incompetent and placed in a home for the insane," Julian supplied. When he read the horror on Lona's face, he added quietly, "Some of the others were given $300 and dropped off under bridges. Endl was lucky."

So this is what Julian meant about these Pathers being different. Obviously they were different from Fenn, Gamb and Ilyf, who'd made it through the entire Path and graduated.

In this house, the residents hadn't graduated. They'd been thrown out because something in their brains prevented them from staying on Path.

Like Lona.

Even while these Strays were different from Fenn, they may not be that different from her.

"I wasn't remmersed." Harm's feet made thumping sounds on the steps as he skipped up from the basement. He was the only one who didn't always use Path speak – who sometimes managed to refer to himself as an individual. "My brainwaves were perfectly synced with Julian when I was on Path. They said I was an exceptional candidate for immersion in the Path, that I would have been able to sync with anyone. It was my Off Path behavior that they said was a problem. Off Path, my test patterns were . . . undesirable."

Undesirable. Whatever that meant.

"Harm and Ezbrn found each other first," Julian said from the head of the table. "At Path Expo West. They had come – well, they had come to find me. They recognized each other from their sector."

"But that is where we realized that our first instinct—" Harm gestured to everyone seated around the long table "—All of our first instincts, that is – might be to seek out things related to Julian. Conferences. Events."

"Which is how I found you," Julian said. "At the Expo."

Right. Except they hadn't come searching for him. They had come searching for a way to break free of him.

"We wish We could go back." Endl was now using her fork to trace matter-of-fact patterns into her forearm – criss-crossing shapes that left trails of red behind them. "But We can't. And even if We could, Julian says We shouldn't. We know that. The Path leads you astray, away, today, parquet."

"Endl. Don't embarrass Julian." Ezbrn reached over, pulled the fork out of her fingers and firmly pressed her hands into her lap."

"I'm not embarrassed." He looked embarrassed, though.

"Julian, is it our turn downstairs yet?" Affl tugged on Julian's sleeve.

"I think it is, Affl-Apple!" He scooped Affl up in his arms and blew a cheek raspberry that made the child squeal. Affl wriggled off his lap and skipped to the door.

"Can you do it by yourself?" Julian half-rose from the table.

"Yes. We're not a baby like Nick."

"I know that! You're getting huge! As tall as a brontosaurus!"

When the child's back was turned, Julian's smile wavered, then disappeared. He took his hair out of the ponytail at the base of his neck, sighed, then put the ponytail back in again. His eyes had bags under them.

"What's down there?" Lona asked.

"It's—"

"We'll show you!" Affl was standing in front of Lona's seat, hopping up and down. "Before We get set up. Oh, it's exciting."

Julian shrugged. "You might as well."

The basement was unfinished, a single room with a concrete floor, the perimeter surrounded by wooden shelves holding boxes left behind by several generations of tenants. There was a broken sled, a few bar stools, a box labeled 'Christmas Lights.' In the middle of the room there was a pod.

"What's that?" Lona didn't know why she had asked that. She knew what it was. She just didn't know why it would be here.

"We have to share it," Affl clambered into the too-big pod. "But now that you're here, We could give you a turn!"

"They go on Path?" Fenn asked. He was standing behind Lona, and his hand grazed against the hem of her shirt. His knuckles had a scrape on them. From the lamp and his nightmare. She wondered if he would have another dream tonight.

"We don't go on Path the whole time." Affl traced the worn leather of the pod. Leather. They hadn't used leather in years. This must be an old one. Maybe it was something they had given to Julian as a souvenir. "We can't really do it, since there's only one. But We can do some things."

"It's from an auction," Julian explained. "An estate sale when one sector swapped out their old equipment and bought new pods. It came with some old Pather records and things, but this is all anyone was interested in."

"Today, when it's my turn, I'm going to do Thanksgiving with Gran and Poppy," Affl said. "This year We're making *two* pumpkin pies *and* a rhubarb crumble."

"That's a nice one." Fenn smiled at Affl. "A good memory."

Lona turned around to glare at him for encouraging Affl.

"Look around you, Lona," he whispered.

Affl was getting settled in the pod, and Ezbrn squatted next to her, stroking her arm, like a miniature Coping Technician. Endl had found a Christmas wreath, slipped it over her head and fingered it – a large, prickly necklace. Harm had migrated back to Julian.

"I remember that Thanksgiving," Fenn said. "You can't say it wasn't better than this."

He would turn nineteen in thirteen days.

27

"From what I can piece together, I think it's a combination of a few things."

Genevieve cross-referenced the glossaries in two of her textbooks. "First, they were younger when they were kicked out – meaning they hadn't learned to be independent, like Julian would have in his teenage years. Second, they didn't have the benefit of going through Eighteens, which was specifically designed to acclimatize Pathers to live Off Path. And third – well, frankly, I think that all of them were halfway nuts to begin with."

The three of them – Lona, Genevieve, Julian – were on the back porch of the Julian house. Lona and Genevieve sat on a rusted swing; Julian hunched across from them on a wooden crate. All three watched as Fenn and Gamb organized the younger kids into two groups for a game of Red Rover. Once the teams were set, they linked hands across the patchy yard, taking turns calling each other over, one by one, trying to break the links.

Even with the noise, Genevieve talked quietly. Over the past five days, the three of them had gotten very good at finding empty nooks and talking quietly. They talked about all of the ideas that could save Fenn, Gamb and Ilyf and repair the others, and then about all of the reasons that those ideas wouldn't work.

"But do you think they can get better?" Julian leaned forward on his crate and tried to read Genevieve's book upside down. "With the right treatments? Or will they always have to be around me? Or is being around me actually preventing them from getting better? Or is it more a matter of—"

"I don't have all the answers." Genevieve closed the book. "I'm a freshman in college. The questions you're asking probably couldn't even be answered by a PhD because – in case you didn't understand this – the problems you're having are not exactly standard."

Lona understood that. But it didn't stop her from asking the same question over and over in her head: *Why didn't it happen to me?*

She was underage, just like the others. She'd never gone through Eighteens. Her brain didn't function properly – she'd gone Off Path just like Endl and Ezbrn and Affl. But she wasn't like the other Strays. Lona didn't get distracted by shiny objects like Endl. She didn't worry that the house was going to blow up if her peas weren't organized, like Ezbrn. What made her different from the others?

"I'm sorry." Julian removed his hands from Genevieve's textbook. "I'm just not sure what to do."

"Call CNN? Call People magazine? It's either an investigative scoop, or a human interest story. Maybe they'll build you a better house for all of your orphans."

"Endl did."

"Endl did what?"

"Call the media once."

"What?" Lona turned from watching Fenn swing Affl onto his back for a piggyback ride.

"That's what resulted in her third remmersion. She had two, she escaped, she tried to tell someone, they brought her back and gave her a third."

Genevieve stared at Julian, then picked up another book and scanned the index.

"But maybe if we—" Julian began.

"It's not worth it," Genevieve cut him off, slamming the book shut and tossing it aside.

"I'm just saying that—"

"It doesn't *matter*, Julian. Money and power always find a way to win." She tossed a book to Lona. "Could you try to find something about post-Path integration? One of these should have something."

Lona scanned the summaries at the beginning of each chapter, but the cheering from the yard kept distracting her. "I just hate lying to him," she said. "To them."

"I know," Genevieve said. "But would you rather tell them that their brains are time bombs?"

No. She wouldn't. But yesterday, Gamb had asked her why she thought that no one from Path had reached out to them after Byde or Cadr died, to warn them about what was happening. Lona said that they probably wanted to – they just hadn't tracked down the address yet. He'd believed her and she hated herself for it.

What she'd rather was that Fenn's brain wasn't a time bomb at all.

At least he'd stopped staring at her. She couldn't have

217

handled that, on top of everything else – looking up from whatever she was doing and seeing his face. Ever since she'd told him that there was no need for them to finish the conversation, he'd stopped penetrating her skin with those green eyes.

Her relationship with Genevieve was better, too. It finally seemed like they were on the same team, as they always should have been. Enough shared secrets to bind them together. She didn't know if they would ever be friends, but what they had seemed almost closer – the way she could see the undercurrent of fear in Genevieve's eyes and understand what it meant and what put it there. The way they would huddle together, on the stairway or in the kitchen, trading their observations from the day, wondering whether Gamb seemed sad or whether Fenn seemed preoccupied, or if there was anything – anything – they weren't trying. Lona told herself that having Genevieve as a confidante made up for no longer having one in Fenn. She tried to tell herself that.

"What do you think, Lona?" Genevieve asked now, in response to something Julian had said. "Did anyone ever come in to prepare the older kids for going to Eighteens? Especially when you would have been in your late 5000s?"

"I don't think so." Another whoop erupted from the game running below.

The game was Fenn's idea – psychological training disguised as playtime. Not only did the Strays still use Path speak, but they occasionally had difficulties differentiating themselves from one another and, especially, from Julian.

'Red Rover, Red Rover, send Ezbrn right over' was a

rudimentary way of seeing whether Ezbrn knew who Ezbrn was.

Sometimes to test them, Fenn yelled, "Send Julian right over!" It had taken several rounds of the game before none of them responded to Julian's name. Most of the time, at least one of them still did.

The Strays loved their new guests. They were confused by Lona's story ("What do you mean you ran away?" Affl asked again and again. "Why didn't you want to be with Julian?") but they climbed on Gamb like a jungle gym, and Ezbrn followed Ilyf wherever she went, asking a hundred questions about computers.

Fenn was especially good with them. Like now. Endl had found a bug in the grass, and instead of yelling at her to focus on the game, Fenn called a time out so everyone could come and look at the beetle.

"Has Fenn had any more nightmares?" Julian asked Genevieve. "Since the one the first night I came?"

"No," Genevieve said. "Maybe Lona was right. Maybe being here is good for him. He does seem more rested. Or maybe it was a false alarm. People have nightmares all the time. And he hasn't gotten obsessive like Byde yet."

"Obsessive?"

"That was the second thing that Byde did. The second symptom after the nightmares. He kept obsessively keeping track of things."

"Like Ezbrn?" Julian glanced furtively at the grass to make sure Ezbrn hadn't heard.

"Not exactly. Not *things*. More like days. How many days since he'd been Off Path. How many days old he was. How many days old Julian might have been. It was weird, looking back, but I didn't really think about it at the time." She sighed, and flung another book aside. "But even that could be coincidence, too. Cadr didn't get that way. Czin did, though – not with days, but with time. Always wanting to know what time it was, to the second. It's hard to tell, sometimes, how much you guys are acting screwed up, and how much of it is the brain you were given to work from." She glanced and Julian. "No offense."

"But no more nightmares, at least," Julian said. "That's got to be good."

The scrape on Fenn's knuckles had almost healed. Now it was just raw, pink skin, which Lona could see from here. She noticed other things, too, that she wished she didn't. She noticed how his body moved underneath his T-shirt. She noticed the way that above the scraped knuckles, Fenn had the nicest arms. The most delicate bones in his wrists. The finest hairs on his forearms. The fingertips that had stroked hers twice in Path, four years ago, and once on a subway last week. She'd noticed it all too late.

In the yard, Gamb's side was winning – Fenn's was down to him and Affl, who was more of a hindrance than a help. Half of the time, when a member of the other team ran over, Affl tried to break the chain to wave in excitement, creating an invitation for the others to barge through.

Don't look at Fenn, she willed herself. *Don't think about Fenn. Don't feel for Fenn.*

"Lona." Genevieve said her name like it wasn't the first time.

"Yes?"

"You're being summoned."

Lona had been so busy not looking at Fenn, she hadn't heard Gamb's voice. "Go help them," he called, pointing to Fenn's team.

"Aren't you trying to beat them?" she asked.

"I can't win like this. It's like playing against a team of gummy bears. It's just too sad."

She waited to see if Fenn would protest the offer, but he just shrugged and averted his eyes. "If you want to play," he said finally.

"Make it official, Fenn," Gamb barked. "Do I have to do everything for you?"

Fenn and Affl outstretched their entwined arms. "Red Rover, Red Rover, send Lona right over!"

The sun was hot, outside of the porch's shade. Fenn and Affl's arms hit just below her rib cage; she felt a whoosh of air leave her body. Affl grinned, and dropped Fenn's hand, making a space for Lona between them. "Now it's a game," Gamb said. "Now I won't feel bad when we wipe you out after two minutes." Affl quickly wrapped her hand in Lona's. Her fingers were sticky and small and wriggling. Fenn hesitated for only a minute before holding out his own hand, looking across the yard at Gamb's team instead of at her. It was the first time since their conversation there had been any reason to touch. Lona told herself that if Fenn wasn't bothered by it, she wouldn't be either. She slid her fingers through his as casually as she could, ignoring the way his thumb brushed down the length of hers. "Are you ready?" Gamb called impatiently.

"Ready," Lona called, as she felt Fenn's grip tighten.

Gamb's team took Affl at her next turn, but anyone from the other side who tried to cross between Lona and Fenn failed. Her hand stayed wrapped around his wrist, and his around hers. Lona's arm was sore from the bashing of squirmy kids, but she still didn't let go.

"It's just like when we were kids, isn't it?" Fenn asked, when Gamb called a time out for his team.

"Red Rover was Julian's favorite game." He played it every summer with neighborhood kids, until after the sun went down when they were just blindly crashing into each other and falling into piles.

Fenn hesitated. "I wasn't talking about when Julian was a kid. I was talking about when we were." Sometimes she forgot they'd had childhoods. An hour a day's worth, to do everything normal kids did, so long as they didn't leave the Calisthenics room, see daylight, or stray too far from their big machines. "I was thinking about the time when they brought that doctor in to check our motor skills. Remember?"

It happened several times. Periodically, a researcher or two would pull them out of Calisthenics in small groups, testing that they were able to physically replicate what they virtually learned on Path. Lona remembered demonstrating that she knew how to tie a shoe. They'd had to give her a shoe for the exam. Pather slippers didn't have laces.

But she knew exactly the occasion Fenn was thinking of. It was a fitness test. They had to run the length of the room in an acceptable amount of time. Lona and Fenn were in the same group. The doctor – a gray-haired woman with oversized glasses – blew a whistle and everyone ran. Lona was in her mid-2,500s, then, which put Fenn in his early 3,000s. She was as fast as he was, and they both crashed against the padded wall at the same time.

"Very nice," the doctor said, jotting down the time when the last Pather finished. "You may all go back to your stations now."

Everyone else filed back to the machines. Lona didn't. Without knowing why she was doing it, she broke from the line and ran back across the room. The doctor looked baffled. The Coping Technicians looked embarrassed. The other Pathers looked shocked.

Except Fenn. After ten yards, Lona heard Fenn running behind her, his arms pumping, skinny legs churning. When they both got to the other end, she turned around and expected to see the same elation on his face that she felt on hers. Instead she saw concern. "We ran, too," he panted. "We ran too so they wouldn't get mad."

With Fenn running behind her, it might look like the instructions hadn't been clear – like both of them misunderstood and believed they were supposed to make another pass. With her running alone, it just looked like she was being bad.

"You know what they never tested us on?" Lona asked now, letting herself enjoy the ease of this conversation.

"What?"

"Swimming."

Ironic, the more she thought about it. All the miles they swam in Path, in Julian's body. It wouldn't have been possible to test it, of course. There wasn't a pool in the center, and they couldn't have transported everyone off site. Still.

"I miss the water," Lona said. "At least, I think I do."

"I do, too."

At that moment, a searing pain ripped through Lona's right bicep. Harm barreled into their linked arms. Lona fell backward into the grass, clouds of dust rising around her head.

"Harm. We never sent over for you," she coughed. "That's the point of the game."

Fenn helped her up, then whirled on Harm. "That was dangerous. Don't do that again. Ever."

Harm stripped off the long-sleeved shirt he was wearing over his T-shirt and offered it to Lona. "We apologize. We didn't know."

But he *did* know. They all knew. They'd all spent summers playing Red Rover. He knew the rules. Harm watched Lona dust off the back of her jeans and twist her arm around to see how red the mark was from the impact. He looked curious.

"Did it hurt when I hit you, Lona? Did it hurt when you fell on the ground?"

It had hurt. Her elbow was jammed from the way she had tried to block the fall with her arm. But looking at Harm, the overly casual way he scuffed his graceful toe in the dirt – he wanted it to hurt. He wasn't asking because he wanted to make sure she was okay. He was asking because he wanted to know if he should do it again.

"It didn't hurt. I barely felt it."

"That's wonderful." He laughed. When Lona heard his laugh before, mixed in with the others playing, she had thought it belonged to one of the little kids. It was high and sharp, like a piccolo. It pierced. It lasted too long. She remembered what Harm had said earlier. He didn't have problems staying on Path, not like Lona or Endl. He was declared unsuitable because of his Off Path behavior. It must have been very un-Julian-like. There was only an hour a day that they weren't in Path. What could he have done in an hour?

"Harm." Julian stood up to see why the game had stopped. "What did you do?"

Harm's attention snapped away from Lona. His expression went from blazing curiosity to remorse as he floated to the porch and stretched his hands through the rails. "I was bad and I shouldn't have been. I am sorry." This apology looked authentic. His whole body became an apology, his lithe form curved into an apostrophe of contrition. How odd. He seemed immensely sorry for disappointing Julian, if not sorry for hurting Lona. Whatever wiring existed in Harm's brain was something more complicated than Path had known how to deal with. "I'll try to be good in the future," he said. "I'll try."

People who had to try that hard to be good, Lona thought, usually weren't.

Julian suggested that Harm take a shift in the pod. Endl was next, but swore she didn't mind. "We have Julian in our brain already," Endl sighed.

Lona was fairly certain she was the only one who overheard Ilyf reply, "Honey, I'm glad you have something up there."

Julian made the suggestion casually, but Lona suspected he knew something wasn't right with Harm, and had learned that immersion back into the Path was a way to temporarily un-wrong it.

"Let's stop." Fenn waved everyone toward the house. "We've been playing for a long time. I bet everyone's tired, and we're losing light, anyway."

"And by 'everyone,' you mean you two," Gamb groaned. "And by 'losing light,' you mean 'losing.'"

"We forfeit."

"You for— really? I'll take it. This was a worthy victory." Gamb high-fived the members of his team. "Come here, little loser," he called to Lona. "Even sad weaklings deserve high-fives."

28

Lona went straight to the bathroom to wash the dust off her face and hands, to check a bruise she felt forming on her hip.

"Don't come in here," a voice cried as she pushed at the door, but she'd already glimpsed Genevieve sitting on the edge of the bathtub, her shoulders heaving and her face stained with muddy rivers of mascara.

"Genevieve?"

"Not you. Go away."

"What's wrong?"

"Go *away*."

"We'll figure this out. We'll keep trying." She slipped in and quickly closed the door behind her, taking a tissue from the box and moving to wipe Genevieve's face with it. Genevieve jerked back her head.

"I thought we were starting to be friends," she said. "On the same side."

Lona's hand froze in midair, still clutching the tissue. "What? We are – I am. I don't understand what's going on."

"You don't even know you're doing it, do you?" Genevieve asked. "I used to think you were being coy, but you're not. You're too stupid to even understand what's happening."

"Genevieve. What are you talking about?"

"I'm talking about Fenn. And you. And your glances and your inside memories, and him chasing after you in Calisthenics. Him always chasing after you. Do you think I can't see it?"

Lona's mind reeled. Genevieve was mad at *her*? Genevieve was upset with her for the way *she* acted around Fenn? Genevieve, who shared a bed with him every night? "All I see is him touching you all the time," she said finally. "All the time."

"We were almost there," Genevieve said. "*We* were making a home. *I* was the one who brought them together. Who taught them everything. Who gave him *everything*. When you came – when he *made* us rescue you – I knew this would happen, and I still couldn't say no. I was supposed to be enough. Do you know how long it has been since I felt like enough?" Her voice was hysterical. Lona had never seen her upset like this – pleading and out of control.

"Genevieve," she said, trying but failing to keep her own voice calm. "You were the one who told me that he needs you."

"Yes. He needs me. What a verb. He needs. I would rather have the one he has for you."

She clutched the tissue box as if it might float away. "The one he has for me?" she repeated stupidly.

"I'm not going to tell you if you can't figure it out for yourself."

"I don't understand. He chose you. He sleeps in your *bed*."

"Poor little pod person. To think that touching means everything."

"Why are you telling me this? *Any* of this?" If Genevieve thought that Fenn had feelings for Lona, then wouldn't Lona be the last person she would want to tell?

"That's a good question. Why am I telling you this?" She reached for the tissue in Lona's hand and began wiping the grime off of her face, leaving dark brown streaks across the thin paper. Her breathing had slowed, interrupted only by occasional wet hiccups. "Maybe I'm telling you because I think you're stronger than him. Maybe I think that he'll be able to break my heart, but you won't. Because you know what it feels like."

That was absurd. Why would Lona protect Genevieve's feelings, when Genevieve had only barely begun to care about hers?

"Do you feel sorry for me?" Genevieve asked softly.

She did, she realized. When she looked at Genevieve now, with her streaked face and rumpled hair, the way she slumped against the bathroom wall like she was using all the energy she had just to stay upright, Lona didn't feel jealousy or spite, or any of the other emotions she'd felt before around Genevieve. "Yes," she whispered. "I feel sorry for you."

She expected a reaction of anger. Genevieve should tell her now that she didn't need the pity of a pod person. Instead the other girl smiled, faintly and sadly.

"Good," she said. "I told you. I told you that I would do almost anything to preserve what I have with Fenn. Confiding in you. This is almost anything."

"That's . . . I don't understand."

"I have to go back to school. I'm telling Fenn it's because of my grades. It's true – I've missed so many classes that

229

they're going to put me on academic probation unless I ace my final tests. But I also have a couple of professors who might be able to give us some help, if I can find a way to ask questions without them knowing what I'm saying."

"When are you leaving?"

"Tomorrow morning. I'll be depending on you."

She was depending on Lona to keep secrets. To solve mysteries. To not want Fenn. Lona was depending on her for almost all of the same things.

Genevieve looked pale; her lips were light around the edges from where she'd pursed them together. Lona knew she must look the same, because she was making the same gestures of worry, had the same agonized loss of appetite. The two of them were entwined. After all of those hours of practicing together in front of the mirror, she could finally see herself in Genevieve.

Julian was sitting in the living room when Lona went back downstairs. It was late. The lights were off; she didn't see him until he called her name.

"You're still awake," he said.

"So are you."

"I stay up and listen to the house. I wish it had more room for everybody."

"The kids don't mind. Affl told me they get lonely if they sleep alone."

"Affl. Affl is my favorite. Is it egotistical to have favorite versions of me?"

"Do you still think of us as that. Versions of you?"

"Not really. I think of you as – as my wards, I suppose. My children. My thousands of children."

"Luckily less than a dozen of us live with you."

Julian smiled. "It's better with you older ones here. You have no idea how much of a difference it makes."

"Really?"

"It makes everything easier for me."

Lona sat down on the edge of the couch. It smelled like mildew and coughed up small puffs of dust whenever she moved.

"I forgot, this is where you've been sleeping, right?" Julian started to stand up. "I'm taking up your bed."

"It's fine. I'm not tired anyway. Go ahead and listen to the house."

"Drama in the corridors?"

She wondered if – no, she *knew* that – Julian had overheard at least part of her conversation with Genevieve.

"Something like that."

"Do you want to talk about it?"

"Is it okay if I say no?"

"We all do what we need to do."

"Shhh. Do you hear that?"

Julian stiffened next to her. There was a noise coming from directly above them – the bedroom where Fenn and Genevieve slept. A wail. It sounded like a keening animal, sad and cracked. She thought it was the wind at first, blowing through the drafty walls. But the noise persisted, shifting shape, growing more desperate. There were foot-steps, then – someone getting out of bed and talking, low and soothing.

Fenn was having another nightmare, and Genevieve was trying to comfort him. Until now, if she'd had to pick one of Genevieve's body parts that she was jealous of, it would have been her long legs or her shiny hair. Those were stupid things. Now the only thing she was jealous of were Genevieve's hands, stroking Fenn's cheek.

29

Talia had never liked the way that Julianbase was ordered. It was easy enough to look things up by day, if you knew what the day was. The organizational methodology also worked fine for important people in Julian's life – you could look up 'Nick Zaber,' for example, and any major events involving Nick would come up. Some events were already pre-programmed into the database, which gave an advance alert if someone was going to die or be injured or undergo another major event. Quadrant 4, for example, was about to be a disaster – one Pather was heading into the hospital for Julian's tonsillectomy, another would experience Grandpa Pierce's first stroke, and a third was going to be rejected from Julian's first choice college.

What Julianbase didn't have, however, was a good way of looking things up by key word. If you wanted to remember what day Julian got a detention or gave a presentation on the Underground Railroad, there was no way to easily track it down. This is what Talia wanted to do now: look up a certain event. Specifically, when Julian went to the zoo, was selected by the walrus keeper to be a special assistant, and got to help feed Wallace and Mimsy. It was for some kid's birthday party. It happened when Julian was four. What was that kid's name? Adrian? Avery?

She wanted to look it up for Djna. He'd been here a little over a week now; the Coping Technicians said he was adjusting to his accelerated Path well and getting lots of remedial attention. But Talia couldn't help but worry about him. She wanted to find that birthday party because the day was considered an eleven, and she wanted to know how long he would have to wait.

"Talia?" The knock on the doorframe was timid.

"Yes?" Talia didn't bother to look up at Sanjeeta. She didn't want to lose her place, clicking on the descriptions for every single day between 1460 and 1824. She also didn't want to get sucked into helping Sanjeeta oil a squeaking pod or polish a visioneer, or whatever else she was about to be asked to do instead of trying to find this birthday. *Aidan? Aspen? Abbott?*

"Talia." Sanjeeta gingerly sat down on the swiveling chair belonging to the next desk over. She was too short for her feet to touch the ground; the chair started rotating listlessly to the right, taking Sanjeeta with it. Talia was trying not to laugh about it when Sanjeeta said, "Your mother called."

Suddenly the room was freezing. "Are you sure?"

"Am I . . . sure?"

Sanjeeta looked confused. Most people's first reaction upon hearing their mothers had called would not be disbelief. Talia shouldn't have been caught so off guard. She did vaguely know that her mom had the number. Some friend who'd thought she was doing Talia a favor confessed years ago that she'd passed it on. Talia's mother had never called, though, and Talia stopped returning that friend's emails.

"She asked for you by name. She said to tell you your dad is very sick. He's in a hospice."

Sanjeeta reached out toward Talia's arm to deliver her default gesture of reassurance. Talia shrank back. She didn't need a government-contracted Toucher to comfort her. She'd needed that when she was twelve, not now.

"I see."

"I'm so sorry."

"Is that all she said?"

The CT pulled back her hand, picking a piece of lint off of her own blouse, as if that was the intention all along. The exchange was obviously not turning into the bonding session Sanjeeta envisioned. "She said you could call her, if you wanted. That she's still at the same number. That's all she said."

"Thank you."

The other woman didn't move. Well, she moved – the chair continued to steadily rotate her away from Talia, feet swinging in the air – but she didn't move to exit the room.

"Thank you."

Sanjeeta hesitated, then nodded sadly, as if she understood some people liked to grieve in private. She took longer than she needed to hoist herself out of the seat and drift to the door. Giving Talia enough time to change her mind and decide she needed someone to talk with after all.

"Sanjeeta, actually, could you do something for me?"

"Of course." The way she stopped was almost greedy.

"Could you see if anyone else on the shift remembers this

day I'm trying to locate? Julian fed the walruses at the zoo? Some kid's birthday? Anders or Abner or something?"

Sanjeeta cocked her head. "Jeffrey Kim?"

Jeff. That was it.

"Right. Thanks."

"Why did you want to know?"

"No reason. Well, just one – I think that day is coming up for Djna. I thought he would like an eleven." She sounded like an idiot. "You know – help his brain waves stay on track."

Sanjeeta looked concerned. "Do you have any reason to think they're not on track?"

"No. Not from my end. I was meaning to ask you the same thing, though. Does he seem to be adjusting appropriately? As you would expect?"

"I think he's doing just fine. Are you sure I can't do anything else, Talia?"

"Jeff Kim. That's all I needed."

"Good, then. Take care."

When Sanjeeta left, Talia typed Jeff into Julianbase. A picture of a Korean boy with a gap between his front teeth popped up. That's right. Jeff and Julian met at summer swimming lessons, the first time Julian was ever in a pool. And he turned four on June 2, which was in less than a week.

Talia closed the tab and walked down to the bay, into the electronic white-noise hum. Out of the corner of her eye, she saw a Coping Technician watching her suspiciously. She didn't usually come down here unless it was time for rounds. Sanjeeta shook her head at the man in warning.

Don't. Talia imagined her saying, *She just found out her dad is sick. Give her some leeway.*

Djna's pod was a perfect fit. Talia had done well. His spindly elbows were properly supported; his neck was cocooned against the headrest. He was watching Julian listen to story time at the library.

Talia crouched on her haunches, examining a strap she already knew worked fine. "Hey, dude. Angelina Ballerina, huh? Wait until you get to Shel Silverstein. Way better."

The other kids sitting around Julian were smiling. The librarian did good voices.

Talia's mom did good voices. If she thought back to before she hated her mom and loathed her dad, her mom did all of the voices. She would read the books over again as many times as Talia wanted, and unlike the parents of some of Talia's friends, she never tried to skip paragraphs. Sometimes they would read so many stories that her mom would forget to make dinner. Instead they would have reverse breakfast. Banana pancakes. Talia still made banana pancakes every Sunday. It was just a habit. It had been years since she thought about where the habit came from.

"You don't even need funny voices with Shel Silverstein. *Where the Sidewalk Ends* is funny on its own. A different kind of funny – you'll see. Julian reads that next year. You know what else you'll like? Feeding the walruses. At the zoo. That's not next year – that's next week. Really soon, you're going to have a really good day. It's not exactly like the aquarium, but walruses live in the water too. And they make funny noises. Way funnier than fish."

Djna's mouth turned up at the corners. If Talia was back

at her desk, she could have pulled up his chart and compared it to Julian's, to verify that their humor receptors were both activating at the same time. She couldn't do that from his pod.

"Getting into the story now, huh? That's what's happening?" She rebuckled the strap for the third time. Her fingers moved slowly.

"Or are you . . . are you getting into the fish? Like at the aquarium? Djna?"

This kid was a Mona Lisa. She couldn't tell whether he was smiling or not. Probably not. Julian had no relationship to fish. He thought they were gross. Turned down all of Grandpa McKay's invitations to go fishing on the weekends.

"Djna? Djna? Djna?

"Gabriel?"

She wasn't making it up. She didn't think so, at least. It was a small smile, but it was there.

30

There were endless ways to keep busy. There were Strays to care for. Julian meticulously taught Lona the particular needs of each one, like how Ezbrn got upset by wrinkled clothing, and how Endl loved pockets but would never empty them on her own. There were news sources to monitor, for anything related to Path. There was Genevieve to call, quietly, with updates – to hope that she had discovered something and to learn that she hadn't. There was normalcy that had to be carefully orchestrated so Fenn – and the others – didn't see how anxious she was. Fenn still didn't know he was having nightmares. There was no point in telling him. He couldn't control them and they'd only make him worry.

Lona worried all the time. She worried in her bones, in her sleep.

Two mornings after Genevieve left, she woke up already tense in her body. She'd slept through the night, which meant Fenn had too because his screams hadn't wakened her. She could sense someone was sitting next to her, even before opening her eyes. It was him. He knelt on the floor, hands folded in his lap, a few inches from her nose.

"What are you doing?" She scrambled to a seated position.

He lifted something up from the floor next to him. A blue shopping bag that bulged in the bottom. "Everyone else is still sleeping. I thought we'd go on a field trip."

"What kind of field trip?"

"Secret."

"Should we invite Ilyf and Gamb?"

"No. This is just for us. If you want to come – you don't have to. But I hope you will."

Of course she wanted to come. She couldn't help wanting to come, especially since Fenn looked so happy, like he was holding an eleven behind his back, waiting to give it to her. But her brain wouldn't let her stop thinking of Genevieve, crumpled in the bathroom, begging Lona to be worthy of her trust.

"I shouldn't." She watched his expression fall. He awkwardly began to rise to his feet, backing away from the suitcase.

"Of course. I understand. I just hoped that after we played Red Rover, you might be less upset with me. I thought this would be – but of course. Never mind."

Then again, it couldn't be wrong to do something that would make Fenn so happy. Wasn't that the point of all of this? To keep them happy? Even Genevieve would have agreed with that. She was almost sure of it.

"You know what? Let's go. As long as we're not gone too long."

"You're sure?" His face broke into a tentative smile.

"Let's go."

* * *

The sun was up but the house was quiet when they walked out the front door. Fenn paused to grab granola bars and the keys to the van on his way out. So it was a far away field trip, one that required driving.

This was the first time they'd ever been in the car alone. They were *almost* alone the day she escaped from Path, except for Gamb and for the fact that she'd been unconscious. Both things put a damper on that experience.

"Where are we going?"

"Still a secret."

His eyes darted down to the blue shopping bag tucked near his feet.

"What's in there?"

Fenn shook his head. "Seeecret."

They passed through several residential neighborhoods until the landscape turned industrial. Fenn didn't drive like Julian. He kept both of his hands precisely at ten and two on the steering wheel, braking well before he needed to. Fenn drove like Julian's grandmother.

"Did you have driving lessons in Eighteens?"

"A few. Am I bad?"

"You're cautious."

"This is a real car on a real street."

"With real people in it."

"And a really beautiful day." The sun was a show-offy blue. The neighborhood they were in now could have been one from Julian's childhood – stores and strip malls and four-lane roads. It looked like the stretch that the Tru-Mart was on, where Julian's dad would vow to never shop at least once a month because of its bad environmental practices, before relenting for the low prices. Fenn checked his directions again, then swung the car into an office park, stopping in front of a big, boxy building.

BRIGHTWOOD RECREATIONAL CENTER, the sign said. PUBLIC POOL.

"I know that you've been mad at me," Fenn started. "I wasn't even sure you'd want to come. But when I found out that this was nearby – I thought that you might like to go swimming."

Julian swam in two kinds of pools: the kidney-shaped pool at his grandparents' retirement complex, where wrinkly men in waterwings dogpaddled across the width. And the rectangular lap pools he spent hours of the rest of his life in, lap after lap, staring down at the black lane markers painted along the bottom.

The rec center was a lap pool – indoors with fluorescent lighting, a tile floor, six lanes, and a bored-looking teenage lifeguard slouched in his chair, twirling his whistle around on his fingers. Since it was almost June, there were probably already outdoor pools open. He looked profoundly annoyed not to be working at one of them. Lona was glad Fenn chose this one. It was calming to be here. Familiar. If she closed her eyes and smelled the tinny chlorine, she could almost hear Coach Armand yelling about someone's messy flip turns.

A heavyset woman in a skirted suit diligently swam freestyle in a far lane; a couple of moms read magazines on the deck while their kids bobbed in the shallow end. Other than that, the pool was empty.

Fenn wore a pair of navy blue trunks, the baggy kind Julian and his teammates layered on to increase drag during training. She had never seen his chest before, or his legs, or even his arms much beyond his wrists. She wondered what it would feel like to brush her hand across the flat plane of his stomach, skimming from his chest down to his torso. Her face flushed hot and she could feel red spreading across her cheeks.

Lona wore the contents of Julian's mysterious shopping bag, which turned out to be a fairly hideous floral-printed suit at least two sizes too big. "I thought you would like it better than a bikini," he said, apologetically. He was right, but what she really wished she had was a huge T-shirt. Fenn's nakedness made her acutely aware of her own.

"Let's jump in!" Fenn folded his shirt carefully on a deck chair, then stood expectantly at the ledge.

"I don't know. I don't know if I can swim." It was one thing to learn how to read music or do quadratic equations in Path. It was another to learn how to propel oneself through the water without drowning. In her mind, she pictured the feeling of water between her calves as she snapped them together in a frog kick. She pictured the buoyancy of her body – the way it should slowly rise to the surface after she dived in the pool. Should. What if she dived in this water and sank to the bottom like lead? The lifeguard was patrolling the deck now, holding a flotation device across his chest. If it was too bad, he would save her.

She edged toward the pool, dipping her foot in, feeling the comfortable numb that came with the cold. It felt like it should, almost exactly – the lapping and tickling, and the way droplets of water felt like pinpricks on her skin. Experimentally, she flicked her toe up in Fenn's direction, spraying his calves with water.

"Lona, you just—" His benign expression was replaced by a smile as he realized that she'd splashed him on purpose. He retaliated with an armful of water aimed at her midsection. Soon they were both shrieking, wet enough from splashes that it made more sense to jump in the pool than to stay out of it. Lona dived off the side, headfirst – a flat racing dive that wasn't as elegant as what Julian would have done, but still made a sort of sense to her body. She hit the water on her belly, feeling the sting of contact and the disorientation of weightlessness, and emerging with nostrils full of water. *Right. Exhale when you dive in.* This felt like home, in ways that her other Off Path experiences hadn't. Maybe it had to do with being in the water. Water was a foreign substance. Swimming in it left all human beings – not just Lona – quite literally out of their element. It was an equality of strangeness.

They swam until their fingers were pruny. They took turns timing each other around the pool. Lona proposed they see who could do the most somersaults; Fenn suggested a breath-holding contest. She could stay here, doing this, all day. The weightless water, the humid air, the dimness that made time feel unimportant. It was a different world in here.

After a half an hour, one of the boys from the group of kids asked if they knew how to play Shark. His mother

244

peered over her magazine long enough to give Lona a sympathetic look saying she didn't have to join in. Shark had always been fun for Julian, so Lona and Fenn lined up by the side of the pool and waited for the shark in the middle, a bossy seven-year-old named Micah, to yell 'Go!'

"I thought you said you *played* this before," Micah grumbled when he caught Lona on her first pass across the pool.

"I have. Sort of. Not really." She ignored his disapproving expression and continued to overexplain. "It's harder to swim underwater than I thought it would be."

"Well, now you have to be my helper shark." He pointed to a spot in the middle of the pool. "Just try to catch people and not mess up, okay?"

"Okay."

Lona was the shark assistant for only a few rounds. Then the surly teenage lifeguard blew his whistle and announced that the pool was closing for his thirty-minute break. Everybody paddled to the side. Micah and his friends left, under protest, with their mothers. The lap-swimming woman gathered her swim fins and assorted other props, heading for the showers.

"Do you want to go?" Fenn stood uncertainly in front of her, her towel outstretched in his hand. "Or stay?"

"I want to stay."

His skin was covered in goosebumps from the cold, which made Lona more aware of her flowered suit bunching up in all the wrong places. She grabbed the towel and wrapped it around her shoulders. "Is that okay?"

"I want to stay, too."

The lifeguard appeared to have left the pool entirely for his lunch break and, against all protocol, turned off the main lights. If a manager walked in, he would definitely be fired. Lona and Fenn sat by the edge of the water and dangled their feet in.

"This was fun," she said.

"Don't you love the weightlessness? And that moment when you first jump in and your scalp gets wet?"

In the low light, the blue of the water looked iridescent. Neon. "Have you been to a pool before?" Lona asked.

"Yes." He paused. "Genevieve brought me to her health club once. It . . . wasn't like this. There were all of these women standing around in white uniforms. If you wanted a towel, they used a pair of tongs to get one for you from this hot-air machine. The towels were all heated and smelled like mint. It was . . . nice."

"Well. It was nice of her to take you. Minty towels."

She wished she had a minty towel right now. She would use it to smother this conversation. Her stomach panged at the mention of Genevieve. But she wasn't doing anything wrong, she reminded herself. She and Fenn were just talking. It would be impossible to live in the same house and never talk. The figure eight that Fenn made with his toes in the water collided with the figure eight that she was making with hers.

"Lona. I want to talk to you about the day on the train."

Her toe faltered. Could he never stop bringing it up? Did he never want her to outlive her embarrassment?

"It's fine. You don't have to worry about us." She used 'us' in the Pather sense. It just slipped out. She'd meant, 'me, alone' not 'us,' like 'you and me together.' But explaining that now would be awkward.

"I know you were mad at me. I know that you haven't been Off Path very long and seeing that couple – I know that what they were doing must have seemed disgusting. I'm sure it was uncomfortable for you to know I'd done that before. And I'm sorry."

Lona replayed his words in her head, at full speed, at half speed. What was he talking about? He thought she was mad at him because she thought kissing was *scary*?

"I just keep forgetting that this world is so new to you—" He broke off. "I'm trying so hard to respect your feelings. I wish you felt differently." He paused. "There," he said. "That's all I wanted to say."

"Fenn," Lona said slowly. "I wish things were different, too. I wish I didn't hate the idea of you kissing Genevieve. I'm sorry that I do; I can't help it. I wish—" Her eyes were filling with embarrassing tears. She cut herself off. She'd almost said, *I wish I didn't wish it were me instead.*

Fenn was still.

"Did you say that you don't like the idea of me kissing . . . Genevieve? That's the part you don't like?"

She nodded, miserably. Fenn closed his eyes and nodded his head slowly back and forth. "I'm so stupid."

"Why?"

"Do you know how I first met Genevieve?"

"She came to your graduation. She said she had rooms to rent." Why were they still talking about Genevieve?

"She said that. But the first thing she said was, 'What a nightmare.' Everyone else was asking if we'd like to participate in studies, or if we'd thought about religion, or our souls. Genevieve said, 'What a nightmare,' and she asked us if we wanted to go get pizza. She was the first person to seem like she wanted to know us apart from what we were."

"Right. I get it." She stared at the middle of the pool, at a shiny object below the surface. Someone had dropped a watch, or a necklace, maybe.

"I was so grateful for her. For a long time, it was easy to confuse being grateful with something else." Fenn's eyes weren't looking at the pool. They were staring at her; he craned his neck to see her face.

"When I figured out that they were two different things, I thought it would still be okay. I thought being grateful could be enough, or I could make it be enough. And I could, almost . . . Until . . ."

He swallowed, hard. The muscles in his jaw clenched together. "I really didn't mean to do this today. I know it's too fast. I know it's not fair."

It took a moment for Lona to realize what he hadn't meant to do. His hand was on her face, first brushing her hair from her forehead, then running the tips of his fingers over her cheek, and then lightly, so lightly – so lightly that what she was feeling might have been the movement of electrons rather than the contact of skin – he touched her lips. She felt the faint, fluttering pulse in his fingertips, the same feeling on the same fingertips that had stroked her arm for the first time four years ago. Now he was

248

cradling her face with both hands and it was his lips that were touching hers, barely brushing. Barely moving at all, except that she noticed that their breath was synchronized, rising and falling at the same time. She wondered if their heartbeats were matching, too, and reached out to Fenn. When the palm of her hand landed on his chest, he gasped.

"I'm sorry." Lona jolted back.

"Don't be sorry for that." Fenn took her hand and gently moved it back to his heart, which was beating faster than hers. A tiny droplet of water fell from the curls of Fenn's wet hair, snaked down his neck and over his olive-colored skin until it came to a rest on the top of Lona's index finger. *Water-tight barrier.* She remembered an ancient Chemistry lesson. They were closer than water molecules.

"I shouldn't," Lona whispered.

"I have to," Fenn said. His hand moved around to the back of her head, running his fingers through her damp hair and moving his mouth toward hers again. "Unless – unless you don't want me?"

When their lips met this time it was harder. His mouth molded to hers and his body molded to hers, pulling her closer into him until the way that she could tell that their heartbeats had finally synced up was that her chest was pressed against his. Path could never have replicated anything that felt like this. He kissed her eyes. He kissed her nose. He kissed her mouth again. She tasted his lips with the tip of her tongue and he groaned, and before pulling himself away and resting his chin on the top of her head.

I have never been this close to another person, Lona thought. Not just in a kissing kind of way. In any kind of way. There wasn't ever a reason to touch like this or breathe like this, in tandem with someone else's body. Not just with someone else's body. With Fenn.

"I'm going to tell her," he said.

"What?"

"Genevieve. I'll call her tonight."

"You can't." Lona lifted her head from beneath his chin, panicking. "Don't you care about her?"

Fenn's chest expanded and fell. "I do care. I don't care the way she wants me to. That's the problem. That's always been the problem."

"No! After everything she's . . . it's not fair to her."

"No, what's not fair is that I had to turn eighteen to realize I'd been in love with a person I've known since I was two," Fenn said. "That Genevieve had to teach me what it meant to feel romantically toward someone, and I learned it just in time to realize that I didn't feel it toward her. *That* is what is not fair."

"In love?"

"I know it's all messy, but I think that's how it is Outside. I think sometimes people get hurt, and it's bad, but it just happens and no one can help it."

Her ears were still stuck on the first sentence. "Love. Do you . . . do you think that's what you feel?"

"Have I been dumb enough not to say it a hundred times? I am in love with you, Lona Sixteen Always."

In love. The missing verb. Fenn loved her.

There was no shortage of love in Path. Julian's parents loved him, deeply and unconditionally. They loved each other, too, but it was steady and chaste. The Path version of their relationship was passionless. In love was what happened in Mrs. Dwyer's Shakespearean sonnets. It was abstract. Lona hadn't been able to picture the real feelings until now.

"Do you remember when you smelled the grass?" Fenn asked. "The real grass? How it made you realize that the grass in Path was wrong?"

"Not wrong. Just fake."

"Sometimes I think that what I feel for you is the first real emotion I have ever felt."

"Are you sure it's not because of Julian? That we have—" How had Genevieve put it? "—inside memories? That we had the same experiences?"

"Lona." When Fenn said her name, it didn't sound like a random grouping of letters signifying dates and locations. It sounded like a name. "I have thought of you every day since I went to Eighteens. It has never been because of what we both saw in our visioneers."

Fenn must have mistaken her silence for uncertainty, because he hurriedly began to backtrack, his sentences coming out disorganized and distinctly un-Fenn-like.

"I'm not expecting to you say the same thing . . . or feel the same thing. I just – I wanted you – it just feels good to say it to you. Are you upset?"

"I'm not upset." Just like with Fenn's grass, she was feeling something for the first time, in its purest, undiluted form. Today, they could be Jackson and Caroline on the train, except more, because Lona swore she would never take the magic of this feeling for granted. "I'm happy."

31

On the ride home, her cheeks hurt. She worried, until she realized it was because she was smiling. Another muscle group that Path hadn't exercised well enough and had forgotten to test.

Her hair was wet and the sun was drying it; her muscles felt spent and sore. There was water caught in her ear, and she periodically shook her head, more because the sensation was new and interesting than out of any real attempt to dislodge the drop.

And Fenn. Fenn was alive, and here, and saying that he loved her.

"Do you know what I'm thinking?" she asked.

"What are you thinking?"

"I'm thinking that everything feels okay right now."

"Maybe we should just keep driving, as long as it feels that way."

There was a solution she hadn't thought of. Drive away. Leave everyone. The Fenn that was in the pool would never try to kill himself. This Fenn was too happy, she was sure of it. She slid her hand into his hand. This felt good. This felt right. Maybe they should do that. It wasn't fair, but everyone would survive. Why did she have to be the person responsible for figuring how a massive governmental experiment had wrecked its participants? She was sixteen.

"Do you know what I'm thinking?" Fenn asked.

"What are you thinking?"

"Six thousand and nineteen."

"What?"

"Six thousand and nineteen," he repeated cheerfully.

"That's . . . days?"

"That's how old you are. Assuming that you came to Path when you were just born, that's how many days I've known you. Considering that I would have been two years old at the time, and had to develop rational thought, it is probably a reasonable estimate to say that I've been in love with you for 5,024 of those days. And now I'm just six days from my nineteenth birthday. And everything is perfect."

"Perfect," Lona said. "Perfect."

"So should we keep driving?" He was teasing, but there was a part of him that wanted her to take the suggestion seriously.

"No. We should go home. Right now."

She kept his hand in hers. She squeezed it tightly.

Byde counting days. Cadr counting time. Fenn knowing the precise duration they had known each other. Pointless math none of them should have been able to do so easily.

It wasn't fair for happiness to disappear so quickly.

She wondered how soon she could get ahold of Genevieve to tell her that Fenn had just begun displaying the second set of symptoms that would lead to his death.

32

"I don't understand what you're saying, Lona. You want Fenn to go . . . back on Path?"

Lona worked to keep from hitting Julian. What didn't he understand? Why was he wasting time repeating her words? "If people die when they go Off Path for too long, then isn't the solution – temporarily, at least – to keep them on Path longer? Some of the kids here have been away for months and months, and they're not showing the symptoms that Fenn is. You just plug them in downstairs a couple times a day."

"They're not—" Julian lowered his voice, even though the door to his bedroom was closed and everyone else was outside. "They're not exactly *well*."

"They're alive."

Surely he could see this wasn't the time to be picky.

"Lona, there is no more Path to plug him into. It was supposed to end at eighteen."

"But *you* didn't end at eighteen, Julian. You have more memories. I bet you're still equipped with LifeCapture."

"So what if I am? What if I could download my life for Fenn? What would he find? He'd find a regular guy whose regular life was going on fine, until he was randomly selected to represent the perfect life."

"It's what he's used to."

"And then after that, you'd find a guy who spent five years adjusting to the fame, five years enjoying the fame as a third-rate celebrity hack, and five years wondering about what a huge, colossal mistake he'd made in ever agreeing to do it at all. You would find a guy who took pills, drank too much, acted like an ass and couldn't manage to hold down a longterm relationship. And then you would find that guy wondering whether all of it – the drinking and self-loathing – was a lovely trait that he had managed to pass down to thousands of his non-biological progeny. Oh, but don't worry – you won't have to worry about that for too long, because then the little versions of you will start killing themselves. So then you get a whole new basket of problems to start worrying about. Sound good?"

Julian opened a drawer of his bureau and pulled out an armful of T-shirts, rolling them into smaller shapes and stuffing them into a duffel bag.

A duffel bag. Lona was too upset when she first burst into Julian's bedroom to notice it, but there was a half-full black bag sitting on the bed. Next to the bed, a rolling suitcase was already zipped up.

"What are you doing?"

He didn't answer, just opened a second drawer and grabbed a bundle of socks, shoving them in a side pocket.

"Are you taking a trip?"

"Something like that." He avoided her eyes.

Where would Julian go that he needed two suitcases and all of his clothes?

"You're leaving."

He brushed past Lona to go to his nightstand, sweeping a bunch of toiletries into the bag without bothering to sort them. He winced, examining his fingertip, which was red with a spot of blood. He must have nicked it on the nail scissors before they went into the duffel. Julian sucked on the finger, using his other hand to work the zipper closed.

"This was your plan all along wasn't it?"

Finally, he answered. "I have to go, Lona. If I don't leave now, I never will."

"You never thought we could be any kind of revolution. You just wanted some babysitters."

"They like you. They trust you. It makes more sense for you to be with them than for me."

"Leave the freakshow behind to run itself."

"It's too much. Don't you get it? I'm proud of you for not giving up, not letting this beat you. But I can't."

Lona felt like she was seeing him for the first time. "They depend on you. They worship you – Julian, they need you in order to survive, and now you're leaving them."

"I was hoping that with all of you here—"

"That you would be able to go back to a normal life?"

"You're one to talk about betrayal, Lona." He slammed a drawer shut, hard enough that the handle rattled. "Genevieve tells you how much she loves Fenn, and you wait a whole two days before running off with him to the pool."

Her heart skidded to a stop. "That's different." She and Fenn were supposed to be together. If she'd known how he felt about her, she would have told Genevieve not to depend on her for anything. If she'd had the right vocabulary, she never would have let Fenn leave Path a year ago without telling him to wait for her. "I didn't understand things then."

He looked at her meaningfully. He didn't understand things, either, when he first came to this house and undertook this responsibility. "Lona," he said. "I'm tired."

"You're worthless."

"I know."

The way his shoulders crumpled, it looked he was a balloon she had popped. He took one deep, ragged breath, and she could see the way his chest caved in on itself. He wasn't worthless. He was just empty. The man literally gave half of his life to Path, and here Lona stood in his bedroom, asking for the rest of it.

Apologize, she ordered herself.

She couldn't make herself apologize, though. Because she wouldn't have abandoned them. Even earlier today, when she had the chance, when she and Fenn were in the car, she chose to go back.

"I'm sorry," Julian whispered. He slung the duffel over his shoulder, and grabbed the handle of the other suitcase. "Tell everyone I'm sorry."

Lona crossed her arms in front of her chest, and stared past Julian, out the window. She would not acknowledge his apology. Only when she heard the front door open and shut did she allow herself to sink onto the bed, slowly so her knees wouldn't collapse under her.

What next? She needed to figure something out. She would make this work. She would—

"You forgot," a voice said, from the landing on the stairs.

"You forgot to tell Julian about the third set of symptoms."

Fenn. Fenn was standing on the stairs.

She remembered to close Julian's door for their conversation; she forgot how well sound traveled from the upstairs bedrooms to the couch downstairs. Shouldn't she know that better than anyone?

"Maybe you didn't forget," Fenn continued. Maybe Genevieve never noticed it. I didn't think of it, until just now, when I realized it happened to me this morning."

Lona rose to her feet and tried to look nonchalant. "Third set of . . . what? Can we talk later? I was just helping Julian get some clothes together. To donate."

"Let's not lie, Lona, any more than we already have."

Lona sat down again, hard, succumbing to the hopelessness of the situation. "When did you figure it out?"

"When you did, probably. All of the clues were there. I just had more of an incentive to ignore them. Or if you want a more specific answer, I started to suspect something ninety-seven hours and thirty-four minutes ago. I can do that now – see my life clearly in hours and days. Why do you think that is?"

They both knew that the answer to that.

"Because you're dying."

"Who else knows?"

"Genevieve. She was the one who first learned."

She waited for Fenn to yell. Anger could be such a purifying emotion. Julian's mother taught her that. Sometimes she came home after a failed surgery and locked herself in the basement bathroom to scream before dinner.

259

Fenn needed to explode with all the bitterness she hated in him when she first arrived. They would fight. And then they would move on.

Instead, Fenn turned and walked toward his room. Saying nothing, acknowledging nothing.

"Fenn. What are you—"

He stopped, but didn't look at her. "We're fine."

"We meaning you and me, or we meaning you?" She sensed it was a Path 'we'.

"We, like me. I am fine."

"What about—" she followed him into the hall. She wasn't used to talking to his back. Fenn never turned away. Not from her, at least. Even when Fenn was angry, he didn't turn away from her the way he was doing now. "What about you and me?"

In that moment she hated him. For introducing a world where there was a you and me, and making her want it. For making her into a person who would have to ask this question.

"We are . . . nothing. We can't go back to the beginning. I think I just need you to leave me alone."

We are nothing. The words physically stopped her, like a barrier.

"Fenn, wait."

She searched for something she could ask that would make him stay, even for just a minute longer.

"The third symptom of Byde's. What was it? Genevieve only said there were two."

"It's happiness, Lona. Before Byde disappeared, before Czin disappeared – both of them said life couldn't get any

260

better than it was right then, at that moment. That's how I felt, at the swimming pool. That life was perfect. Maybe that thought was depressing enough to want to die."

He paused again, outside of his room.

"My picture was on the news."

"What? When?"

"Now. That's what I was coming up to tell you. I'm wanted for questioning about a security breach. Yours, too. You are wanted for instigating a dangerous rebellion."

So. They decided Lona wasn't an endangered child anymore, but the leader of something. The leader of the Strays. Fenn went into his bedroom and closed the door behind him. In case Lona hadn't gotten the message, he locked it, too.

33

We are nothing, his voice said, again and again. Sometimes it was her own voice, replaying in her head. *I am nothing. I am nothing to him.* She thought about going after him, knocking on the door until he opened it again. She didn't because he wouldn't, and also because she knew she didn't deserve forgiveness. Not after the way she'd lied. She didn't even deserve to be in a place where she'd lost him. He wasn't hers to lose to begin with. Everything Julian had said about Genevieve was right. She was disgusted with herself.

Lona went to the phone. Her fingers were heavy on the keypad, but she had to tell Genevieve what had happened. At least some of what had happened – the parts about Fenn overhearing her conversation. But the flickering light at the public pool – did Genevieve need to know that, too?

"Hi," Genevieve said. Lona's stomach twisted in relief and shame at the sound of her voice.

"Genevieve, it's—"

"I can't come to the phone right now," the voice continued. It was her voicemail. "I'm in exams from six to ten every night this week. Leave me a message and I'll call you back as soon as I can." Lona looked at the clock. A quarter past six. Genevieve had just turned her phone off, and wouldn't turn it on again for hours, if she remembered to at all before going to bed.

"It's Lona," she said anyway. "Come home when you can. Genevieve, it's really bad."

Now was not the time to fall apart. Now was the time to think. She fumbled in the darkness for the basement light switch. The fluorescent bulb lit up the pod in the center of the room. For a second she moved toward it. What could it hurt – to curl up for a minute and fast-forward to some encouraging memory? Julian winning the most valuable swimmer award for his team. Julian pouring Mountain Dew on Seth's head, after he'd harassed Curtis one too many times in the locker room.

But that wasn't what she came down here for. She scanned the boxes on the shelves until she found the blue box tucked up in a corner. The files that came with the pod when Julian bought it from the estate sale.

Julian said there were records, but the yellowing pages crammed into the box weren't anything useful. An instruction manual for the operating the pod. Service requests for broken equipment. A calendar of Calisthenics schedules for a month of August.

"Dammit," she muttered. She swept her hand along the bottom of the box just to be sure, and that's when she felt it, tucked under a folded flap of cardboard.

She tugged it out: a slim, silver jump drive marked *Admission Records*.

The jump drive wouldn't have been part of the official

record-keeping system. It was probably just a backup some techie made during a system upgrade. It didn't matter where it came from, though, so long as it still worked.

A computer sat in the corner of the room. Not fancy like the computers of the Monitors, just a basic desktop. But it had the port Lona needed, and when she stuck the drive in, the computer whirred and began to load the contents.

The first page to appear was the boy facing the sun. What a stupid logo. In real life this boy would just go blind.

Fenn had given her this idea, when he said they couldn't go back to the beginning.

They could, though. This was the very beginning. This is where their lives started. Maybe if she learned where they came from, she could learn where they needed to go. It was something. Better to do something.

When she clicked the file's 'Find' function, a gray box appeared in the center of the screen. It was empty except for a blinking cursor.

NAME?

The keyboard was dusty; it felt gritty underneath her fingers as she typed.

FENN BEGINNING

The page that loaded next looked like a scan of an old admission form. It was pale green, and covered with rectangular boxes in which the person who'd done the intake wrote information in block print.

AGE AT TIME OF ADMISSION, the box had prompted. Whoever had filled it out – a person who crossed their sevens with horizontal lines and made perfectly round 'O's – had written *7 months*.

Fenn hadn't immediately been placed in Path. Fenn had had a family for seven months. What happened to them?

She scrolled lower. REASON FOR ADMISSION. It wasn't necessary to read every word. The important ones glared off the page: *Untreated fractures. Bruising on abdomen, arms. Mark of belt buckle on thighs.*

"Oh, Fenn,"

This was snooping. Even if she was doing it to help him, this was still wrong. She and Fenn had shared almost every part of their existence, but she didn't know how he'd feel if she knew about the seven months they didn't share. She didn't know how he'd feel if he knew, either.

The first rectangular box was empty. It was the box labeled ORIGINAL NAME. He had no original name. He was seven months old by the time he was brought to Path, but his parents never bothered to give him a name.

Ilyf and Gamb's files were less depressing than Fenn's. Less depressing, but no less sad. Gamb's parents died in a car accident a few weeks after he was born; there was no other family. He'd been born with a severe heart condition. *Unplaceable*, the box said. Ilyf's parents were political exiles. They were deported, then assassinated; Ilyf fell through the cracks and into Path. Gamb's name had been Charlie. Ilyf's was Charlene. She wouldn't tell them, though. If they found out, it would just result in more bickering.

"Lona?" Affl's voice sounded like it was coming from the kitchen. "Lona, Fenn won't come out of his room. And We can't find Julian."

"He's not here," Lona called up the stairs. "Julian's . . . not here."

"But We're scared. Is he coming back soon?"

"I'll be up soon."

She faced the monitor again, clicking back to the search screen.

HARM BELIEVE

The person who filled out Harm's file had loopy, cursive handwriting in purple ink. They dotted their Is with little circles. It was nothing like the purposeful handwriting from Fenn's form – it looked like the penmanship used for a personality quiz in a magazine.

Harm's name had been Benjamin. His mother brought him in after he bit her breasts while nursing, bit them so hard they bled. *And laughed*, the notes said. *Mother wants it noted that boy 'laughed.'*

Lona could hear the doubt in the admission officer's notes, could see how this was something written down just to pacify the parents. Lona believed it, though. She didn't know what Harm would have become if he had never been admitted to Path. It wouldn't have been good.

The cursor blinked in front of her. A message appeared: *You appear to have been idle for a while. Close system?*

Did she need anything else? Had she learned anything useful? Did the fact that someone broke Fenn's bones when he was a baby make him more or less easy to save now? Was there residual instability in Gamb's once broken heart?

Her work was done. She didn't need to do any more searches. And yet she couldn't close the computer. There was one more thing she wanted to look up.

LONA ALWAYS

It was a form like everyone else's. Scanned in on the

266

same pea-green paper as Fenn's. Ilyf's was beige; Gamb's peach. They must use different colors for each of the sectors. At the bottom, the signature of Lona's admitting worker was in blue ink, not black. After three minutes of scrutizing the page without actually reading it, Lona knew everything there was to know about the paper, except for any of the contents.

Begin at the beginning.

AGE AT TIME OF ADMISSION, the rectangular box asked. Even handwriting, similar to that on Fenn's form, recorded hers: *Approximately two hours.*

She had been ready for her file to uncover repressed memories about the violent deaths of her parents, or horrible abuse. But it didn't. Because there were no memories to repress. Her file was exactly one page long. Under REASON FOR ADMISSION, it said only: *Baby was left at entrance. No family could be found.* Under HEALTH AT TIME OF ADMISSION, it said, *Healthy. Umbilical cord still attached – doctor called for examination.*

That was it. No additional medical records. No next of kin. Nothing from the courts. The space for her original name was blank. She had never been anybody before she became Lona and Julian.

This was a good thing. This was neater. Simpler. Having no past was an excellent way to make sure it never caught up with her, to always move forward. So why did her chest feel hollow?

Maybe it was because as much as she'd feared a past like Fenn's, she secretly wished she would be somebody. Not somebody important. But somebody's daughter. She secretly wished she had meant something to someone. Instead her parents had abandoned her and disappeared into the night. She doublechecked the recorded time of the official admission. 2:30 a.m. Somehow that made it even worse. Her mother couldn't even wait until the morning to get rid of her.

But it was fine. Now she knew. It didn't mean anything.

Lona wrapped her fingers around the silver drive, feeling its cool plastic against her palm. She would put it back where it came from – probably safer than carrying it with her. She looked one last time at her file. What nice handwriting this 'T.N.' person had.

Wait.

She clicked back over to Fenn's records. The handwriting wasn't just similar. It was the same. The same 'T.N.' person admitted both her and Fenn into Sector 14. She checked Fenn's time of admission. 3:42 a.m.

It should have been a CT who processed this, since CTs were the ones who interacted more with Pathers. But there were fewer CTs on duty in the middle of the night. There wasn't as much need to comfort everybody when everybody was sleeping. So it could have been a Monitor who had performed the initial intake.

Lona scrolled to the bottom of Fenn's file. There was a page she missed, the first time she saw it. It wasn't a part of the official records – it wasn't green like the other pages. It looked like a plain piece of notebook paper that someone photocopied and scanned in.

'This is my first intake,' the note said. 'I am afraid I behaved against protocol and brought the baby with me to the control room while waiting for the on-call Toucher to arrive. I know I should have requested the EMT keep him in the ambulance, but he was so cold, and the EMT would not turn up the heat. He stayed in the control room for less than one hour, and I wrapped him in my sweatshirt. The on-call Toucher arrived at 4:27 a.m. If there are any questions, please contact me. Here is my home info.'

There was a phone number, an address, and a signature.

Fenn was Talia's first intake. They started the program at the same time. On Talia's first intake, she disobeyed rules in order to keep him warm. Just like she disobeyed protocol on the day Lona was supposed to be remmersed.

Over her head, Lona heard a rumbling. It sounded like a quiet stampede. A stampede of housecats. Followed by muffled cries of relief.

"Julian," someone said, probably Affl. *Julian. Julian.*

She pictured the scene upstairs. The wrapping and rubbing and cooing. She unplugged the drive and tucked the box back on the highest shelf, behind the Christmas wreath.

While she was downstairs it had grown completely dark. Inside, scattered lamps cast shadows on the wall. Just one lit the front room, in the corner, far enough away from where she stood that the group of children huddled in front of the window looked like one being, with many limbs. Lona flicked on another lamp. Ezbrn turned around and shielded his eyes.

"We heard the car and thought Julian was coming home," he said. "But it was just someone visiting across the street."

"He's never been gone this long, except for when he was finding you. Do you think he's finding more of us?" Affl looked hopeful.

Endl sat down on the edge of the couch and, as Lona watched, calmly dragged her fingernails along her neck, leaving dark pink tracks behind. "Endl, don't hurt us," Affl pleaded, tugging on the hem of Endl's pants, but Endl was staring off into a point in the distance.

Harm glided from his post near the door, went to Endl, and gracefully pried her fingers away from her face. "Stop it," he said. Lona was relieved by the gesture until she saw the way his eyes couldn't leave the welts on Endl's neck.

"Endl," he said. "How does that feel, when you scratch yourself? Does it hurt?"

Julian had not gone to find more of them. Julian had found enough of them, and now he was leaving. Now that Fenn was angry at Lona, he probably would want to leave, too. And next week, unless Lona could do something, Fenn would leave all of them for good.

Gamb and Ilyf would be back at the house soon. They'd just gone out for supplies. Gamb would be back for twenty-five days longer than Fenn would be back, and Ilyf for a couple of months after him.

Then there would be no one left but her.

"Lona," Affl asked. "When is Julian going to come home?"

"Oh, who cares?" She was channeling Melissa, trying to sound like the babysitter did when Julian's parents were leaving and Julian didn't want them to. "We don't need Julian."

Affl's eyes were big and round. "Yes. We do."

We do. Lona thought. But they couldn't have him, and she couldn't change that. So instead she wrapped her arms around the tiny body and stroked Affl's white-blond hair. It was soft, like feathers. Affl leaned into her.

"I was Julian for sixteen years. And then I left him. Do you know what that means? It means that I was led astray, but I found my own Path."

Affl started to look up at her, but Lona brought her chin down on Affl's head to make the gesture impossible. It was better for no one to be able to see her face right now.

"You don't need Julian. I will take care of you now."

34

"What is this on my desk?"

"Nice to hear from you on a Saturday night, Mr. Greevey. At 11 p.m."

"Don't jerk around with me, Talia. Is this a letter of resignation?"

"If it's a sheet of paper, and it's on your desk, and it's saying I have resigned, then it is a letter of resignation."

"I think you need to reconsider."

"Do you think that because you're worried that the non-disclosure agreement I signed with my employment expires when I quit? It doesn't. I'm still not supposed to talk."

"I'm worried about losing your institutional memory, Talia. You know a lot of things about how this establishment runs."

"That's a nice way to put it."

"You could tell the press anything you wanted, Talia, and they wouldn't believe you, any more than they believed that Endl kid when she escaped from Sector 4 last year. That's the thing about running a place for damaged youth. People understand that they're damaged. It's got to rub off on the staff, too. If you understand me."

"Look. I just need a change of scene. As hard as a moral

argument might be for you to understand, I'm just not sure I believe in the work as much as I need to."

"I think you believe in the Pathers. The children, I mean. I think that you care about them. And frankly, with all of the crap that's up in the air right now, it just looks bad for me to have a senior employee quit."

"Touching."

"Talia, we can do this—"

"Wait, hold on. Someone's at my door."

"—the easy way, or—"

"The hard way, I get it. My doorbell is ringing. I'll come in on Monday. I owe the program that much. But I don't think it's likely I'll change my mind."

Talia opened the door.

Lona asked if she could come in.

35

She had grown, Talia thought, the girl standing on her stoop under the blinking porch light she kept meaning to fix. Was that possible? To grow in three weeks? Or was it just that Talia wasn't used to seeing Lona standing? The clothes she wore didn't fit her well. The shirt was too big in the bust; the sleeves were too long. It was a thin shirt for this weather, anyway. She must be cold. She was still wearing her hair pulled back, the way Talia had always seen it. It was shinier, though. Someone had been giving her access to better shampoo than the generic stuff provided in Path.

"Is this your signature?" Lona held up the pages she'd printed from the intake files. "Is this you – were you the Monitor who admitted me to Path sixteen years ago?"

If they were going to have this conversation, it was probably better not to have it on her public stoop, Talia thought. She stood aside. "Come in."

Lona scanned the interior. Talia was still at the same address from eighteen years ago. It should have been more cluttered or lived-in. Instead, the front room was carpeted in sterile beige Berber, and the walls were bare except for a single bland painting of a seascape. She couldn't imagine anyone buying that painting. Maybe it came with the house. Next to the painting was a bookshelf containing paperbacks with broken spines, and a television, turned on but muted. There were no photographs, though, or knick knacks or anything else particularly personal. The house looked like an extended-stay hotel for business travelers.

There was, however, a cat – a meow coming from a pile of gray fur that was exactly the same color as the blanket it sat on. The cat arched its back in a stretch and then mewed again in Lona's direction.

"Moosh," Talia said. "He doesn't get many visitors. But will probably let you pet him."

"I don't know if I can. I might be allergic."

"You're not."

Lona held out her fingers for the cat to sniff. Moosh leaned his head into her hand, petting himself against her palm.

"Would you like something to drink?" Talia cringed. Why was she offering a beverage, like Lona was a friend stopping by to socialize and not a fugitive minor on the run from her legal guardians? Then again, Talia didn't have many friends stopping by to socialize, either. It was odd she remembered the niceties. "I have orange juice and some kind of berry spritzer."

"Do you have anything hot? It's cold outside."

The kitchen was separated from the living space by only a cheap laminate countertop. Talia found a box of ginger tea in the cupboard – when did she buy that? – and a few loose packets of instant hot chocolate. Lona pointed at the cocoa, and Talia put a mug of tap water in the microwave.

Abetting, she thought. Right now, Lona was just paying a surprise visit. Once Talia gave her the hot chocolate, it probably entered the territory of aiding and abetting.

"You don't have any kids?" That's what made this house so sterile, Lona realized. People who were Talia's age tended to have kids or spouses or something.

"No."

"Why not?"

"I don't think I would pass the screenings. Though, to be fair, I've never applied to find out."

"You don't like kids?"

"I didn't think I'd be a very good parent."

"Naturally they let you be in charge of all of us."

Talia raised an eyebrow. "I was only in charge of the computers that were in charge of you. It's different."

"Was? Did you leave?"

"I turned in my resignation last night. Though they are trying to convince me to stay."

"You need to stay." She unintentionally clutched the fur around Moosh's neck. The cat stopped his self-petting to look up in concern.

From behind the kitchen counter, Talia folded a dish towel into smaller and smaller squares, using her thumb to set creases. "Lona . . . this is very dangerous," she said when the towel wouldn't become any smaller. "Why did you come to my house?"

"Why haven't you called Mr. Greevey and told him that I'm at your house?"

Talia was silent. Moosh had forgiven Lona and climbed onto the back of the sofa to bat the end of her ponytail.

"I'm hoping you haven't called anybody because I'm right about you," Lona said. "But if I'm wrong I'll leave now."

"Right about what?"

Lona stepped away from the cat and handed Talia the intake forms. The page on top was her handwritten note.

The microwave dinged. Talia ignored it. She read her note, then turned to the first page and read from the beginning. Then she read the whole thing again.

On her third pass, Lona began to feel like she was intruding on Talia's privacy. She squeezed into the kitchen and took the mug out of the microwave, adding in the powder and the tiny marshmallows. There was no spoon, though, so she washed one from the sink while Talia read and read.

Moosh jumped on the counter when he heard the running water, climbing in the sink and drinking from the drip. Lona stirred her hot chocolate and petted the cat, trying to seem uninterested in what Talia was doing until she heard the rustle of the papers being set down on the counter.

"I remember that day. I was only twenty. It was my first day. I was so scared of messing up protocol."

But she had, Lona thought. On her first day, she messed up protocol to help an infant she didn't know.

"Why did you?"

"The ambulance driver was a dick."

"You cared about Fenn."

"He was just a baby."

277

"And me, too. I think you cared about me." She shivered and sipped her hot chocolate. It got so cold in the nights here. Who would have thought that it was May?

June. It was June second. Fenn turned nineteen in four days.

"Tell me what you're doing here," Talia said.

She did. All of it, everything from the moment she left Talia's van until the moment she knocked on Talia's door. She told the things she didn't tell the other Pathers, that she couldn't articulate to Genevieve, that she wished she'd told Fenn. She talked about Fenn's nightmares and Julian leaving, and the fact that the moment Genevieve confided in her, she had betrayed her.

When she was done she felt empty, exhausted. If Talia were a Coping Technician, she might have tried to touch Lona to offer comfort. Lona couldn't have borne that right now. It would have shattered her. Instead, Talia rose and walked toward the back of the house.

Was this her sign to run? Talia could have been getting a telephone. Or a portable remmerser, whatever that would look like.

Instead, she opened the coat closet under the stairs and pulled out something soft and navy blue. Talia shook out the hooded sweatshirt, wordlessly handing it to Lona. After Lona put it on, Talia reached over and efficiently rolled up the sleeves. Lona saw creases in the fabric from where Talia made the same adjustments for herself. The hoodie was heavy and fell halfway down to her knees, but felt nice.

"Better?"

"The worst part is that I was trying to protect everyone. I was trying to protect Fenn, and now he'll never talk to me again."

"It's possible that's true." Talia's response should have hurt, but somehow its brutal honesty made Lona feel better – like someone was acknowledging the full despair of the situation.

"Why did you want to resign?" she asked. "You said you were going to quit today. What happened?"

Talia looked startled by the topic change, then appeared to think hard before answering. "I started to think about my mother."

The way she tripped over the word – it was like she didn't have a lot of practice using it. "What about your mother?"

Talia hesitated, then changed directions. "To really believe in the Julian Path, you have to believe that some things in real life are irrevocably bad. That alternate realities are needed, because the realities provided are . . . shitty."

Lona was confused. "What does this have to do with your mom?"

"Let's just say that not all childhoods Outside are perfect either."

"Your mother was bad?"

"My mother didn't protect me."

"Oh." Lona hated the Path because she was sure her life right now would be better if she'd had real parents. Talia had loved it because she believed the opposite was true. "But you don't believe things are irrevocably bad anymore?"

Talia sighed, a long and pained noise. "A few days ago

she called me. And a few days ago we got a new Pather who deserved a chance to live out his own screwed-up life, and who I didn't protect any better than she did me. And everything seemed pear-shaped."

Lona took another sip of her hot chocolate. She wouldn't make Talia's distress worse by trying to comfort her. A few seconds later, Moosh mewed. Lona looked over; he was pawing at the door.

"Does he want to go out?"

"No. He only goes in the back yard, never in the front. That's weird."

The cat mewed again, louder this time. There was a faint noise, the sound of shoes scuffing on concrete as Moosh began to howl.

"There's someone outside."

On her last syllable, the doorbell rang.

"Get in the closet," Talia whispered to Lona, motioning to where she'd just gotten the sweatshirt. "That will be Mr. Greevey, coming to talk me out of resigning."

What if he'd seen her come in? Lona pressed against Talia's jackets and winter coats, trying to disappear in the fabric without making any noise. *What if he could sense that Talia wasn't telling him everything? What if he hurt Talia?*

"Where is she?" The door flew open; Lona could hear it slamming against the wall. The voice was angry and familiar and getting closer.

"Lona, you can come out," Talia said. "And you should have more faith in your friends."

*   *   *

"What are you doing here?" She was almost as stunned to see him in Talia's living room as she had been to see him in her visioneers.

"You didn't leave me a choice. In the middle of the night? By yourself? Did you think you could leave a note saying where you'd gone and someone *wouldn't* come find you?"

"I wasn't trying to scare anyone."

"You terrified us."

Relief spread through her body like warm liquid, at seeing him, at hearing him yell at her instead of ignoring her. Fenn's hair was wet. The cold wind must have turned into cold rain. Talia noticed it, too. She opened a drawer and pulled out a clean dish towel, tossing it over the countertop. Fenn caught it reflexively, looking up in the direction it had come from.

"Did you want some hot chocolate?" Talia asked flatly. "Or tea?"

"If you think I would drink *anything* you offered me—" He broke off, seeing Lona's half-empty cup on an end-table. "Lona, you didn't drink this, did you? We have to leave, now. Whatever she put in it could kick in any minute."

"She didn't poison me, Fenn."

"Just like she didn't try to trap you in the Expo."

"I've been in the room with her the *whole time*."

"And she never turned her back to open the microwave or get out a mug?"

Talia silently crossed the room, passing between the two of them and picking up Lona's cup. She took a long gulp of the lukewarm beverage and set the now-empty container back down. "Most people," she said, "don't have drugs capable of knocking out human beings in their kitchens."

Fenn stepped in front of Lona, rearranging their standing pattern so that Talia was not between them. "Go outside and slash her tires, Lona. And take her phone."

She couldn't leave with Fenn. She couldn't let him harm Talia, either – which he would most certainly do. He was already taking a step closer. She reached out to Fenn's arm to stop him, but Talia spoke first.

"Have you gained or lost any weight since leaving Path?"

"Have I – what?"

The question was so incongruent, it stopped both Fenn and Lona, throwing Fenn mentally off balance. The three of them were motionless again, Talia's arms folded in front of her body. "Even a few pounds?" Why was Talia asking this? If it was a diversionary tactic, it was the strangest one Lona could think of. "I'm not just screwing around. This is important."

Fenn looked unsure, but seemed to decide the question was either harmless or weird enough to answer. "A few. Gained."

"What about drinking? Not a glass of wine with dinner, but heavy alcohol? Have you been drinking or doing any drugs since leaving Path?"

"No. What's this—"

"I would have been surprised if you had. So many anti-drug messages are embedded into the Julian Path."

Fenn glanced at Lona. She shrugged. She wanted to be able to reassure him that Talia was on their side, but she didn't know what these questions had to do with anything, either.

"This is all good," Talia said. "You haven't sped it up at all. With your weight gain, you might have even slowed it."

Out on the lawn – a crashing sound, a clattering like cymbals. Fenn and Lona both jumped, Fenn instinctively grabbing her hand. "Sorry," Talia said apologetically. "Raccoons get into my garbage every week. I must not be closing the lids right. Tomorrow's trash day."

But the noise once again tipped Fenn's curiosity back to fear. He pulled Lona to the door. "She's crazy, Lona. I don't know what she's talking about."

"I think it's the drugs, Fenn," Talia said.

"What?"

"Everyone who goes on Path is given a drug cocktail. Some are stronger than others, or different blends, but everyone is given one. It's the only way to assure a level of immersion deep enough for the long hours required for Path. The drugs stop when you turn eighteen."

"I've been eighteen for a while," Fenn began.

"The drugs stop being administered," Talia corrected herself. "But they don't stop working. It takes a full year for the effects to wear off completely. Maybe longer if you've gained weight, maybe shorter if you're on other drugs. But in general, a full year."

A full year. Just in time for a birthday.

Lona felt dizzy. The drugs designed to keep all of them in Path after a while became the drugs that kept them alive. Genevieve was more right than she'd known when she said that the Strays were going through withdrawal without Julian. She just hadn't known that all of them were. Byde

283

died of drowning. And of a drug addiction. And of over-exposure. Over-exposure to the outside world.

Lona bet they put them in the flavor tabs.

She swallowed hard. "Are there more drugs? Or if we found a way to put Fenn back on Path, and then later, Gamb and Ilyf, then could—"

"No," Fenn interrupted. "I won't become a pod person again. I'd sooner die."

"You *will* die, Fenn." Didn't he understand that she would rather have him hooked up to a machine than gone for good?

"Even if you were willing to go back in Path, I don't know if that would help," Talia said. "The drugs have a cumulative effect over time – you can't just stop and start them. And even if you could do that, you would need a precise dosage, which Path engineers probably haven't studied because nobody thought they would have to be dealing with Pathers past their eighteenth birthdays. And even if someone had studied it, if you found them, I'm sure they would want to bring you in for some in-patient—"

"No," Fenn said. "There's no guarantee that these theoretical engineers could help. And if they couldn't, I don't want to spend my final days as a lab rat."

"If you won't let us bring you in," Talia said, "I don't know how much I can help."

"You can't help at all."

Fenn sank into the arm chair covered in the soft gray throw. Moosh leapt into his lap, emitting a rattling motor of a purr. Fenn petted him with shaky hands.

"Talia?" Lona asked "Would you heat up the hot

chocolate? Or tea? Fenn is shivering and he doesn't realize it."

As Talia assembled the drinks, Fenn turned to Lona.

"Stupid," he said.

She knew he was angry with her but the insult still seared. They never called each other names.

"How could you not know I would come for you?" he said. "I always come."

36

They pulled up to the house just before dawn.

Ilyf walked out on the porch. She was alone, and her mouth was a thin, hard line.

"Good morning, Ilyf." Lona closed the car door and waited for Fenn and Talia to appear next to her. She couldn't blame Ilyf for being upset. Fenn wouldn't have been able to leave without telling Gamb and Ilyf where he'd gone and why. Ilyf would know by now what secrets Lona had been keeping.

But when Ilyf spoke, she sounded less angry and more distressed. "You need to come inside now." She waved her arms, beckoning them along. "I don't know what's wrong, but he won't let me in."

Behind Ilyf, the screen door opened again. Affl flew down the steps. "Lona! We thought you wouldn't come back."

The others followed. Endl, who carried a spoon and some underwear, and was wearing only one shoe. Ezbrn, staring at the ground as he danced over the sidewalk, trying to avoid cracks, or step on cracks, or whatever else he had decided was necessary today. Harm, whose shining eyes were equal parts welcoming and devouring. He had, inex-plicably, bound his right arm to his side with what looked like packing tape. It didn't make him any less graceful, as he slid down the porch. "We had some trouble," he said in his crisp accent, "being good today."

"Did you get hurt?" Maybe the tape was a bandage.

"No. We made sure We didn't hurt anyone."

Ah. The tape was a preventative measure. Handcuffs.

Then, all of them were on Lona – arms wrapped around her legs, cheeks rubbing against the fabric of her sweatshirt. She'd said she would take care of them. And they'd believed her, all of them. Endl was pressing something into her hand. The spoon, the mouth of it, cold against her hand.

"Lona," Endl and Ezbrn whispered. "Lona."

"I did come back. And I brought someone else, too."

From the corner of her eye, Lona saw the frozen, queasy expression on Talia's face. It was what her own face must have looked like when she first arrived at this house. She wanted to apologize and explain that she didn't have any control over the Strays' behavior. She resisted the impulse. Talia might be on their side now, but for eighteen years she'd been on the other side – the one that created Ezbrn's obsessions and Endl's madness. Talia might be good, but sometimes even good people didn't deserve an apology.

Everyone was here except one person. "Where's Gamb?" Fenn asked, simultaneously realizing what Lona did. From the upstairs window of the tiny front bedroom – the one outfitted with the cheerful red bunkbeds and the train bedsheets meant for children – from the window of that room, the screaming began.

Gamb's nightmare had started.

* * *

Lona raced up the stairs, feeling Fenn and Talia on her heels. Behind them, Ilyf frantically explained. "He just said he was tired, but he didn't answer when I knocked, and the door was locked – I didn't even know you could lock it—"

Fenn rammed against the heavy oak door. It shuddered but didn't splinter. He pulled back and tried again with the same result.

"Fenn, it's too heavy," Lona said. "We can't get in unless we—"

"Break the knob." Talia read her mind.

"We need something heavy. Julian's tool kit. In the kitchen."

Ilyf turned and sprinted down the stairs. Lona heard her slamming cupboard doors as she searched for the shiny blue tool box. She watched the hand on the hall clock drag itself around the clock face. Gamb's cries grew softer. She thought softer would be better. It wasn't. It just sounded like terror had been replaced by desperation, then defeat. The cries she had to strain to hear were infinitely more horrifying than the loud ones before.

"I have it, I have it." Ilyf began yelling before she was halfway up the stairs, thrusting a hammer up to Lona. It took four swings before the handle, now dented and malformed, finally crashed to the floor. Ilyf rushed into the room ahead of her.

Gamb's forehead was sweaty; so was his neck. His T-shirt stuck to his chest. He was gasping, like a fish on a boat deck, and his body was contorted, bent backward at the waist, pained and grotesque.

"Breathe, Gamb, you giant idiot." Ilyf was half yelling, half sobbing. "Breathe."

He was still wheezing, choking on the air instead of inhaling it. In the gray light of the bedroom, his face had begun to turn dark. He was going to die, right here. Not of a suicide, but of a nightmare.

Ilyf reached down and, with uncharacteristic tenderness Lona had never seen, placed her hand on Gamb's chest. "Breathe," she said softly. "Just concentrate on raising my hand with air, because I swear to Christ, Gamb, if you die, that means you forfeit and I win all of the games, ever."

Gamb opened his eyes. Just once at first – just a blink – but then again and again until it couldn't be coincidence, slowly focusing on the figures surrounding him in the room.

"Gamb?" Fenn asked. "Can you see us? Can you understand me?"

Gamb's features were still slack. His neck looked like it wouldn't support weight, but he managed to weakly nod his head. "Ilyf," he whispered. His voice was a dry crack, a rub of sandpaper. "Ilyf. Why are you always yelling at me?"

Talia was standing by the foot of the bed. Lona had momentarily forgotten that she was there.

"I heard that noise before," she said, unable to look away from the scene in front of her. "That screaming. I've heard it. It's the sound you all made the day you woke up from Path."

Lona dumped the doorknob into a waste can where it clanged unceremoniously against the tin.

"Yes. This is what the company you work for created. Now we have to fix it."

"Fix it?" Talia repeated.

This was the part Lona hadn't gotten to last night.

She'd been afraid Talia wouldn't agree, until she met the Strays. This was the part that she thought it would be harder to turn down from here, with Fenn and Ilyf and Endl, than it would have been to turn down back at Talia's house.

Now she could tell it. Talia wouldn't turn anything down now.

"Sector 14," she said. "We're going to shut it down."

37

The air had that feeling in it – that feeling like if Lona lit a match, the whole house would explode. What she just proposed was the kindling.

Not just save her friends. Shut down the Path. Disrupt the whole program. Release everyone. Shut down the Path. Shut down the Path. Julian and Sarafina used to play a game. They would pick a word, a boring word like 'blanket' or 'calendar,' and take turns repeating it over and over again until the syllables were divorced from their original meaning and the word sounded gluey and strange. Lona never understood the appeal. 'Blanket' meant 'blanket' no matter how many times you said it.

Now she was understanding the game, though. 'Shut down the Path.' To the others, staring at her with open mouths, it would sound like alien speak, like a nonsense concept.

Talia was the first to recover. "You want to close down Sector 14?"

"Talia. Ilyf figured out how to break into my system remotely. Could you figure out a way to do that for all of the pods in the bay at once? Disrupt the transmission and bring them out of Path?"

"It would mean overriding the schedule that's already in place for each quadrant, but I could do it. It's not the technical issues I would worry about, though."

"In the nighttime, most of the Coping Technicians go home, don't they?" Lona pressed on. "And how many Monitors are on duty?"

"Just one. Even with the new protocols, at night there's usually just one."

"And you have access to all of the pods? Is anything hidden?"

"I'm the most senior employee," Talia said. "I have access to almost everything. No protocols are really secret in Path."

Path was hidden in the way things are when they deal with something uncomfortable or unpleasant in a society. Hidden out in the open. No one wants to find these things, so they don't have to be hidden at all.

"But my access also isn't the problem," Talia insisted again.

"The problem," Ilyf supplied, "is what happens when you abruptly take two hundred Pathers Off Path."

Lona remembered the nothingness in her visioneers the first time that Ilyf had broken in. She remembered the panic that spread through the bay. It's not like once Talia interrupted the transmission, everyone would hop out of their pods, cured. They would be confused, feeble, hysterical. They would be lost.

"That's why they will need something waiting for them, when the feed first cuts off," Lona improvised. "Something to bridge the gap – a message reassuring them about what is happening."

What they needed was Julian. But Julian was gone.

"Something in their visioneers?" Ilyf asked.

"Yes. I've wondered if—" She'd rather not say this in front of everyone, but as there was no alternative . . . "—I think that seeing Fenn in my pod is part of what helped me adjust so quickly. I wanted to see him again, so I wasn't as scared as everyone else. I was excited."

Nobody else seemed to notice the smile tugging on Lona's lips as she remembered what it was like to see his face after so long. Next to her, Fenn quietly reached down and laced his fingers through hers.

That, Ilyf noticed. "What about touching?" she asked. "Talia, unless you have a bunch of professional Coping Technicians you can blackmail into helping us, everyone who's waking up will need to be comforted with some kind of touching."

"I'm seeing a problem with this logic," Talia said.

Gamb snorted. "*A* problem?"

Talia ignored him. "Lona was already friends with Fenn. She knew him. He was already special to her. It's natural that would be comforting."

That was a problem. Whatever was inserted to help the Pathers couldn't be a simple message of consolation. It had to be something with meaning. Something that wouldn't merely soothe them, but inspire them to be curious about what waited for them on the Outside. But Lona didn't know what waited for each of them Outside. That was the problem with Outside. Everyone had their own path.

"It should be Lona."

Affl. Affl was standing at the door, with Endl and Harm and all of the other Strays. They had been listening.

"It's the logical choice," Ezbrn said. "Lona was the only one to escape on her own. Lona would be a good model to follow."

"And Lona said. Lona said she would take care of us. Lona can lead us on the right path," said Affl.

When Lona said she would look after the Strays, she meant these Strays, the ones in this house. She meant she would see to it that they were fed properly and not neglected. She hadn't anticipated becoming a symbol for all of the Pathers of the world.

But all around her, people were nodding. Gamb and Talia, and Fenn locked his eyes into hers and gave her one, slow nod.

Endl caught the last word of Affl's sentence and turned it into a refrain. "Path, math, wrath, bath, half, laugh, calf path."

It was after six. Lona's body sank into what had become a familiar brand of exhaustion. Bone weariness layered with adrenaline. The desperate urge to close her eyes battling with the deep, pervasive feeling of guilt that she should be pushing through, taking action, staying awake.

"You should go to bed," Fenn said as she swayed in place. Talia was downstairs making pancakes for everyone else.

"So should you. You've been awake as long as I have." Fenn looked uncomfortable, averted his eyes. "What? You don't want to sleep?"

"I knew I was having nightmares – I mean, I knew because I heard you tell Julian about them. But I didn't know what they looked like until I saw Gamb." He looked embarrassed.

"I'm afraid to sleep. Unless – do you think you could come with me? Sit with me just until I close my eyes?"

"Of course I will." She followed him into his room, watching as he curled into the bed.

The last time they'd spoken in this house, she was on the other side of the locked door because she'd hurt him. Lied to him. He did come to find her at Talia's, but just before that he said they were nothing.

"I shouldn't have lied to you," she said, lowering herself gently onto the edge of the bed. The sheets were made of flannel. She knew that silk sheets were supposed to be more desirable, that linen stores were always bragging about high threadcounts and Egyptian cotton. But flannel was so comforting. Why would anyone sleep on anything else?

"I don't want to talk about that."

"I think we should." If they didn't, they would become trapped in another cycle of misunderstanding, like the one launched when they saw those stupid kids kissing on the train. They wasted days on that misunderstanding.

"No we shouldn't. I understand why you did it and I forgive you. But I don't want to argue about it anymore. If I'm going to die, I don't want to spend another minute not being with you."

It would have been so easy to lean down to him right now, and feel the softness of his lips on hers again. To feel his mouth on her collarbone, where only his fingers had touched before.

That desire warred with another emotion. Guilt. Gnawing guilt about what she'd done to Genevieve. Julian never would have betrayed someone like that. Julian *did* betray people like that, she reminded herself. Abandoned them all.

But her Julian, the Julian she'd followed on the Path for sixteen years, never would have done something like that. He never would have watched someone's heart bleed and then stolen the thing they most needed to make it stop. Duty and kindness were ingrained in her. *The Path is in you.*

She pulled the flannel sheet over Fenn's shoulder. He caught her hand in midair, gently turning it toward him and kissing the middle of her palm, the place where a school-fair psychic once told Julian his head line intersected with his fate line.

She fell into him. *No,* she corrected herself. She didn't fall. She chose to jump, stretching out on the soft flannel sheets, feeling the warmth of Fenn's body and her heart beating against his chest. She chose to ignore what would have been the moral thing to do.

I am a terrible person, she thought, before Fenn's lips eradicated her ability to think. And then, *I am finally free from the Path.*

38

She'd spent her life with Julian's brain piped into hers. It was only fitting, this reversal. There was an odd sort of balance, a satisfactory completion to the fact that she was now preparing to enter his brain, to be piped herself into the other Pathers of Sector 14.

Fenn was flat when he appeared in Lona's Path almost a month ago. Two-dimensional. She was too stunned to notice it much at the time, but if she'd paid closer attention, Talia assured her, she would have realized that he didn't seem to be a part of her Path so much as he'd seemed to be superimposed on it – like a Julian mask worn at Halloween. Ilyf did the best she could with the equipment and skills she had. It was impressive, but Talia had eighteen years of knowledge, and a black camera bag full of all sorts of interesting things.

They were in the basement. All of them were in the basement – all of the Strays, Ilyf, Gamb, Fenn. Everyone was here but Genevieve. Genevieve still hadn't come home, and hadn't even called. It wasn't like her. Lona hoped it was for good news reasons, picturing Genevieve and one of her professors writing complicated equations on a blackboard, coming up with a solution that would fix everything. Maybe she had independently figured out that it was the drugs that went wrong, and also figured out how to right them. Maybe. Now that her betrayal of Genevieve was complete, Lona both awaited and dreaded her return.

All of them watched as Talia opened the camera bag and removed a small plastic case. Inside, a sheet of small, round stickers marched four by four down the waxy paper. The stickers looked silver at first, but when Talia peeled one off, it turned shimmery and clear, disappearing on her finger. She leaned over to Lona and started applying them to her face.

"Dimension sensors," she explained, affixing one to the tip of her nose. "They're used when something is inserted."

Dimension sensors. Some had been on display at the Expo. Most of what Pathers saw was transferred directly from Julian's LifeCapture. They already perceived it as three-dimensional. But Lona would be an intruder in their visioneers. She would seem out of place without these sticky dots to help the camera read the different planes of her face.

When something is inserted. She could have guessed by now that this had been done before. Probably not with people. Maybe with brand names. Why should some companies get free publicity just because Julian liked their products? Everything from the laundry detergent Julian's dad used to the soda Julian drank after school was probably dimension-sensored.

Talia finished stickering Lona, then she and Ilyf retreated behind the camera to take readings and make adjustments.

"Ready, Lona?" Ilyf counted down from five. But when

she reached one, Lona was still standing in the middle of the basement. Ilyf's head appeared above the camera. "Is something wrong?"

"I don't know what to say."

The people who developed the Path took years to figure out the right way to create a sense of comfort and intimacy. They probably had teams of psychologists, social scientists, market researchers. She had herself, a group of defective teenagers, and one chance.

What could she convey to two hundred Pathers that would, in a matter of seconds, break through years of immersion?

"Say the food's better out here," Gamb offered.

"Say they can come meet us all!" Affl clapped her hands. "And We'll all be friends!" Lona looked at Harm and Endl. No. She would not say that. She could think of few things that would be more horrifying to most Pathers.

When she appeared in the visioneers in Sector 14, it would be at the same time for everyone. Some people would be with Julian in school. Some would be with Julian's parents, or at swim practice. If someone had interrupted her Path – appeared standing, fully clothed, in the swimming pool when she was in the middle of a set of sprints – what could they have said that would have resulted in anything but panic?

"What would *you* say, Fenn?"

"I would tell them . . . I would tell them about the grass."

The grass. The way the grass smelled so springy and green.

"That's . . . that's great, Fenn." Gamb rolled his eyes.

"'Come on into the world, guys – we have *grass* here!' But telling them about the *food* is a bad idea?"

It was great, though. In Path, they had always been told that Path was perfect and that Outside was something to fear. That wasn't true.

At the same time, she couldn't say Outside was perfect, because that would be equally as unfair, setting up expectations that could never be met Outside.

"I'm ready now."

A ripple of silence made its way through the Strays, past Gamb and Ilyf and Harm. She'd always felt like Harm's eyes were consuming her. Now she felt like all of their eyes were. Not like a wolf would eye its prey, but like a starving dog would eye a plate of scraps. Like she was the last chance.

She wasn't the last chance, she reminded herself. She was the only chance.

"We are Lona Sixteen Always," she started. Was that a bad start? Maybe she shouldn't have used the plural. Her voice cracked in the middle of her name. Start over, she instructed herself. Breathe.

"We are Lona Sixteen Always. Our parents are Holly and David. Our home is at the end of a block, with a driveway We learned to ride a bicycle on. We are Julian.

"But before We were Lona Sixteen Always, We were someone else. We had other parents. They lived on another street. We never thought who that person was mattered, because our life was the Path.

"I am off the Path now," she continued. "I went astray. I am Outside – and when they tell you that Outside is scary,

300

they are right, but they tell you the wrong reasons. Outside isn't scary because there's so much misery. Outside is scary because there is so much happiness, you don't want it to slip away. Because you have to fight to figure out what is important to you, and how to hold onto it. The Path is safe, but it is not life. The Path is in you. But you are not the Path."

The red light was still on.

"I can't think of anything else to say," she said.

When Talia shut off the recorder, the first person to speak was Endl.

"Yes," she said. For the briefest moment, her eyes were clear. This might be the real Endl – the version of the girl whose memory wasn't ragged with bullet holes. Endl as she might have been if she had never been given the perfect life. "That was good."

39

June 2

MEMO: Path 20th Anniversary Celebration

Dear Committee Member:

The inaugural planning meeting for the celebration gala honoring the 20th Anniversary of the Path program has been canceled until further notice. There will be no response to media inquiries. Failure to comply will result in immediate job termination.

We thank you again for your continued investment in the Path, and look forward to many years of brighter futures.

Sincerely,
Bonnie Gray, Secretary to the Architect

40

So this is what it looked like, from the outside. Nothing, really. A granite building. On the side, Lona could still see the outline of faded letters: NEW YORK AVENUE SPORT AND SPA.

The new sign said DEPARTMENT OF HEALTH AND FAMILY SERVICES, but it was tiny. Just a placard, copper turned green. Lona could barely read it from her spot behind Talia's seat.

The parking lot was gated; an automatic bar raised and lowered when someone punched a code into a keypad. Talia leaned out the window, tapping numbers in a succession that sounded like the beginning of *Do You Know the Muffin Man?* The code was only five digits long, so it stopped with 'Muf.'

Next to Lona, stuffed in the back of the van with everyone else, Endl was shaking. Lona stroked her arm. "Remember this?" she asked the girl. "This is what you'll do to everyone inside. Help them." Endl reciprocated, stroking Lona's arm back with her right hand, and Lona tried to ignore what Endl was holding in her left, which appeared to be a dead bug.

Across from her, Fenn sat between Ezbrn and Affl. His knuckles were white. She'd always thought that was just an expression. White knuckles. But it wasn't, because his were. His role was more dangerous than all of theirs. It was the one he insisted on.

"How are you?" she whispered to him.

"Fine." His body was rigid, palms against knees, eyes fixed on the spot above Lona's head. Fine, he said, but then didn't speak again.

Ilyf sat in front with Talia, checking and rechecking something on a small, hand-held computer. Gamb was entertaining Affl and the other small Strays. Harm was . . . Harm was here. That was the most certain thing she could say about Harm. She worried about bringing him along; in the end the only reason he came was that she also worried about leaving him behind. He'd seemed off since Julian had left. More off than usual.

"Hello, Lona," he said to her now, as he caught her looking at him. "Is everything all right?"

She looked away.

The van slowed. Talia peered into the back. "We're almost at the blind spot for the security cameras. Fenn – you should get out now."

No, he shouldn't. She didn't want him getting out of the van. She wanted them to keep driving. *Could it really have been just a few days ago that he'd proposed just that?* That she'd sat next to Fenn and shaken water out of her ear, and joked about driving on, not coming back? Too late for that now. Now it was act or die. Act and die.

Fenn climbed toward the rear exit. Affl was crying. Affl was crying, even while murmuring that everything would be okay, that no one should worry.

"Wait!" Lona didn't know why she had said that. She

didn't have anything to say, at least not that could be said in front of a van full of people. She was just stalling. "Don't do this. You don't have to do this."

Fenn grimaced, bracing himself against the open doorframe. "If I'm going to die, it's better this way, isn't it?"

"This day is a one." What a stupid, trite thing to say. The words tasted salty. She hadn't realized she was crying. But Fenn smiled, impossibly, at her stupid line.

"But you're my eleven."

Then he was gone, jogging back toward the floodlights surrounding the security fence, until all Lona could see were the pale outlines of his neck and hands against his dark clothing and hair.

The parking garage didn't have another keypad, just a scanner for Talia to press her badge into. It was manned by a security guard that Lona could hear but not see, now that Talia pulled the front partition of the van closed.

"Hi, Marvin," she said.

"Hey, Talia." A flashlight shone across the front seat onto Ilyf. "Visitor?"

"Intern. Erin Dannenbring. From George Mason – it's her first day."

"Is that why you're driving the van?"

"No, the van is because my truck broke down."

"I thought maybe you were sneaking in a boyfriend."

"Ha."

Talia rolled up the window and slid into a spot, pretending to search for something in the console while muttering softly to the back end.

"You have the walkie-talkie, right?"

It was a clunky square thing with a stubby antenna, sitting in between Lona's feet. The technology of it seemed ancient, but Talia told her that sometimes the simplest technology is the least likely to break down. Then both of them had considered the irony of that statement in light of their current mission, and burst into nervous laughs. "Remember to keep it on channel four for internal emergencies," Talia said now. "You'll hear the alert."

Then, more loudly: "This is technically not the main entrance, Erin, but only the people who walk to work actually use the front. So for all intents and purposes, this is where you'll come in every day. Marvin can get you a pass . . ."

Talia and Ilyf exited the van, closing their doors and clicking softly toward the building. Lona should have said goodbye to them, just in case. It was hard to keep track of how many people she might not see again. She strained her ears, hanging onto any last wafts of Ilyf and Talia's conversation that she could hear from inside the van. When she could hear no more, there was nothing left to do but wait in silence.

"You know what I just realized?" Gamb said, talking softly enough so that the younger Pathers couldn't hear him. "Fenn's birthday is in just a couple days. If he dies tonight, it will still probably be classified as suicide. That's what they call it, when someone pisses off law enforcement on purpose because they don't have the guts to kill themselves. Suicide by cop. Ironic, huh?"

It was ironic. Everything that was happening could

have been in one of those ironic tragedies Ms. Dwyer had them read last spring. That's where the word irony came from – named after some Greek character, perfected in a bunch of Greek plays. Oedipus doesn't know that he is the murderer of his father that he is trying to catch.

Ha ha ha.

Lona tried to picture where Talia and Ilyf would be in the building, mentally walking them through the floor plan as she remembered it from her one pass through with Talia. Now they would be walking past the vending machines. Now they would have reached the control room. Now they would be relieving the current Monitor on duty, repeating the fake story about the internship.

And what about Fenn? Now he would be spotted in the footlights. Now he would be caught. Now he would be dead. Better not to think about Fenn.

She started over. Now Talia and Ilyf would be walking past the vending machines.

Her brain must be moving faster than real time. It felt like hours had passed. Needles shot through her right foot. It was good to have the pain. The pain would keep her alert.

She had done Talia and Ilyf's mental walkthrough three times. It shouldn't be taking this long. Something had gone wrong. The other Monitor – Paige, Talia said her name was – should have already exited the garage in her car, but Lona hadn't heard anything.

She'd just decided to pull back the curtain partitioning

off the front seat, when a staticky crackle made her jump. "We have an emergency." A panicked female voice – Paige – hissed into the walkie-talkie. "Code Four. I mean, Code Five. Code— Fenn Eighteen Beginning has breached the security fence. I saw him when I was leaving and I think he's trying to get in the building."

That's what had gone wrong. Paige must have walked to work today. She was leaving through the other entrance. If Fenn was by the security fence, then he was maybe two hundred yards to where Talia's car was parked in an alley. He could run fast, certainly faster than Paige, whom Talia said was a smoker who always wore high heels. But in order for the plan to work, he couldn't start running yet. He had to wait for—

As if on cue, the walkie-talkie in Lona's hand buzzed again.

"Is the suspect alone?" Marvin's joking tone disappeared. Outside of the van, she heard the hard soles of his shoes run toward the garage entrance.

"I can't tell," Paige cried. "But I think he has a weapon." He did. A taser. Lona wished he had something stronger, but Julian had taken his revolver with him, and Talia's taser was the only option they could arrage on short notice. "I think it's a gun."

Lona barely had time to think about how little Paige knew her weapons before Marvin broke through on the line again.

"Don't worry," he panted. "I have a gun, too, and I'll shoot first."

"No!" Lona fought her way through the mass of Stray

bodies toward the rear exit, and was stopped only by Gamb, grabbing her arm roughly.

"You can't," he said. "Not yet." She shook him off. "Lona." He grabbed her arm again, this time hard enough to leave bruises. "Do you want to ruin the whole plan?"

How dare he be reasonable now, for the first time since she'd met him? Fenn caught. Fenn dead. Fenn with half of his face blown off, lying on the pavement and staring at her with one green eye. She didn't care if she ruined it all.

"If he's armed, you should have backup." It was Talia's staticky voice, right on cue. "A Coping Technician – they're trained for this. I'm paging Sanjeeta." Talia grew muffled as she barked orders to Sanjeeta on an internal line. "She's coming out now. She'll be there in thirty seconds. Did you copy that? Thirty seconds."

The thirty-second warning was not for Marvin or Paige. It was how long they had to wait.

Talia and Fenn had lured away from the building everyone affiliated with the Path program – Paige, Sanjeeta, Marvin – except the ones who were trying to overthrow it.

Lona and Gamb helped the smaller Strays out of the van, filing underneath the security camera no one was left to monitor. Affl reached up to take her hand.

Talia had drawn a rough map of the interior in case she got lost, but Lona's feet knew where to go. The further they went into the bowels of the building, the more quickly they moved. She wasn't being guided by her own memory. The building was making sounds. She was being pulled along by the breathing of the pods.

*   *   *

Ilyf sat at a computer, her fingers flying so fast over a keyboard that she didn't acknowledge Lona and the others when they streamed through the door. Talia was at her own desk, looking up just long enough to verify that all of them made it safely through the building and into the room.

"You need to get downstairs. We'll only have a few minutes before they come back."

"Fenn," Lona began.

Talia shook her head impatiently. "Fenn is faster than Paige and Marvin."

"But—"

"They won't expect him to have a vehicle in the alley. They'll have to go back for a car. Go, Lona. You need to go."

"But even if he loses them, couldn't they find him at your house? When they realize you're involved in this, your house is the first place they'll look."

"He's not going to my house," Talia broke in. "He's going to my mother's."

Before Lona had time to register surprise at that revelation, Talia waved her off. "Get to the bay."

Talia would launch the Path interruption in stages. She had to. There were ten Strays and ex-Pathers, minus Ilyf helping out in the control room, minus Fenn running outside. That left eight, and dispersed between the two hundred Pathers who would be pulled out for the first time, eight was not very many.

It would have been easier to do this right after Calisthenics. They could have started by extending the Off Path time by fifteen minutes, and then, after a week, extending it

310

fifteen minutes more. If they could do it gradually, maybe none of the Pathers would react too badly. Their memories of Julian could be like memories of a town they used to live in – something they looked back on fondly, as part of another life.

But that would never work, Talia explained. Calisthenics were when the largest staff was on duty. Even if Talia could go down the line waking people up, the Coping Technicians would be there lulling them back under almost as quickly, like cleaning up messes with a sponge.

Besides, Lona wanted them awake now. Now, when it would be all of them, when the mass of frightened children would be too big for protocol to deal with, when it would be too hard to round them all up and erase all of their brains. Now, when all of them together could get enough important people to notice, and help them figure out a way to save Fenn. Assuming Fenn still needed to be saved. Assuming he was alive.

Lona checked the big wall clock on the far side of the bay. Talia would break into Quadrant 1 first, at 12:17 a.m. Lona's recording took forty seconds to play – they timed it to the second – and then she would move on to Quadrant 2. They would go until they got caught. Talia wasn't sure when they would get caught. It depended on how fast Fenn could drive.

Lona drifted to the center of the quadrant, watching Affl skip around the perimeter. Affl didn't seem to realize this was a terrifying mission. Maybe that was a good thing.

Lona came to a pod that was smaller than it should have been.

Oh wait.

She hadn't been drifting at all. Her flesh memory had drawn her to her pod, only it wasn't hers anymore. Now there was a boy inside. Skinny, late 1000s or maybe early 2s. She looked at the ID. Djna. She would save Djna.

"Hey, Djna. I'm going to be the one here when you wake up."

12:15

12:16

Lona wasn't sure what it would look like when Talia launched the program that put Lona in their Path. Maybe she wouldn't notice anything from the outside. Maybe this wouldn't work.

12:17

Djna's tiny legs jumped in his footrests.

It had begun.

The boy's brows were knitted together in concentration. His feet twitched in his footholders, his neck jerked in his headrest. The vital stats screen in front of his pod showed his heartrate increase, and then increase again. What if it kept going up? Lona hadn't considered that option. What if his heart exploded?

But no – it was stabilizing now, higher than before, but steady and strong. And his finger – his right index finger was twitching, and his middle finger, too, and then his whole right hand was leaving its arm rest and reaching out toward something.

My face. He was reaching out to touch the face of the Lona that was in his visioneers, while she was standing in front of him, waiting for him to wake up. She clasped her hand to her mouth to stifle a giggle, but wasn't fast enough.

Her laughter echoed over the whooshing machines – the only human sound in the room.

The only human sound.

She should have heard footsteps, or skipping steps from Affl and tuneless hums from Endl. She didn't hear anything at all. When she turned around, she saw why.

Three broad, shovel-faced men were a few steps away. They had badges. And clubs. They'd used their clubs to corral together five of the Strays and Gamb. Someone was missing. Who was the missing one? It didn't matter. The ones they did have cowered on the floor. Gamb, the largest, was bound with plastic twist-ties. Riot handcuffs. What they showed on the news when cops corralled unruly protesters.

A small figure lay lifeless in front of one of the men. Affl. Affl, crumpled in a heap, blood trickling from her forehead. They didn't need to beat the smallest one. Affl could have been restrained with one hand. That injury was just for fun.

"Lona," one of the men said. They knew her name. Of course they did. They were here for her.

"Ezbrn, get Affl and come to me." What was she saying? And how did she sound so firm when she said it? One of the men smirked. How amusing, to see Lona Sixteen Always, pretending that this plan was still working.

"Endl. Untie Gamb."

"I don't think," said the man who knew her name, "that you understand what's going on here."

"I do. We're leaving. You're leaving us alone." Ezbrn and Endl didn't move toward her. They were petrified. A club raised in the air, ready to crush down on their skulls.

But there was also another flash of movement, from behind the pod next to her, springing like an uncoiled snake in the direction of the first man's face. Harm. Harm was the Stray she hadn't accounted for before, and now he was leaping onto the men with sticks. The unleashing of demons.

There was a spurt of red. It hadn't come from Harm.

Lona could see Harm doing things to the men with the badges that she wished she could un-see. She was disgusted with herself for being grateful.

She could see Talia up in the control room pause to take in what was happening in the bay, and then immediately turn back to her computer.

Good, Talia. Don't stop until they tear you away.

She could see Endl working on Gamb's knots and Ezbrn dragging Affl away, disappearing in the direction of Quadrant 2.

Then she couldn't see anything.

The time that Fenn had drugged her, her arm had throbbed. It had felt violent, amateur. This time she didn't feel a needle at all. She didn't think there was one. There wasn't a nightstick, either, or anything so brutal. She was being put to sleep by the delicate execution of pressure points on her neck – something that must have to do with optic nerve endings because her eyesight was the first thing to disappear.

She could still feel, though. The nubby sleeve of a wool

sweater brushing against her cheek. And she could hear a polite voice – one that definitely didn't belong to either of the giant thugs with sticks.

It belonged to a man, it was whispering in her ear, and it was saying, "Lona, it's so nice to finally meet you."

41

His hair was brown. A boring brown, gray at the temples. His face was . . . *careworn* was the word people would use to describe it. A collection of gentle lines. He was wearing – she hadn't imagined it – a wool sweater, nubby from too many washings, and a pair of sneakers. He saw her looking at them.

"I was working out when they called me about you." He smiled. "This is all that was in my gym bag. Sometimes when I can't sleep I like to go to an all-night gym. And it turns out that you couldn't sleep either."

She opened her mouth and a squawk came out, a pinched little bird-chirp of a noise.

"Water?" he asked.

They were in a doctor's office. Or something like that. Lona was half-sitting on a beige exam table. To her left was a counter with a jar of cotton swabs, a canister of wooden dowels, a roll of paper towels.

When she'd woken up at Genevieve's, her legs had felt like bags of sand. Now they just felt gone. She had to look down to make sure she still had legs at all.

"Believe it or not, it's something my chiropractor does," the man said. "It loosens all the tension in one's lower half, though I admit the effect is scary. It's the only ninja trick I know. It will get better soon."

He took a plastic cup from the wall dispenser nearby and poured Lona a glass of water. She took it without thinking. "Who are you?"

"I suppose it's not fair for only one of us to know the other, is it?" the man responded.

His voice was familiar. She'd heard it before.

The other item on the counter was one she didn't recognize. It was white and cylindrical. It looked like an electric toothbrush, except that the base it was charging on said 'DANGER. HIGH VOLTAGE.'

A doctor's office would have charts of the human body. That's what Julian's doctor had. Human anatomy charts, food pyramids, and signs with slogans like 'Wash your hands and drown some germs.' This room only had one diagram on the wall. It showed not a whole body but just a skull, in profile. An arrow pointed to the base. Not a doctor's office. A remmersing room.

She refocused on the man in the sweater.

"I heard your voice in the convention center. You were the voice in that video about Path."

"That was me, yes."

It still wasn't the way she thought she knew him, though. When she'd first heard his voice in the convention center, she'd thought even then that it sounded familiar. She couldn't think of where the first time would have been. It was familiar in a way she couldn't place. "But you do more than that?" she asked.

"I am the Architect of the Path. I built it. I created it.

My company runs most of it. You can call me Architect, if you like."

She shook her head.

"Or you can call me Warren."

She didn't want to call him that, either. She didn't want to call him anything. She jabbed the fingernail of her left thumb as hard as she could into her calf, hoping to feel something. Her flesh seemed cold and dense beneath her prodding, but her leg felt nothing at all. She looked down to make sure she had pressed as hard as she thought she had. A bloody half-moon crescent appeared below her knee. She'd broken the skin.

"Ouch," the man said.

"I can't feel it."

He sprang from his chair and retrieved a cotton swab from the counter, rummaging in a drawer until he found a Band-Aid and some rubbing alcohol. He swabbed the wound and blew on Lona's knee.

Such an odd, personal gesture. *Maybe he's a doctor, and can't help but patch people up*, she thought. That would explain the alcohol and the Band-Aid. Not the blowing, though. Blowing on scabbed knees was something a parent would instinctively do, not a doctor.

"There," he said, straightening back into his chair. She realized, too late, that she should have attacked him when he was inches from her body. "All better now." He smiled. She noticed for the first time that his eyes were red and a little bloodshot. "It's nice when things can be made all better." He looked at her. "Like the Julian Path."

"The Path doesn't work for everyone," Lona said.

"No, there are exceptions. Your friend Harm, for example."

Harm. She had seen something hanging from his teeth in the bay. She closed her eyes, trying to erase that memory.

"Harm is a really interesting case. I've never seen anyone's brain patterns adapt so well on Path. He genuinely loves Julian and wishes he could be him. But Off Path, he reverts to his natural tendencies, which are problematic. His brain clings so stubbornly to its original wiring – if his sector was under Pequod's management, we would have studied him, not banished him."

"Is that what you want to do with me? Study me?"

"Under better circumstances, that's exactly what I would do. You have such a remarkable mind. The way you gained a sense of self so quickly after leaving Path. They way you had the internal strength to run. You're far more interesting than Harm, in some ways. Of course, you have your mother to thank."

"My – what?"

"She herself was an extraordinary woman."

His last sentence was a punch in the stomach. Her mother. If she was left at Path when she was a few hours old, how would he know anything about her mother at all?

"Did you know her?" she blurted out. "Were you there when she left me?"

"You're curious."

Of course she was curious. He had found the only thing in the world that could distract her from these surroundings. Her real mother. *The other one*, she had told Talia in the van a decade ago.

He looked intrigued by her curiosity. She didn't want

him to be intrigued. She didn't want him to think of her as a science experiment. She would not give him the satisfaction of asking for more information. Nothing to acknowledge that he had the power to hurt her any more than he was already planning to. It was better to use this time to make him think of how the Pathers who died were people, not lab projects.

"Three people *killed* themselves. That's not a successful program."

He rubbed his eyes, hard, and ran his hands through his hair until it stuck up in slept-in tufts from his head.

"It wasn't supposed to happen, Lona. I didn't mean for those two to harm themselves. I didn't mean for any of them to die."

Why had he phrased it that way? Like two of the deaths were separate from the third? Why hadn't he just said that he was sorry for all of their suicides? It was an odd way to phrase something, from a man who seemed precise in his language. She couldn't figure out why he would have done that.

Unless – of course. Not all of them were suicides.

Only two.

Something had always been off. She hadn't realized it, because it didn't make sense to look at the deaths of Byde, Cadr and Czin individually. It made sense to look at them the way people thought of Pathers when they were alive. As a collective. As a We.

Jumping off of the Wilson Bridge would have been an easy way to die. Not easy – none of it would have been easy. But all that someone would have needed were rocks. And gravity. And the determination not to save yourself at the last minute. The same with a train. Dying that way would have been terrible, but it didn't require any props. No equipment.

But a gunshot wound to the face. What Lona knew about guns came from police shows Julian watched. She didn't know much, but she was as much of an expert as any other Pather would have known. Even if someone stumbled out of Path and into a legal gun dealer, would anyone sell a gun to a person with their background? Would she have known how to find an illegal one? It didn't make sense.

Which meant.

Cadr.

"Cadr didn't kill herself, did she?"

"Cadr was responsible for her own death." The politeness in his voice was gone. For the first time in the conversation he sounded unhinged.

"But she didn't kill herself."

"Cadr figured out what happened to Byde, and after he died, she was going to make a scene. She came to me, threatening things that would have closed down the whole program."

"So you shot her."

"I didn't want to. It wasn't planned." He leaned toward her, placing his hand on her still-numb knee, pleading. Repulsed, she shrank back as far as she could. "This program is about helping children, Lona. What she was going to tell people would not have helped children."

Cadr was a child, Lona thought. *All of us were.* She wanted his hand off of her. Almost as soon as she thought

321

that, she felt a twitch in her leg. Was it involuntary? Had he felt it? Could she do it again if she tried? She focused all of her energy on the lower half of her body, but couldn't make the leg move again. She did feel pressure, though. She was beginning to be able to feel the imprint of his hand.

"What about Czin?"

Had Czin been pushed in front of a train? Was Genevieve's lie to Fenn correct all along – that the deaths had been not suicides, but perverse acts at the hands of a man who thought that his actions were for the common good?

"Czin. Czin was especially sad." He truly sounded regretful. Lona couldn't decide if that made him more or less hideous. More. "Honestly, I don't know whether Czin would have killed herself if Cadr hadn't died. But once Cadr did, Czin had two deaths to cope with. It might have pushed her over the edge. We can all be pushed over the edge. The human mind is so complex and we're only beginning to figure out all of the ways it can react to the Path. We'll be better. With future classes."

Talia's medical explanations about withdrawal. Genevieve's relentless scouring of her textbooks. None of it mattered. Because when it came down to it, some Pathers were strong and some weren't. Some were able to adjust and some couldn't. Czin died because she lost Cadr. Cadr died because she dared to look into what had happened to Byde. Byde died because the drugs ran out of his system before he was ready to live without them. Back and back and back, to the moment when some Monitor in Sector 4 placed Byde in his very first pod. And Fenn – where did Fenn fall in this chain reaction? Fenn had lost three friends.

And what about her? Julian said she was stronger than the others. Could her strength last?

The Architect had finally removed his hand from Lona's knee. He wasn't even looking at her anymore. He was looking at something that he had taken out of his pocket. A photograph. Lona could only see the back, and the way it was weathered around the edges. Was it a duplicate of the photographs that Fenn kept under the rock? Did the Architect at least have the decency to make himself remember the three people who no longer existed because of him?

"I'm sorry," he whispered to the photo. "I'm trying."

Finally, he flipped the picture around and showed it to her. "Do you see?" It wasn't one of the ones that Fenn had. There was only one figure in it, and that person looked younger than any of the dead Pathers.

What she did see, out of the corner of her eye, was the door at the far end of the room begin to open. Just a crack. A small enough crack that it could have been due to a cross breeze. But then four fingers wrapped around the door. And behind them, an eye.

The Architect pushed the photograph closer to Lona's face. The figure was a small boy. He sat behind a table wearing a party hat. In front of him was a birthday cake. It had five candles on it. The boy held up five fingers, one already covered in icing.

"Liam wanted pie. We told him that cakes were for birthdays."

Liam could be a Path name. But Pathers never had birthday parties. Where had she heard that name before?

"We would have let him have pie," the Architect said. "If we had known."

Known what? She couldn't focus on what he had or had not known, because behind him, the door was opening wider. A face appeared. Julian. Julian had found her. He raised his index finger to his lips, eased the door another silent inch open again. Now all she needed to do was keep the Architect from looking at the door.

"He looks happy, though," Lona said, as Julian snaked along the side of the wall, closer to Warren's turned back. "Even if he didn't have pie."

"Doesn't he, though? He would be happy about the work I've done."

It was possible this man wasn't evil. It was possible he was completely insane.

"He would?"

His expression darkened. "Of course he would. Liam is the whole reason the Path even exists. To make sure other children have the childhood that my son never did. He would have understood what needed to be done."

"I don't know if he would have understood. He was five."

"He was my son. I know what my son would have understood." Shaking his head sadly at Lona, he picked up the electrical prod, flicking a switch along the side that made a light at the base turn from yellow to red.

"Don't worry, Lona," he said as she swiveled her head away. You're not dying. You're getting a new beginning."

"I got one of those when I left your program. This isn't a beginning for me. It's a do-over for you."

The Architect reached around Lona's neck and probed the area where her spine met her skull, landing on a spot just below her occipital bone.

Behind him, Julian raised the gun to the Architect's head and pulled back the hammer, a sharp, metallic click.

"Warren," Julian said calmly. "Put that down."

The Architect looked only slightly surprised. Without turning around he smiled wistfully at the sound of Julian's voice. "Julian. How are you?"

"I'm fine, Warren. Why don't we sit down and catch up, and let Lona go?"

"I don't think so. It's for everyone's own good, Julian." The metal prod grazed the back of Lona's neck. "It's the only way to save these children."

"No, Warren," Julian said softly. "It's the only way to save the program. There's a difference."

The metal was icy. She could hear it vibrating, like there was something trapped inside, fighting to get out. She was going to die, or her memories were, and either way she would be gone. She searched for a memory to hold onto. The swimming pool. Diving into the water at the swimming pool, feeling the material of her bathing suit stretch as she hit the cold. Wiping the chlorine from her eyes to see Fenn. Diving into the water. Chlorine. Fenn. *Remember this.*

The door Julian came through burst open again, and another person flew through it. *Fenn?* Lona's muscles tensed with the hope and dread that Fenn would have come to help her. But it wasn't Fenn. It was Genevieve, and she wasn't bothering to sneak around the side like Julian had. She charged directly toward the Architect, putting herself in the path of bullets and currents.

"Genevieve, stop!" Lona used her arms to launch herself from the table, and her right foot automatically shot out in front of her to break her fall. She could control her muscles again.

There was a loud bang. Julian and the Architect were wrestling for the gun, and one of them had just shot a bullet into the ceiling above Lona's head. "Get down!" she yelled at Genevieve, who ignored her and screamed something that another shot made it impossible for Lona to hear.

Genevieve moved in the wrong direction. Not toward the door, but toward Julian and the Architect, who still had their hands on the grip. Two shots had been fired. How many bullets would a standard revolver like this contain? Twelve? Fifteen? And they'd shot off only two?

While Genevieve was running in the wrong direction, she was crying the wrong thing.

"Daddy," she wailed. "Daddy, please don't."

Another shot went off.

42

Someone was screaming. Lona wished they would stop. She closed her mouth and the screaming ended. It was her.

The first two shots had ended in crumbles of plaster, showering the floor and Lona's hair. There was no plaster explosion after the third shot. There was Genevieve, lying on the floor, and there was red. The stain spread from her abdomen.

Lona staggered to Genevieve and knelt on the floor. She was breathing. She opened her mouth. A bead of blood appeared at the corner. Something inside her must be punctured. Of course it was. Her whole body was punctured.

"I'm sorry," Genevieve said.

Across the room, the wrestling match between Julian and the Architect stopped. They still held the gun, both of them, all four of their grown hands wrapped around the grip.

"Genny?" The Architect craned his neck, trying to get a better view of the still figure lying on the floor. "Genny?!" He must have loosened his grip, even a small amount, because suddenly Julian had the gun, and was barreling the other man over with his shoulder, knocking him to the floor and straddling his chest.

Lona turned back to the girl lying in front of her.

You were supposed to apply pressure to a wound, but was that true when the wound was in the chest? If Lona pressed down where the bullet had entered, Genevieve wouldn't be able to breathe. She tried to peel back Genevieve's shirt, to see how bad it looked underneath. The material made a sickening, wet sound, sticking to Genevieve's skin with a paste of blood.

"Stop." A hand clutched her wrist. Genevieve's eyes had opened. "Don't."

There was too much blood, and it was coming out too fast. From her lungs, a hollow whistle.

"I wanted to tell you. All of you. But I was too selfish. And it got too late."

Lona was furious in spite of herself. Did it get too late after Byde had died? After Czin? How many people had to die before it officially became 'too late' for Genevieve to tell them that she was the daughter of the man who actually knew how to help them?

Genevieve's eyes pleaded with her. Or maybe it hadn't been any of those reasons. It had become too late when Genevieve realized she was in love with Fenn. And when she decided she would be someone she wasn't in order to be with someone who might be harmed by who she was. If that was the truth, then Genevieve wasn't hiding herself from Fenn, but hiding Fenn from her father.

It was little difference.

"Genny?" Beneath Julian's knees, the Architect struggled to get up. "Is that my daughter over there? Baby?"

Genevieve ignored her father's calls. "Just tell Fenn. I know he can't forgive me." She stopped to suck in another breath. The hollow sound was replaced with a gurgling. Something sticky and viscous was filling her lungs. "But I love him. Tell him."

She was shaking. Shivering. Was it shock? Blood loss? Her shiny hair was splayed out on the ground behind her head. But she didn't look beautiful anymore. Her skin was sallow. There is no beauty in death.

"He loves you, too," Lona heard herself say. "He told me."

The grip around Lona's wrist tightened. "He did? When?"

"When you were gone. When you were gone he told me that nothing could ever happen between us, because he loved you."

"He loved me."

She hoped that Genevieve would believe this lie. It was the least that she could give. But if she didn't believe it, she hoped that Genevieve would understand that it was meant to be a gift.

"Genny? Genny?" The Architect's cries sounded like a mewing kitten. "That looks like my daughter but it can't be her," he babbled to Julian. "She's away at college."

Julian looked at Lona for guidance.

"He didn't know," Genevieve told Lona. "I didn't tell him either."

Lona nodded at Julian. He rose from the Architect's chest, retrieving the gun from where it had fallen, keeping it trained on his back. The Architect didn't run toward

Genevieve. He stepped cautiously, like the path that lay ahead might be strewn with land mines.

He sank to his knees opposite Lona the other side of his daughter, kissing her forehead. "We'll call an ambulance, Genny. You'll be okay."

"I'm sorry, Daddy," Genevieve said. "I was trying to do your work. For you and Liam."

That's why the Architect's voice sounded familiar. She should have heard it. His way of speaking – his vocal inflections and his cadence – he'd passed it all on to his daughter.

Pieces of the Architect's story were knitting themselves together with pieces of other stories that Lona had heard. A son who had died and left his parents stricken with grief. Trying to patch up holes with new children. Why had Genevieve been at Fenn's graduation to begin with? It seemed it wasn't to celebrate Path's first graduating class, but the man who had created it.

Genevieve's blood spread, trickling out of her mouth, pooling around her father's shoes. When he lifted his head after kissing his daughter's face, his mouth was dark with it.

"Stay here, Genny," the Architect cried again, shaking his daughter so hard that her head snapped roughly to the side. For a second, her eyes flew open, but they weren't sharp with awareness, just pain.

"You're hurting her." Lona said, but he kept shaking.

Lona reached over Genevieve and shoved him. "You are hurting her. You are *hurting* your daughter." She pried his hands away from Genevieve, twisting his fingers sharply. He looked down dumbly at the hands that Lona had just released. Then he buried his face in them and began to wail.

"Neve." Lona whispered the name that could have been Genevieve's if she had been raised in Path. Underneath the rusty scent of blood, Genevieve smelled like linen and gardenias. "Neve, you don't have to hold on anymore. If you need to, you can go."

Genevieve smiled. Not wryly or sardonically, the way that she had in life, but sweetly, the way she she might have as a child. Then she was gone.

Lona looked at what remained of the man sitting across from her. Crying. He dared to cry because the chain reaction that he had started had ended in an explosion. His nose was running and red. It was disgusting. In his pilled sweater with his blobby, blotchy face he looked pathetic, not intimidating.

"Where were we?" she asked. "I think you were in the middle of erasing my brain."

He slapped her. She could feel the welts from his nails rising on her cheek. She could taste Genevieve's blood, transferred from his fingers to her lips. She deserved it.

"Lona." Julian had collapsed on the other side the room. He was hurt, but only in the shoulder. A flesh wound. It looked painful, but he would live.

She crawled to his side.

"Julian."

"Is he—" Julian tried to stand. Lona pressed him down again.

"He's not going to do anything. Genevieve is dead." Julian winced. He knew. "How did you find us, Julian?"

331

"Genevieve called – when you left her a message saying to come home, she knew it was time to tell her dad. But she couldn't get hold of him, so finally she just came back. But by then you'd already left, and when he did return her call, he left a message saying he was in this neighborhood, and she knew the only thing in this area was—"

"It's okay." She could see how much energy it was taking him to recount this complicated story, full of coincidences and confusion that she might never fully be able to put together.

Julian cut the timeline off and reached for her hand. "I'm sorry I left."

"Why did you come back?"

"Genevieve made me."

"Forced you?"

"Not like that. In a good way. I wouldn't have done it on my own. She tried to guilt me, but then – then she just said that every path has an end. This was the only way to get to mine."

"Your path isn't ending. It's just a shoulder wound."

"This part of my life is over. This is the last chapter. This was the last thing I needed to do to get off this path."

His eyes filled with tears when he looked at Genevieve's lifeless form. "Oh God. Oh God, it's so awful. All of it. Lona, is this the worst thing we've ever seen?"

She shifted her weight so that she was facing the same direction as Julian, so they shared the same perspective just as they would through a pair of visioneers. She scanned through sixteen years of shared memories, every incident she'd ever experienced through his eyes. She'd never thought about it: she had Fenn and all of the other Pathers to help her be Julian. Julian had only himself.

"That was the worst thing we've ever seen."

It was the last memory they ever needed to share.

It felt like a goodbye.

The roll of paper towels on the counter next to Julian had a country pattern, with pioneer women raking at the ground. Lona unrolled a wad of them and held it to Julian's shoulder, watching the women in bonnets slowly turn red. She started to rip off more sheets before deciding to just press the entire roll into Julian's arm.

"I need to go find Fenn. We don't know what's happened to them, and he needs to know what's happened to Genevieve, and—"

And I need to see him.

Julian grunted and tried to stand up again.

"You stay here. Find a phone and call an ambulance. You need to talk to them when they get here."

"No. No!"

Julian wasn't trying to follow her – he was pointing behind her, trying to get her to look.

She turned back to the corner where she'd just left Genevieve's body. Genevieve was still there. Her father wasn't. He lurched across the room, holding something in his hand.

"Don't," Lona begged, but it was too late.

He had already taken the electric prod, and already used one hand to find the soft spot at the base of his skull, and clear the hair away. He had already pressed the button, which emitted a crisp, electric noise.

The Architect had remmersed himself, erasing all of his bad memories, and all of the good ones along with them.

43

It should be light outside by now. It should be mid-afternoon; it should be tomorrow. That's how much time it felt like had passed since she woke up on the Architect's chair. Like she had aged several lifetimes. Lona left the building squinting in preparation for the sun, but the sky was still dark.

There were only two cars in the parking lot. One was Julian's; Lona used the keys she'd taken from the Architect's pocket to unlock the other. The digital clock inside said 2:42. She'd been gone less than three hours.

Back inside, Julian was dealing with the Architect, with a grown man who now had the faculties of an infant. Julian said that coming to Lona was the last thing he needed to do. But in one way or another, maybe he would always be picking up the pieces that his own Path had left behind.

Right now, the Architect would be like Lona was when she was first left at Path, by a mother he said he knew. What would he have told her, if she'd been more pressing about asking him? Why didn't she when she had the chance? Now it was a link to her past she would never have, an answer she would never know.

There was static coming from the floor of the Architect's car. Muffled voices. Lona felt around the floor of the passenger seat until her hand closed on something boxy and plastic. She must have been holding the walkie-talkie when she was taken.

Her fingernails looked grimy. She looked closer. Not grimy. Bloody. She had Genevieve's blood on her hands. Wasn't that a saying, too? Something that meant guilt? Genevieve would still be alive if she hadn't tried to save Lona. If she hadn't succeeded in saving Lona. The walkie-talkie was made of solid rubber. She depressed the 'talk' button and held it to her mouth.

"Hello?"

She let go and waited. Nothing.

"Hello? It's Lona. Is anybody – there?" She almost said 'alive,' but she would force herself to be optimistic.

More static. Then the sound of shuffling, of something being knocked over or dropped. Then, breathless: "Lona? Lona, it's Talia. Lona, are you okay? Come back right now."

It seemed like too much work to respond with words. Anything that came out of her mouth right now would not be coherent, might not even by human. Instead she put the key into the ignition and slid out of the parking lot and onto the quiet street, lit by a single streetlamp and the twenty-four-hour neon glow of Wok Don't Run.

In the background of Talia's message, someone else had been talking. Someone begging Talia to find out where Lona was, to let him go find her. Her brain could only manage the most basic of concepts now. The simplest, truest concepts. One of them was that it was good to hear Fenn's voice.

Newly awakened Pathers huddled together in small groups, leaning on each other, whispering. There were lots of them, but the bay still had the stunned stillness of an emptied battlefield.

"We were warming up for the Christmas concert and Nick fell off the risers."

"We just got our best time in the fifty butterfly."

"We were about to get on the plane for vacation in Colorado."

She wondered when they would all stop talking like that. Probably never.

Some were not in groups at all, but still sitting in their pods, looking more confused than upset, as if the screen had suddenly gone dark in a movie theater but they didn't want to get up until they were sure the usher really wasn't coming to fix it. Around these people, in particular, she saw ex-Pathers and Strays – Gamb, trying to make someone laugh. Affl, curled up on a large Pather's lap, patting his shoulder gently. Endl, sitting side by side with a boy about her age and staring companionably into space. She did not see Harm.

In addition to those expected conversations, though, she heard new ones. She heard, "Do you think someone will come and take us Outside? A Coping Technician?"

She heard: "I hope so."

Conversation stopped when she walked past. Children,

even the ones she knew, looked at her with shyness and awe. It made her feel self-conscious. To them, she was the one who'd ended one of their worlds, but simultaneously given them the possibility of another. Up in the control room, Talia sat with a small boy in her lap. Lona recognized him as the one from her pod. Djna.

Her heart thumped when she saw the figure standing next to Talia, his palms pressed against the glass as he scanned the bay. When she tried to move up the stairs, her knees felt like they would buckle. Instead she raised one hand in greeting, watched as relief spread through Fenn's face and waited for him to come to her.

He was alive. Seeing him was like stepping into a scalding bath after coming in from a frozen night. Soothing but painful. She didn't realize how numb she'd become until she felt the sharp pinpricks from the heat. She wished Fenn's face could have awakened just some of her emotions. Just the good ones. Just the relief and giddiness and the profound sense of gratitude that she got to see him again. But as he sprinted down the rickety fire escape, she felt all of them, unsheathed like knives. Joy, guilt, elation, sadness.

The sleeve of his shirt was torn, like it had been caught on something, and his face was smudged with dirt, but otherwise he looked unharmed. When he wrapped his arms around her, he smelled like grass and hot asphalt and gasoline. Real things. She clung to his shirt, a soft flannel cotton, and to the dark, soft curls on his head. She could heal herself with these things.

"It's over," she mumbled into his shirt. "It's over."

He ran his hand lightly over the back of her hair. "I was so scared I would never be able to do this again." He pulled back slightly and looked into her eyes. "I didn't know they took you until I was already with Talia's mom. I called from there and Talia said you were gone. I didn't know where to go. I didn't know how to find you."

"Wait, Fenn."

"The police are coming. Talia called them herself. There will be reporters and crowds. We can stay if you want, but if you don't, I'll go wherever you want me to."

"Wait," she said again, stepping backward out of his embrace. He shouldn't speak any more until he knew what had happened. If she let him keep talking to her, she wouldn't be able to tell him the things he deserved to know. "Fenn. Genevieve is—"

There were euphemisms she could use that might spare him pain right now. Genevieve didn't make it. Genevieve is gone. Genevieve is lost. There had already been too much avoidance and too many secrets.

"Genevieve is dead. She was shot. She was trying to help me."

Fenn crumpled into himself. Somehow, without moving at all, he became much smaller. He reached out a hand to steady himself on the stair railing.

"Are you—"

"I'm sure. I saw her at the end."

"How did it happen?"

"An accident. I said goodbye. I told her you loved her."

"I never," he said, "I never loved her as much as I should have."

What an awful kind of pain that would be. The inverse of losing someone you loved more than you knew.

Lona knew the second kind. It was what she felt when Fenn left her the first time, for Eighteens. It was what she felt now, knowing that the parents she'd never met were now unknowable.

She would tell Fenn the rest later, about Julian and the bullet and the broken family. She would tell him all of the rest.

"There's good news, too, Fenn." It felt crass to present it this way. As if Genevieve's death could be balanced out with dessert. But this news was important, too.

"You don't have to die. The Architect said. There is a choice – the medicine puts you through withdrawal, like Talia thought. But there's a choice."

"A choice?"

"More than a choice. More like . . . a will."

"Czin wouldn't have chosen to die."

"By the time it got to Czin, it was impossible to stop. But you know now. Now you know and you can stop it."

She wanted him to hold her again. She needed it, badly, and he did, too. For comfort. For making up for years of not touching anyone. But the gesture seemed so exorbitant to ask for now, so selfish when so many people would never get to have that kind of human contact. She reached for his arm instead, running her hand from shoulder to elbow, watching the goosebumps that appeared in the wake of her fingers. Stroke, stroke, stroke. Then she clasped her hand over his, the one that was still resting against the railing. He laced the fingers of his other hand through hers.

It was appropriate, in a melancholic way, to be back in the bay with Fenn, touching him with the simplest of gestures. Holding onto each other, holding each other up.

"What do we do now?" Fenn asked.

What did they do now? Become normal? Go to the movies? Get married? Maybe some of them would. But Lona couldn't wrap her brain around a future that mundane.

"Now I need to find my parents." Saying it out loud, it made perfect sense. It was the thing that Lona needed to do before any other futures became possible. There had to be other records. Or blood tests, DNA. There had to be reasons that the Architect mentioned her mother.

The light around them was growing dim. Dark, even. The intercom emitted a low beep.

"It is time to return," the familiar voice said, "To the Pa—"

It cut off in the middle, abruptly, like the voice had something in its throat. Lona looked up into the control room to see Talia with her hand on a button, preventing the automated system from finishing the scheduled message.

She was Lona Sixteen Always. It was June. In six months would be the first birthday she would not share with Julian. She could have a cake. She could have presents. She could have her own wishes.

Fenn was eighteen. But not for long. In three days he would have a birthday, and he would be the oldest living graduate of the Path.

In three days he would be Fenn Nineteen.

His last name would stay the same. Fenn Nineteen Beginning.

"Let's go outside," he said. "I want to see you away from here."

Holding hands, they picked through the Pathers at the back of the bay to a rear emergency exit. Outside was a small courtyard with a few wooden benches.

"Careful," he said. "It's still dark out."

It was. But the path was extremely well lit.

MONICA HESSE

Monica Hesse grew up in the cornfield American town of Normal, Illinois, spending most of her childhood pretending to be Laura Ingalls Wilder or Anne Frank. She is a feature writer for *The Washington Post*, where she has covered everything from political campaigns and the Oscars to the cultural meaning of Doritos. She lives in Washington, DC with her husband and a big black dog named Sheba.

Follow Monica on Twitter: @MonicaHesse